BANG GOES THE WEASEL

By Robert H Page

Any crime requires good planning. A good plan could have a hundred steps. Not all plans turn out as the planner had envisaged. This is the beginning of a tale of obsession, lust, greed and corruption where death is all around and where the end game was never in the plan at all.

PART 1

CHAPTER 1

It had taken her some time to settle and finally drop off to sleep. It's funny how when you are happy you sleep well and dream happy dreams. But now it's 2am and she hears the noise again. The first time she dismissed it as just a routine night time noise. This time it sounds more like it was in the yard, below her window. She doesn't move, intent on going back to sleep but by now she's lost track of the dream she was having, and which involved her favourite rock singer and a king-sized bed. She closes her eyes, gets comfortable and tries to get back to that warm place. But it's too late, the dream has faded away, and her thoughts turn to the activities of the day just gone.

She'd met with Sadie, the nearest thing she had to a friend, whom she'd met at school that year. It was her last year at school. Very soon she'd be 16 and able to do what she wanted. Her father, Nathan Montgomery, had other ideas. Annie wanted to leave and go travelling; backpacking, anything to escape from this place, her life and, moreover, her father. Her oppressing father who controlled every aspect of her life. From when she got up, what she ate for breakfast, all aspects of her schooling even so far as to include private tuition in those subjects she didn't excel in – namely maths and physics. He had set the bar very high indeed. She was under immense pressure day in and day out. In the evenings, when she didn't have private tuition, she had piano lessons, singing lessons and, worst of all, cooking lessons from an old maid who once had a cooking show on the TV. The hag had moved into the same area to retire but, due to a boating accident, had lost her husband shortly after. Shame that. What was to be a retirement of laughs and shared times turned into a sad, lonely existence. Her only escape was back into cooking. She also liked being close to young people as she said they made her feel young. Annie was a polite student but usually wished she were somewhere else. Her father was old fashioned and very strict – not that that is such a bad thing she thought. The young people of today have far too much freedom. In my day…. well. But it wasn't about her, it was about him, always about him; who he was, his social standing, his job.

Annie's replay of her boring day faded away for good at the third sound. She found herself suddenly wide awake and sat bolt upright in her tiny bed listening intently to the night. Not the night outside her room but the night inside the house. The third sound had sounded like a squeak; not a very loud squeak but nonetheless an audible one and a recognisable one. The very same squeak her back door made when opened. She hadn't consciously noticed this particular squeak before as it was quiet compared to the average daytime noises of traffic, planes passing overhead, the television and the local boy racers' sub woofers. But now, in the middle of this dark night, there it was. She recognised it and knew what it meant. Someone was inside the house.

CHAPTER 2

Bruce Bourne's story had started several months earlier. He had gotten up with the birds again. His new job wasn't what he had hoped. He was finding out that working for an Indian company was completely different to an American or English company. The culture was different. The way it had been set out to him during the recruitment process was not how it was turning out. He'd been there 18 months now. At first, he was working from home as was his plan when he joined – work from home more, see the family, try and hold his marriage together and earn more money so he and his wife could travel more and not worry too much about the everyday things like paying the mortgage, bailing out the kids etc. He'd wanted to spend the evenings making the house and garden look nice and the extra cash would allow him to do this. After the first couple of months he'd been expected to drive to the office most weeks – and at his own expense. Sometimes it was a Saturday or Sunday when one of the Indian managers or VP's were in the UK and wanting to meet the troops over a meal and preach the latest mantras. He was currently travelling to the other end of the country every Monday, working all week and returning home Friday evening, tired and grumpy. The weekend wasn't long enough to recharge his batteries or his mood and then Monday came around and the same again. He'd had enough. His wife was on the verge of moving out, surely this time for good. He called his recruitment agent.

"Hey James, how's it going? Have you found anything for me yet? It's been three weeks now and I'm sick and tired of all this travelling. I hardly see my family and I never get to do anything around the house." James tells him he is doing his best and that he has the feelers out for two or three good opportunities in the City. One of them would like to see Bruce on Wednesday at 4pm in Birmingham. Bruce agrees, wondering what he will tell his boss that he needs to quit work early in order to drive to Birmingham. At least it is something. He has light at the end of the tunnel. He decides to wear his blue suit. With or without tie? Well it is an interview so with tie – but not a blue one, maybe the yellow spotted one. Maybe not.

His wife, or rather soon to be ex-wife, Barbera, or Barb as her friends called her, but definitely not Barbie, was two years older than him and they had met at, of all places, a church. Neither of them went to church but Bruce had been cycling past a church and she had driven past him and nearly knocked him off his bicycle, only missing him by the narrowest of margins. She had in fact gotten so close to him that he'd been forced too close to the pavement and the near side pedal had caught the kerb sending him sprawling onto the pavement. He wasn't hurt, more upset at her lack of driving skills! He had told her as much.

The next time he saw her was in a pub, the Golden Ball. At first, he didn't recognise her, but he knew he'd seen her before, he just couldn't recall when. She was attractive and short with red hair. She noticed him looking at her and came over. "Hello again." Again, Bruce thought…. They chatted for a few minutes as Bruce struggled to recall where that had met previously. And then it clicked – she was the dozy bitch who had knocked him off his bike a couple of weeks back. "I'm ever so sorry about the other day" she said. "You sure look like you have made a full recovery." she went on to add. "Yes, thank you – I'm fine. And no damage to the bike either I'm pleased to say. "That's good." she replied. For a few seconds neither of them knew what to say. Before it became awkward, she said, "Let me buy you a drink." Bruce was on his own waiting for a friend who was typically late and occasionally didn't show. "Thank you." he replied. "Somersby? Pint of?" she said having noticed his nearly empty glass. "Yes please – thank you." He acknowledged. She briefly returned to her friends who seemed impressed at her ability to pull a guy so quickly; which was in fact something she had never actually done before. She finished her spritzer and went to the bar and a couple of minutes later returned with the drinks. "I'm Barb." She said. "Bruce" he replied. "Bruce Bourne."

CHAPTER 3

Devizes stood very still in the silence. The door had made a slight creaking noise. He knew he'd have to stand in silence for some minutes to be sure he remained undetected. His thoughts went back to Manguang as they often did. The heat and the noise there were unbearable and meant that only once in two whole years did he sleep well. His thoughts gravitated back to the events of exactly one month ago.

By this stage he had put up with incarceration for over 700 nights and that wasn't the worst of it. The heat was intolerable accompanied by the smell of filthy bodies, piss and shit. Barlinnie was a five-star hotel in comparison to this place. But he'd had it lucky. He'd seen people disappear never to return. Most of his fellow guests were from the surrounding areas. Rumours abounded that bad behaviour resulted in being stripped and thrown into water then electrocuted until they were unconscious. This cured many behavioural problems; and for some permanently. The so-called staff were far worse than many of the inmates. He could also speak a little Sotho which helped. He had always liked to be one step ahead of his adversaries at all times. He was lucky, not being an especially good-looking man, but being menacing and being able to handle himself. This, coupled with being a foreigner, had allowed him to evade the rapes often bestowed on the prettier looking fellers. But he planned to escape it all and soon for he had a plan. He'd been working on it for months; observing the other inmates, the staff and the routines of day-to-day life.

His plan was simple, very simple but it relied on two things;

two things beyond his control. Every day he waited and observed in the hope that soon both these things would transpire at the same time and open the gateway to his escape. Twenty-seven days later, on Friday the 13th they did and now he was sat in a bar, free again. "And the rest, as they say, is history." said Devizes to his audience. His audience were a bunch of small-time criminals who looked up to Devizes. DoDe they called him which was short for Dominic Devizes. Devizes never used the name Dominic as he didn't feel it suited a man of his skills or capabilities. Neither did DoDe for that matter but the name had stuck with him for years now. Most of his drinking buddies in the bar that night had known him that long. They heard of his conviction for rape and murder whilst on a collection run and were surprised the authorities over there had actually caught him. And even more surprised that he couldn't persuade one or more officials to let him go. It transpired that his victim was said to be the daughter of one of the local officials who was actually well liked even by the police there. Bad luck and it had cost him two years of his life. He still maintained that he had never raped the girl and that she was a most willing partner. A few even believed this.

But those two years hadn't been wasted. Not only had he planned his eventual escape he'd also been planning for the future; a future that would take him up to a new level in every respect. But he wouldn't be sharing those plans with anyone. Not until they were work in progress. And the whole country would know by then.

The first phase of his plan was driven by unfinished business. The merchandise he was bringing back had never been recovered. This meant only one thing. Either that pretty bitch had taken it from under the police's noses before making an almighty scene, diverting attention away from her, or her father had bribed the officials, or sweet talked them, and taken the stuff himself. Even if the girl, most likely a prostitute, had tried to keep hold of them, no doubt her so-called father would have taken possession of them. Missing goods meant angry bosses and prison was their playground. The bosses had gotten to him in prison, but their chosen operative wasn't a match for Devizes, and he had taken him out in front of several other inmates. This was what had earned him the respect he so badly needed to gain his starting position on the ladder of power. When they knew you could kill, and had seen it happen in front of them, it scared off most of the low life petty criminals and smugglers sharing his accommodation. They couldn't prove he did it as no one would talk but the manner in which he killed him scared even the toughest ones to the point that they left him alone fearing they'd end up the same way as the other English guy. This other guy was only serving 2 years whereas Devizes was to serve life. The records in there were poor. They were both English, they looked alike and no one knew either of them. It was easy to change identities with the newcomer. He identified the dead man as himself, no one argued. No one viewed the body – that was that. Very simple and very effective. So simple that no one back home would ever believe the story. He then kept his nose clean and served his 2 years and was released on Friday 13th. The second phase of his plan was to commence this very night. This was the part where he got even.

At least five minutes had now passed in silence and he had heard nothing. He would take no chances though. It was still possible she had heard the squeak and trouble awaited him. However, he had been here before and knew exactly where his quarry was located. He also knew exactly what to do, it was all planned in meticulous detail, written down only in his head, refined over the two years he languished with little else to do but make plans. Slowly he moved from the door towards where he knew the bedrooms were and specifically towards Annie's room.

CHAPTER 4

Annie sat very still hardly daring to breath. She had no enemies especially since moving to the UK with her mother. The events of 2 years ago aided her mother's legal battle with her father for custody of the then 15-year-old and tipped the balance firmly in her favour. Returning to England offered a much safer place to live away from the events of the past and it also offered more educational opportunities together boding for a better life. That was how her representatives laid it out. Her father, now deemed a target, didn't have a leg to stand on. He said he loved Annie and when she was younger Annie was definitely a Daddy's girl and a tom boy to boot. But when she grew into her teens she turned into a beautiful young woman and all that changed. Her mother, with her wealth, could offer her exactly what she wanted and needed; namely some spending money, fine things and a one-way ticket to England. She'd worked hard on her spoken skills and had done a veryy good job at eradicating her South African accent that she'd picked up in her younger years over there. But right now, she was listening. Listening intently, like she'd never listened before. Her internal volume was on full. She could hear her blood pumping through her veins and the rapid beating of her heart.

Only now did she desire a weapon. She had never learned to shoot. The UK is a far cry from South Africa and indeed the USA and most other places for that matter. In the UK it isn't the norm for people to have firearms by their bed unless they are the hunted, or the indeed hunters. Gang members carried knives but that was a different world. Now she was almost certain that she was the hunted and the hunter was close by. This was confirmed by another squeak, longer and quieter, as though someone were closing the door behind them, quietly, slowly, deliberately.

She may not have had a gun, but she had a knife; call it insurance. It had been in residence since the day they moved in. Close at hand, accessible and cold. She retrieved it from under the mattress. It was no ordinary knife, this one had purpose, a 6" hunting knife. But would she have the courage to use it? She may find out soon.

CHAPTER 5

Bruce is busy trying to remove what appears to be a small coffee splash from his tie when the Asian girl returns and tells him they are ready for him now. As instructed, he takes the lift to the 23rd floor. He looks both ways knowing his destination was in one of two directions but not wanting to give a first impression of being a fool, even though that was how he felt. He spotted a sign with the company name on and turned right from the lift. At the door was an intercom. First, he tried the door, but it was locked so he pressed the call button on the intercom. For a few seconds nothing happened and then he heard a faint buzzing sound and he realised the door was now unlocked. He tried pulling the door handle only to realise he should have pushed. Why do they put handles on the push side of doors he wondered? By the time he pushed the door it was locked again, and he had to press the call button a second time. He could feel his face turning red. "Great start" he thought to himself.

As he went through the door the peace and quiet from the lift area changed to the hubbub of a busy office. He hated offices. He hated being in the same place, the same seat, the same faces 5 or 6 days a week, week in week out. But needs must. He needed the money. Barb liked nice things and nice things cost money. The house, the cleaner, the gardener they all cost money. Money that Bruce soon wouldn't have unless he landed a new job. He reckoned he could go on another couple of months, but his debts were piling up. If he got this job, along with a bit of negotiating on the salary, he could be back on his feet within a year. And he needed it to happen to both keep his sanity and keep his wife, who was now threatening to leave.

Bruce had been in the building trade all his working life. At the age of 14 he helped out at a local site where they were building a new mall. Not a large mall but a smaller, more exclusive one. Ironically the very same mall was now his wife's favourite place to spend his money. He carried bricks up and down, he mixed cement, he learned the basics of many elements of the building trade in the two years he helped out there. When it was finished, he felt a certain pride that his sweat and tears had gone into this fine building. A building that would be appreciated not only by all the folk living in his village but also people further afield who liked to do some up-market shopping. He took pride in this. He also found that he had new aspirations not to be a just construction worker anymore, but to help design and project manage the construction of such buildings. He went to college and earned himself a Master of Architecture at the Marylebone campus. He'd saved his earnings from working on the site and, together with a small amount of money from his father, plus his wages from an evening job, he managed to afford to live in the relative squalor of London. Soon he grew to like London. He'd seen the seedier sides and the nicer sides of both the city and the people who inhabited and visited it. He liked the diversity. It was a far cry from where he had grown up.

His father had been glad to see the back of him. Bruce always felt that he reminded his father of his mother who had left them when Bruce was three years old. His father had never tried to find her. Bruce wondered why. Once he was old enough to understand that couples break up, he found that he would have liked to have heard her side of the story. He'd heard his father's side many, many times over the years. This seemed to grow and mutate as his mother became worse. The story had changed and evolved, but Bruce had been gifted with an excellent memory. He detected these subtle changes and knew exactly what they meant.

"Mr. Bourne – welcome to City Developments, my name is Lauren." Lauren was young, maybe twenty-five, slim and quite tall but her finest feature or features were a very fine pair of breasts. Bruce's eyes were momentarily fixed on Lauren's top trying to decide if he could see the outline of her nipples or whether it was part of the Brunel-esque structure that formed the underwiring of her bra. That unknown force of gravity that only affected the eyeballs had a firm grasp on him and it tool all his strength to raise his eyes to meet hers. "Thank you" he said. She also had beautiful brown eyes, as to be expected given the colour of her skin. Her hair was a deep brown and lustrous; shoulder length and it smelled very fresh and inviting. "Mr. Khan will be with you in a moment."

"Thank you" Bruce said. Lauren went off to bring him a coffee. Bruce waited patiently, getting a little hotter as the moments passed and his apprehension mounted.

CHAPTER 6

No more sounds came from the other side of the house for nearly four minutes. It seemed like twenty to Annie. She kept checking the clock on the bedside and was beginning to doubt herself when she heard movement that she knew had come from the lounge. She had a large vase on the table in the middle of the room. Annie loved flowers, particularly lilies, and she had purchased a large bunch the previous day. She hadn't cut the stems short enough and they had started to droop. Whoever was in the lounge had brushed past the flowers in the dark, catching one and causing the vase to move slightly across the glass top of the table. Whilst it wasn't a loud or particularly distinctive sound, Annie recognised it immediately and she felt certain that someone was in the lounge. That meant she didn't have much time, two minutes at most judging from his stealthy movements, before he crossed the hall, passed the spare room and the bathroom. Foolishly she'd left both doors wide open and her bedroom door was closed but not fully, leaving an inch or two to allow the circulation of air and for her to hear the doorbell or an intruder. She wished the doorbell would ring but she knew it wouldn't. She was on her own with just the knife for consolation. Time passed even slower as she counted the seconds straining to hear the next clue to the progress of the intruder.

She listened intently trying to focus on the silence, but her mind wandered back to her childhood. Annie had started playing truant from school. But even the letters that were sent to her father didn't persuade him to spend time with her, he just berated her and constantly reminded her of the money he was spending on her education and that if she quit school or didn't get good grades she'd be on her own and the money would stop. This did nothing to either improve her view of life in general or to instil any values or love towards him. She knew that she didn't have the means to go it on her own even though that was exactly what she wanted and needed to ultimately do. If she could travel and then get a job somewhere waiting tables or working in a shop or a hotel then maybe she could make a new start in her life. But the thought of working didn't make her feel happy either. She liked the easy life and she'd gotten used to it. She preferred to take rather than to earn.

Initially she hadn't wanted to come to the UK. But her father had never really paid any attention to her needs. If his job deemed it a requirement to live someplace else, then they packed and left. She had never lived in the same place for more than a year. They always rented properties for that very reason. As a young child she'd make friends then they'd be gone. After a while she stopped making friends because she knew sooner or later, that they too would be gone. As she got into her teens her peers started dating. She had been approached by several young boys attracted by her good looks. As she grew older, she became less receptive to their charms. She'd even been called nasty, derogatory names by boys who couldn't understand why she hadn't entertained them. She had hated her life at that time, and she was beginning to hate everything around her. However, she was no longer the lonely vulnerable child.

Still silence. Maybe the intruder had almost knocked the vase over and was at this moment holding it with a wet hand, or glove, sweating at the near miss he had had. Maybe it was just a burglar. As the time passed, she knew she only now had mere seconds to react. She quietly got out of bed. She didn't have time to dress. Wearing only a thin tee-shirt and shorts, she took a firm hold of the knife. She quietly positioned her pillows in the bed so as to appear like she was still in there asleep under the covers. She then stood behind the bedroom door. She peered through the crack between the hinges but there was insufficient light to see anything through the narrow slit. Conversely the intruder wouldn't be able to see her either. What seemed like five more minutes passed with no further sound. And then it happened.

CHAPTER 7

Mr. Khan was younger than Bruce expected. He looked in his mid-thirties. Somewhere deep inside Bruce's head this triggered a distant alarm bell. "I hope you don't mind me asking you Mr. Khan but how does a person as young as yourself manage to attain such a senior position in such a large company?" Bruce asked. The answer he received wasn't what he expected. Khan and his brother had been left a rather large sum of money from an affluent uncle who had no children of his own. He and Khan's father had been very close. Khan's father used the money to set up a small construction company ten years ago. Khan and his sister, Sidrah, had joined the company upon leaving university. Their father had retired early at the age of fifty due to ill health. Sidrah ran the HR side of the business and he was now CEO. His age defied his gravitas. Bruce knew that this man was special. He just hoped that he felt he himself was special enough too. He asked Bruce about his ideas for building certain types of buildings including exclusive shopping malls for which Bruce was very passionate.

The discussion moved to modern churches, hotels and even safe houses. The latter attracted Bruce's attention. This was something Bruce had never previously had any reason to consider on any of his previous projects or assignments. He thought about the criteria you would place on the construction of such a thing from the perspective of the buyer. "Well aside from aesthetic reasons security would be paramount. It would be essential that the room or area was hidden. If I were to undertake such a project, I would only use a small number of carefully selected workers for this stage and I would build it beneath the basement. Its construction would be done under the cover of building the foundations. The entrance would have to be hidden and only accessible from the basement. Khan listened intently to Bruce's narrative. 'What if it were needed within an office environment?" He asked. Bruce thought this over for a moment and replied "If the office area was large enough and not completely open plan, I'd build it in or around the centre of the office. The entrance would again have to be concealed. Khan thought over this scenario. "How would you provision power Mr. Bourne?" asked Khan. Well I wouldn't. I would provide sufficient electrical wiring and then build the source into the circuit breaker box inside the basement effectively hiding it. I would then wire it myself. I'd also provision enough power locally within the room to provide sufficient power in the unlikely event of a total outage. Using this method no one but I would know the true purpose of the room and no one else would know of the existence of the panic room as Khan chose to call it. Mr Khan seemed to like what he heard as he followed up with several other detailed questions. The discussion around a hidden room lasted much longer than any of the other aspects of their discussions including construction methods, fire resistance and safe exits. The unusualness of this didn't hit Bruce until he was walking down the street towards the car park. Was Khan trying to test Bruce in an area he knew he'd have little or no experience to call upon? Maybe that was Khan's interviewing style. Did Khan have a particular project in mind and was looking for a special person to lead it? Someone he could rely upon for both architectural reasons and other reasons? Bruce couldn't help thinking that there may be a sinister angle to all this. But he soon dismissed this, deciding that he hadn't done too badly after all. In fact, he was feeling quite good about this new role, his potential new employers and above all else making the changes to his like that he so needed. Especially as his marriage was all but on the rocks with this job requiring him to work away from home it would likely mean the end of his marriage and a clean start. Maybe that's what he had wanted all along.

CHAPTER 8

With an explosive crash her bedroom door was flung open at great speed – the intruder had apparently kicked it with the full force. As the door opened in slow motion, she caught a glimpse of him through the gap between the hinges. It was just a silhouette and he looked tall and muscular. She had made the assumption that it was a man due to the excessive force applied to opening the door. Whoever he was, he was expecting her to be hiding behind that very door. This meant that either he was used to doing this kind of thing and knew what to expect or that he had in some way researched her and knew what to expect from her specifically, or that he actually knew her. The door flew open so fast she didn't have time to react. She was gripping the knife so hard she didn't have chance to raise her arms to protect herself and as a result the door hit Annie firstly via the toes then full in the face bursting her nose and most likely blackening at least one of her eyes. The fact that it hit her toes first did in no way slow it down, just spread the pain from head to foot. She didn't scream but simply crumpled to the floor in a shocked heap, semi-conscious. The next thing she knew the stranger had pushed a gloved hand in front of her face, smearing the warm blood coming from her nose. She smelled something familiar. By the time she realised what it was the chloroform had taken effect and her pain had temporarily gone away. She slept, more deeply that she had in over two years.

CHAPTER 9

As Bruce got into to his car his head was still spinning. He thought the interview had gone well. He went through the questions they had asked him in his mind and listened to the answers he had given, those he could still remember that is. Not bad he thought. But nevertheless, some of the questions Khan had asked him didn't sit too well with him and he wondered why.

He had been asked certain detailed questions relating to things Bruce had worked with on previous jobs; quite specific things and, now he thought about it, not many people would have his experience in this particular aspect. Interesting. Maybe he was more suited to this job than he had previously thought. Then a strange thought hit him. What if they already knew about his special skills? This was either a weird coincidence or a better opportunity that he had ever thought; were they head hunting him based on his previous work? He hadn't asked them how many other candidates they were seeing. The speed at which they were working could mean they weren't able to get as many candidates in the short time they had. This project must be important and they wanted to move quickly.

CHAPTER 10

Devizes was pleased with his evenings work. He had succeeded in his mission to capture the girl. She was far prettier than he remembered. In those two years she had turned from a pretty, albeit slightly spotty, girl to a beautiful young woman; and a resourceful one also. He was relieved not to have walked into the room blind and been savagely wounded by the large blade she was holding. He had brought the blade with him as a memento. When the girl was long dead, he would retain the knife and remember the good times they had shared in their brief but enjoyable time together. All of a sudden was feeling hot… and horny.

The girl was still asleep. He sourced more chloroform and gave her another dose that would keep her out for the count for at least another hour or two. He then carefully, and tenderly removed all her clothing one piece at a time. First her slippers. He could see the dark patches of her nipples through the thin material. Eagerly he removed her clothes. He was delighted to find she was wearing nothing underneath and that she didn't shave down there. Bruce liked a nice, well-kept thatch. Shaving it was all wrong to him. He ran his fingers through her hair and hungrily surveyed every curve of her naked body. She was now precisely how he liked women. Young, beautiful, naked and unable to resist him. He could wait no longer. He removed his trousers and climbed on top of her.

Such was his excitement that it was all over in matter of seconds. If she'd been awake, she might have missed it. Whilst he liked the feel of her it didn't match the expectations that he had built up over two long years of lonely nights, sat in a cell, with nothing else to think about except how to get out of there and all the things that he could do to her when he found her. Still it would get better with each time, for now he rested, listening to her shallow breaths.

Before he had made the journey to Africa, he had made plans for his return. He didn't trust banks so had stashed a large amount of cash. He'd chosen to bury it in field that was both desolate and highly unlikely to be built on. He'd seen the movies and box sets where the villains break out of prison, drive to Utah only to find their map takes them to a new housing estate. He wasn't so stupid.

He had chosen a farm where he knew the owners personally but not closely and he knew with some certainty they would never either sell or build there, not in their lifetimes however short they may be. They were quite wealthy and so the trappings of selling the land to builders for lots of money did not turn their heads in the way it would most other people. He used an airtight container within a small metal safe which he buried 4 feet down beside an old, protected tree in a location that would not confuse him on his return. He wasn't sure how long that would be, but he certainly never anticipated it being this long. Whilst Annie slept, he headed back to the farm, which was only some 10 miles away. The traffic was dead at this time of night and he drove fast along the streets. He retrieved the safe in under 30 minutes, working quickly under the cover of darkness. He filled in the hole and left. He would open the safe and retrieve the contents later. This was only one of a number of similar stashes he had made and the second he had successfully recovered. But for now, this one would suffice and serve his needs. He headed back to check on his guest.

After his return to England and the recovery of the first stash of cash he had started to set the wheels in motion for his next exploit. It was a simple kidnapping for ransom. He also called in a few favours from some shady characters with whom he had undertaken some shady dealings in the past. Prison was a great forum for networking and learning new life and career skills, a sort of university but without certificates or pompous award ceremonies. He then set about converting the basement of his modest two up two down terraced house, in the town of Horwich, into a private suite for his new guest to be. Both well-hidden and sufficiently sound-proofed and with the appropriate level of security. A prison in his own home.

He had chosen Horwich because, as a boy, he had grown up in and around Bolton. He attended Smithills High School and orchestrated battles with the rival gangs from the Moor and Grammar schools. These rarely turned as nasty as he hoped and often never even came to the attention of the teachers. When they did, he always evaded capture by the school staff or police by planning an alternative route back to school and not being noticed as missing. He leaned on his peers for alibis in return for leaving them alone. He would also bunk off school, and lead battles with other schools. By the time he himself left school, with only a maths CSE, he was well on the way to becoming the man he was now, whatever that was.

He progressed to going to watch Manchester United and orchestrating trouble at Old Trafford. Here he had more success; occasionally with forays into Europe. He would frequently change his appearance, growing a beard, putting on weight or losing weight. Changing his style of clothing. He became good at passing himself off as different people and speaking with different accents. He had acquired several travel documents to match each of his adopted personas. He liked the escapism of being someone else. He needed to forget who he really was.

His new house guest was still unconscious. He dressed her and put a sheet over her. He then attached the shackles to her legs. These were attached to a metal loop set into the concrete floor in one corner of the room. In hindsight he should have done this before he went to collect his money; that said she couldn't have summoned help or escaped, but she could have been waiting for him with a nasty surprise.

The entrance to his special guest room was in the opposite corner beyond her reach. This way he could enter and leave her room without having to worry about her hiding behind the door again. A trick he himself had used more than once. Abuse followed him and his every move. Through school and into early adulthood – sometimes he was abused, more often he became the abuser. But he had changed. No one would abuse him again. He had proved this to himself without a shadow of a doubt during his enforced stay in South Africa. Now it was time for him to become. As he wrestled with his thoughts, Annie stirred and let out a little whimper. She was then sick down the side of the bed. Devizes left the room and sealed the door and locked both the locks. The room and door were soundproofed ostensibly as a place where he could play his drums without either being annoyed or annoying the close neighbours on either side should he ever find himself in the position of having to explain his extra room. But he didn't speak to his neighbours unless he had to. He certainly didn't invite them in. The last thing he wanted was to have to bump off one of his angry neighbours and be forced to flee.

One thing he had learned was never to leave any loose ends. His chosen builder, a loner from the other side of Manchester, had done a great job of building Annie's new room. When the job was complete, he paid the builder in cash as arranged – no paper trail and, on the pretence of taking him for a celebratory drink in the town centre, he hit him over the head, killing him instantly. He retrieved his cash leaving the wallet and contents and left him in the far corner of a car park where he was discovered in the morning. The authorities had no clue as to what had happened. They suspected foul play but equally well he could have tripped and fallen and hit his head. The case remained unsolved. If only the CCTV cameras had been working. Had this been a murder and had the murderer disabled the CCTV earlier in a premeditated act of preparation? Probably a bit too far-fetched for a small town like this but they would never know for sure. The wiring was old and frayed; a wire could conceivably have worked loose. Alternatively, birds and vermin are known to damage cables of all types. It went down as an accident. Devizes was getting better with each project and he felt good. He was particularly enjoying his current project and he looked forward to the next few days. He would sleep well that night, happy with his progress.

CHAPTER 11

Back to Bruce's story. He'd had his interview and gone home via the pub for a couple. Bruce hadn't been sleeping too well. His dreams were filled with secret passages, cellars and panic rooms. All of which he seemed to be trapped in with no escape. It was hot, he was sweating a little. His sleep was disturbed by the sound of an urban fox in one of the adjacent gardens. He turned over and drifted back to sleep. This time he was looking at his carefully laid out plans for the new building. Whilst he had no idea of what the building was to be, he could see clearly the plans for the single basement room and access. He was completing the work on this room before the rest of the crew came in to start the regular basement, which was effectively a floor above this room, with the ground floor and upwards to the remaining 49 floors. What was this building to be? And for what purpose was the secret room that only he and the owner knew about?

He awoke with a start; this room had been on his mind and in his dreams. He wondered if Mr. Khan had an ulterior motive for this line of questioning yesterday. Did he plan to build a new project somewhere with such a room as a hidden feature, and was he in fact looking for the one person he could trust to build the feature into whatever his perceived project was? And if he did this, would this room also be his resting place? If he were to be locked in, then he would be there for the remaining phases of construction at the very least. When the room was required, they could just remove his body in the night, destroy the plans and the room would be a complete secret. He laughed at his own ramblings. Nevertheless, he remained in this slightly disturbed state until sleep once more overcame him. This time he dreamed about pretty naked ladies who looked nothing like his wife.

CHAPTER 12

Annie awoke. It was pitch dark. Her head hurt and her nose hurt but at least it didn't feel broken. She knew from the pain in her feet that they had probably saved her face from the worst of it. No doubt her big toes would be blackened and bruised. She could still smell the chloroform and it all came flooding back and made her gag. She recalled the man, the abduction. Was it really him? Where was she? What would happen to her? She turned over and threw up by the side of the bed. She could see that she had already done this at least once before when was out for the count. She wiped her mouth, noticing that she was on a bed. Her ankles were shacked in metal bonds. She tried to move them, but they were very secure. They would go one way but not the other – the bonds became tight. They were heavy from the metal from which they had been made. She wondered why she could go one way and not the other. It was pitch black – she could see nothing. She didn't think she had been blinded but nevertheless it was another horrible thing to add to her list of woes. Her current predicament made her hate her father even more. If he hadn't brought her to this country, the safe haven as he called it compared to South Africa, then she wouldn't be in this situation now. Some safe haven. It was his fault. She'd always had a pet name for him – Weasel. A long time ago she overheard a conversation between her father and a couple of school friends who had visited them for a kind of reunion. They'd laughed about their old school nick names and she had learned that his had been Weasel Boy. She liked it and thought of him not as Dad but as

Weasel Boy from that point forward. A weasel by name and by nature.

She needed a drink to wash the foul taste from her mouth. She had no idea how long she had been incarcerated there, wherever there was. There was a dank smell like an old cellar, and she could hear nothing at all. She assumed it was indeed a cellar or mill or the like hence the smell and the extreme darkness. She peered into the darkness looking for a strip of light where a door might be located. She saw none. She listened intently for any sounds. After a few moments, she thought she could hear the distant rumble of traffic. That was all. No sound of movement close by. She thought she was alone. Her attention moved to the shackles on her legs. She tried to remove them but to no avail. Was she in a torture chamber? Was she to be tortured? She didn't mind the thought of dying – she didn't know what she had to live for anyway. She knew she was going to leave school with below the expected, mandated qualifications and thus be disowned and disinherited by her father, but she could cope with that. What she couldn't cope with was her inability to make friends. This too was her father's fault; for taking away all the friends she had made in the past – in her childhood. She was 16 years old and what had she got to show for herself. Fuck all that's what. Maybe she was to be the subject of a ransom demand? Or was she now someone's plaything for years to come? She'd heard similar stories in the news, particularly in the US where young girls of her age had disappeared never to be seen again. One or two had turned up years later having managed to escape from their captors after years of being locked up and treated as sex slaves. She liked the thought of sex – she'd never had meaningful sex, just a couple of quick flings but she thought that was all she needed, nothing more. She felt a little wet below, like she had been raped – but no other things to confirm this like bruising or tenderness down there. She didn't want to think about this right now. Who was the stranger who had abducted her? Was it to do with her father? Where was she? Why had she been abducted and for what purpose? Was it to do with the bad people her father had left behind in South Africa? Just then she heard a noise above. The faint sound of someone moving around. She lay very still, listening.

CHAPTER 13

Devizes had slept remarkably well considering his activities the previous evening. He had returned with the girl at around 3 am and the journey from Manchester had taken just over 40 minutes with hardly any traffic. He knew where the speed cameras were – he didn't want any trace of his journey, so he had planned his route carefully. He avoided the motorway where there were numerous cameras and used the side streets wherever possible. He had mapped out his route previously, so he could make the journey as quickly as possible whilst avoiding having his number plate recognised along the way. She was worth a lot of money to him. Enough, he hoped, to fund a few months of basking in the sun and making up for his lack of freedom the past couple of years. He wanted to go somewhere hot and sunny with lots of pretty birds with which to make up for lost time. And lots of bars needless to say but off the beaten track where he was highly unlikely to meet anyone that may know him. Although he had changed his appearance since his incarceration it was still possible that he may be recognised from the old newspaper pictures. He hadn't made the front page thank God but nevertheless he took no risks. His destination was Carvoeiro on the Algarve. It was originally a fishing village. Between the more popular resorts of Albufeira and Alvor, nestled in the shadow of Portimao, it was a picturesque family destination particularly popular with German tourists. There were a few bars and pubs and only a couple of night clubs. He knew a relatively secluded beach which was accessed down some 100odd stone steps. Most of the tourists didn't know of this beach and parked themselves on the main beach by the bars. His beach was in a cove and more popular with locals at the weekend. Sometimes you could go and there would be no one else around. Other times there may be as many as 20 people paddling and swimming. There were some overhangs in the rocks where you could sit in the shade and while away the hours between swims away from the rest of the world. He liked the sea there. It had a shallow gradient, so you could go quite a way out without it getting more than 12 feet deep in places. He liked to take flippers and a mask and snorkel. If the sea was calm you could watch the fish go by in a world of your own. If the sea was rough, then it was unsafe to venture in but fascinating to watch.

Ransom was his game at this juncture; easy money. He knew the girl's father had money and that he couldn't afford to involve the police lest they delved too deeply into his affairs. He anticipated the process to take no more than a week. By then her father should have conceded to his terms and made the drop and then he'd be long gone and languishing on his favourite beach. Devizes had planned the drop in meticulous detail during his incarceration at Manguang. Whilst he had no writing implements, he had planned and memorised every detail including plans on what he should do if any of the stages went wrong, or should her father go to the authorities which he thought extremely unlikely given his past. He had puzzled on how to ensure the authorities weren't brought in for some time. He knew this man to be ruthless in business and enjoying his reputation as such. His plan was a clever one. He had used one of his old contacts to tail him for a few days. The man, Smithy; his name actually was Smith; had identified certain patterns in his movements on a weekly basis. Devizes didn't want anyone else knowing what he was up to, so he had left it at that, paid the man and then continued the work himself. He followed him to the Lowry Hotel in Manchester on a Wednesday afternoon. The following Wednesday at the same time he followed Montgomery to the Ibis on Princess Street. This time he followed him in. He had been unable to predict his pattern of hotels over the past three weeks so had no choice but to follow the man. Devizes had been wearing a disguise. He had the natural ability to blend in. He was one of those faces that people found difficult to describe. On every occasion that he had seen a photofit of himself it was never a good likeness. The only thing they could get right to any degree of certainty was his height. At 6 feet it was difficult to disguise this feature. He wished he had been shorter, say 5 feet 8. But dwelling on such things was pointless. Being tall had numerous other advantages.

Montgomery had gone to the reception desk and, after a brief conversation, he went towards the lift. Devizes knew he had to take a huge risk and step into the lift with Montgomery in order to see exactly where he was going. Luckily a couple of attractive businesswomen also entered the lift and Montgomery had his attention on their shapely legs in front of him for the whole journey to the top floor. To Devizes surprise, the two women also got off at this floor. They turned left, and Montgomery turned right. Devizes stood by the lift and retrieved his phone from his jacket pocket and pretended to answer a call using his best Polish accent. The women disappeared around a corner whilst he watched Montgomery go through a set of doors and down the corridor. He moved position so as to be able to watch Montgomery. He knew that if he turned the corner at the end of that corridor that he may lose him. He prepared to run after him, but Montgomery stopped at the last room on the right and proceeded to take a cardkey from his pocket and open the door. He disappeared inside and the door softly closed behind him.

Devizes waited a couple of minutes in case Montgomery came out but once he was sure that he was staying put, he waited until the corridor was deserted and went up to the door in question and pressed his ear to it. At first, he heard nothing then he heard the familiar squeaking of bed springs and some sounds that he assumed were sounds of delight, although they sounded more like pigs scrapping over scraps. They hadn't wasted any time in hellos, chit chat or even foreplay. He smiled to himself – he now had what he wanted. He assumed that Montgomery would leave the room first, before his bed mate, so he returned to reception and took a seat. He couldn't risk being spotted by the lift when Montgomery returned, in case he recognised him or found out that he was being watched. He wore a hat so as to appear subtly different to before. Montgomery was a daunting man. He had seen his sort before. He knew that he would stop at nothing to get what he wanted. That was one of the reasons he had thought that he made such a good target for a kidnapping. Time would prove that he had indeed underestimated his quarry.

The liaison transpired to be nothing more than a quicky and fifteen minutes later he spotted Montgomery emerging from the lift and subsequently leaving the hotel in the direction from whence he had come less than twenty minutes earlier. His personal experiences taught him that whilst a man in a hurry was happy to slap his chappy into the sink for a quick wash, his companion, who he assumed to be female, would take a little longer. He waited a further ten minutes then got back into the lift and returned to the top floor. Once again, he stood by the lift, this time under the pretence of waiting for it, and played with his phone. He activated the camera and pointed it down the corridor. He had disabled the flash and muted the phone, so his intentions remained discreet. Several people emerged from the lift and Devizes ignored them, whilst intently looking at his smartphone. No one took any notice of him. A businessman typing on a smartphone is an everyday occurrence. He had seen men and women in their eighties on the train typing away, sometimes even on Facebook. Once he saw two elderly ladies take a selfie on a street corner. As he walked past, he heard them discussing whether to post it to Facebook for their daughters to see. He was gone before he learned the outcome and he now wondered why it had left an impression on him. It was most likely that fact that social media made it extremely difficult for one to hide their whereabouts. Facial recognition could prove very costly. It only took one stray picture on a smartphone to find its way onto a social media site and the authorities could scan it and everyone in it, whether intended and not, and identify some or all the faces therein using facial recognition software. Devizes was acutely aware of the inherent occupational hazard this had become. He was constantly on the lookout for people, particularly younger ones, with smart phones or tourists with cameras.

He heard the closing of a door and saw out of the corner of his eye a person emerging down the corridor towards him. He expected a prostitute or middle-aged woman but, to his great surprise, found it was a young man, dressed in ripped jeans and a trilby; no doubt a few quid better off than when he walked into the hotel. He photographed the man as he had planned to. As he walked by Devizes continued to play with his phone, although he had closed the camera application just in case the man caught a look. As he walked past, Devizes could smell a faint aroma of weed. He had a good idea what this man did if not yet his identity. His plan had worked out better than he expected. He was hoping for Montgomery to be having an affair with a married woman or to be a prostitute user. This topped that by a big margin and would provide a much more compelling reason for Montgomery not to want to involve the police. This guy should be relatively easy to identify if need be. He watched the guy get into the lift and head back down toward reception. After waiting for a couple of minutes he got in the lift and did likewise.

After a good day's work Devizes returned home. He took a short nap to recover his strength. Twenty minutes later he got off his bed and walked across to the bathroom to take a leak. He showered and dressed in clean clothes. He planned to burn yesterday's clothes later today – no loose ends or potential forensic evidence. But first he had to see how his guest was doing. He knew that she would be awake by now and he wanted her.

CHAPTER 14

It was morning, the day after Bruce's interview and Bruce was lying in bed alone, dozing when he heard a knock on the door. His wife had packed a case and gone to her mother's after Bruce told her he'd applied for a job that involved working away again. So far, he didn't miss her one bit. He quickly put his dressing gown on and went to answer the door. "Special letter needing to be signed for" said the jolly postman. It was 8.15am and there was nothing Bruce could see to be jolly about. It was pissing down outside – that fine stuff that gets you wet. If there were any cows nearby, they'd be sure to be lying down. He signed for the letter and closed the door. He went into the kitchen and turned the kettle on and then sat down at the table and proceeded to open the letter.

It was from the company that he had had the interview with the previous day. To get a formal response so soon was very surprising, unheard of in fact. He opened the letter expecting it to be a thanks but no thanks; but if that were the case then why send it so quickly and registered? He briefly pondered the question then decided to find out. Upon opening the letter, he was surprised to read that he was being asked to return there the following morning at 8am sharp to meet the project team for an upcoming project that they were about to start working on. Bruce knew this was a very positive step and, so long as none of the team took against him for any reason, that there was now a strong chance he would get an offer of employment. He would of course enter into negotiations for his package – there was always a deal to be done, especially as they seemed so keen on him. He wasn't a greedy man at all but he had often been taken advantage of on previous projects and had decided to try to become a better negotiator. He had even bought a book, Sales and Negotiation. He'd gotten half-way through reading it before becoming extremely bored. It was to him the perfect cure for insomnia. That said, maybe he should try and finish it today.

He wondered what this team would be like. He switched off the kettle as it whistled its monotone tune just like Radio 1. He knew that returning to bed would result in no further sleep, so he went to his Mac, logged in and went into his browser and navigated to LinkedIn. He clicked on advanced search and entered the company name. He was presented with a list of employees. He went through the list looking for people who he considered may be part of this team, or that type of person. He decided that, since most of these people had excellent CV's and career histories and looked smart, he would require a new suit for the following day. He wasn't connected to any of the employees he found on LinkedIn. But then again, they probably had multiple company names which would make it harder to find them. He checked out his Facebook newsfeed, then went upstairs to shower. For the first time in months he was feeling positive about the future.

PART 2

CHAPTER 15

Detective Inspector Cable had been working this case for over nine months. Counter-terrorism was a long game – very rarely quick wins. It was a war not a battle and whilst they won a few battles they weren't winning the war. He had received more rumblings of an attack at a bar in London, but the sources weren't confirmed. Today he would have to try and ascertain what level of risk this posed and plan accordingly.

His route to work was a short one but the route entailed some five or six sets of traffic lights. He always seemed to get stuck at each and every set. Two were left turns. He often found himself sitting there looking to his right from where no vehicles emerged. He wished that the UK had a similar rule to the US whereby you can turn right on a red light. He wished he could turn left on this red light, but he knew, were he to be caught, it would be another blot on his career and that just wouldn't do at all.

His wife tolerated his outbursts. If he was in the car with her he would always complain about the red lights, the location of pointless roundabouts and, worst of all, those fucking traffic lights on the fucking roundabouts! What's the point in this he'd say and his wife, who had heard this rant so many times before, would just smile and ignore him, or just ignore him. He was turning into Victor Fucking Meldrew – 'VFM'. He was only forty-seven and had been a serving officer for twenty-seven of those years. Both his parents had died some fifteen years ago. His was a small family so no forthcoming inheritances for Bob Cable; not now, not anytime soon, not at all.

His wife didn't work, and Bob was the bread winner and, whilst he earned a good salary, he wished he earned more. He knew there were ways and means by which he could increase his earnings, but he was a straight up kind of guy. He'd never so much as stolen anything from the penny tray and he wasn't about to end up in the pocket of some criminal. He had to keep his nose clean and hope to progress up the long ladder and make his fortune that way, legitimately, but it would be a long, hard slog and he knew it.

CHAPTER 16

Devizes switched on his computer. He went into his browser and entered the IP address of the webcam he'd fitted into the cellar. It was fitted to the ceiling pointing down over the bed. It was equipped with infrared so even in the pitch dark he could see the image of Annie sitting on the side of the bed. She was moving – her hand looked to be up against her ear – she was listening. Could she hear him moving about? He doubted it. Even if she could he knew that, however much noise she managed to make down there by screaming or banging, no one else would be able to hear her. This was the only cellar in this terraced street. Chorley New Road was only 250 metres away and the sound of the incessant rumbling traffic put an end to any chances of her being heard outside. He had built a room within a room within the cellar. He had constructed it himself using breezeblocks and soundproofing material similar to that used in a recording studio, its sole purpose to reduce the sound emanating from within. Whilst it wasn't totally soundproofed, he thought it was more than adequate for his purposes. He only expected it to be in use for a week, tops. Unless he subsequently planned any more such adventures, he would replace the laminate floor thus sealing forever his room and rent out the property again. That way, should he need the room again, he could give notice and return to the property as he had done this time, no one the wiser.

He went downstairs and got himself a glass of water and downed it in one. He wiped his face with his sleeve, got his black balaclava mask, or his terrorist mask as he liked to call it, put it on and proceeded to lift the cellar hatch. He was dressed all in black. He deliberately used a cheap cologne – one of his styles of operating was to wear a particular fragrance with his victim so she assumed this was his fragrance of choice. It would be slapped on thickly so as to definitely noticed and to mask any other tell tale smells which a more sensitive nose than his may detect. He had turned off the lights before he lifted the hatch so that as little light as possible flooded down. The curtains remained closed but nevertheless the light illuminated the floor of the room. He looked into the far corner and saw Annie looking up at him, squinting. The ceiling hatch had obviously been a surprise to her. She must have been expecting a doorway where she may be able to hide behind – or maybe her blooded nose and toes had torn that idea from her head for good.

He expected her to be crying or screaming or shouting abuse at him. To his surprise she just looked at him. He shone his torch into her eyes to disorient her, stop her getting a good look at him and also so he could see what she was doing and to ensure that she hadn't found some sort of weapon or other such trick. He had been very careful to leave nothing in the room that could be used as such, or even dismantled in order to make an improvised weapon. She squinted as the light hit her, but she still looked at him without speaking. He descended down the ladder to the floor below, feeling sure that she couldn't really see him too well.

Devizes used his best London accent, not a corny cockney one but a more common East End type accent and said "Do as I say, and I won't hurt you – too much. I s'pose you'll be wondering why I've brought you down 'ere. Well don't worry your pretty head too much, it's your father who I'm after and you are just a means of getting to him. I have no doubt that once he pays the ransom you can return to your precious little life." Again, she just stared at him. "I'm going out, but I'll be back soon with a sandwich and a drink. There's a bucket over there if you need it. Sorry I couldn't stretch to an en-suite." He expected her to show some emotion – she didn't. No screaming, no tears, and it wasn't plain submission. When he had shone the torch at her he had seen her eyes – empty eyes in a beautifully framed face. They reminded him somewhat of an old acquaintance he had done some business with a few years ago. This guy was a cheap hit man. He was cheap because he didn't do it for the money – he did it because he liked it. Whilst Devizes found this acquaintance a little disturbing, he didn't let it affect his business transaction, but he took a note not to deal with this man again as he felt he was dangerous. He didn't like socio-paths – they were too unpredictable and ruthless and would do anything to get what they wanted.

Annie looked no more than eighteen or nineteen. Her staring eyes and demeanour had somewhat taken away his desire to give her one again. Was he feeling sorry for her? Of course not - she was a spoiled rich kid. With her rich Daddy who would probably give her anything she wanted and even more to get her back. He knew from his visit that her house was no palace but then again how many other girls her age got to live in a place like that – mostly without parental presence. Daddy had probably bought her the place to give her a little independ-ence. He wondered whether he should have done more re-search on the girl; he had focused his attentions on her father as he was the source of the money he so badly needed to turn his life around.

With that he climbed back up the ladder and closed the hatch. Even though he knew she couldn't get to the ladder with her shackles on he nevertheless locked it and placed the rug over the top to hide it. Every one of these terraced places had a run-ner in the hall. It was commonplace and not in the least con-spicuous. It was just a place people passed through. He went back into the kitchen and finished his brew, which was by now getting cold, whilst he watched her sitting on the bed waiting. She sat there almost motionless. Her hand no longer cupped to her ear. Just sat there.

CHAPTER 17

Devizes had put away his black clothing and washed off the cheap aftershave he had used for Annie's deception. He dressed in jeans and a shirt. He put on his jacket and a more refined cologne and went out looking the door behind him. He walked to the end of his street and on to Chorley New Road where he headed towards the town centre. After a blustery five-minute walk, he came to where he had left his car – an old Ford Focus. Silver and distinctly unmemorable due to the number of similar vehicles on the road. He pulled out behind another one the same colour – enough said. He needed some items for the next part of his plan. He always obtained new items, so nothing could be traced back to him and disposed of them immediately after use; never reusing anything so as not to leave any type of trail. He always paid cash – that is if he paid at all. The items were subsequently destroyed when they had served their purpose. Today he needed a new black outfit, something that would burn quickly upon its expiry date, and a holdall just big enough to hold two hundred and fifty thousand pounds in used fives and tens.

He stole the holdall from a sports shop that had no CCTV cameras and a very inattentive, young member of staff serving at the counter. He waited until a group of school kids entered the shop knowing that the staff would be watching the kids. It isn't easy to steal a holdall, but he just walked out with it as though he had entered with it. In it were a carefully selected pair or jogger bottoms and black sports top. He would have taken a pair of trainers too, but none had taken his fancy.

Normally the security system would have detected him leaving the store but all the items he selected were reduced and as such, not deemed valuable enough to have a tag attached to them. As he stepped into the fresh air a sense of relief came over him. He knew that, should he be identified as a thief, he could outrun the shop staff and disappear before the police came. He knew every street and back street for miles around; learned from years of playing truant and walking the streets; for his chosen career a good education. He never made friends locally so that no one would remember him or be able to easily identify him. The local police station was long since closed so the coppers had to come from as far away as Bolton, some twenty minutes away, if they had anyone available that is, and the roads weren't gridlocked. So far so good. He returned to Horwich centre and parked his car in a different location – off the street and inconspicuous amongst all the other older cars in the area with no CCTV of course. He bought himself a couple of pork pies and a sandwich. He ate the pork pies whilst walking back to his terraced prison. Pork pies were one of the things he had really missed whilst interred. Since his return his diet had comprised pork pies and curry. A thought crossed his mind – could he possibly be identified by the smell of his breath, or even his farts? Maybe he should vary his diet he thought, vigilant as always. He smiled – his attention to detail was becoming... too detailed! He went into the kitchen sniggering to himself and put the kettle on again. This time he'd have a coffee.

He drank his coffee then went to the cupboard and retrieved a bottle of energy drink. He took this and the sandwich he purchased earlier into the hall where he collected a sheet of blank, plain paper and an everyday blue biro. He donned his black outfit complete with cologne and then returned to the hallway. He pulled back the runner and unlocked the hatch. He opened the hatch and shone the torch in to see Annie sat in the same position as when he had left her. Assured that it was safe to go down he did so and placed the sandwich and drink on the bed beside her. She must be famished by now. "These are for you." He said. "I'll bring more this evening. But before then I need you to do something for me." When she spoke, her voice surprised him. It wasn't the delicate, childlike, terrified for her life voice he had expected but rather a deeper voice which sounded like it came from a different body altogether, a bit like Cat Deeley. She was about 5 feel 2 inches, slim with amply proportioned breasts that Devizes's eyes lingered on for some time. "Which do you want first then? Do I write the ransom letter for you or do you wanna fuck me again?" Devizes was taken aback. He gathered his thoughts, cool as always. "Which would you like first?" he said in a matter of fact East End voice. "Fuck me first" she said "then I can mention it in the note to him. Not that the bastard will give a shit." Further taken aback Devizes didn't know what to say to this. Was this some kind of game she was playing in a bid to secure her freedom? He pondered this question for all of 15 seconds, which was the time it took him to remove his trousers. He kept the black long-sleeved jumper on so as not to reveal any of his tattoos or tell-tale scars that could be used to identify him even down here.

She watched him casually, in the gloom, as he had placed the torch on the floor to give some ambient light and allow him to make sure she didn't try anything. She knew she was tethered and, even if she managed to kill him, she'd never get out of there. First, he removed her tee shirt to reveal her well-shaped breasts which he gave a gentle squeeze. She adjusted her position, so she was lying in the middle of the bed and he removed her clothes leaving her naked. She made no attempt to struggle or kick him in the balls which was his worst fear. If she had done, he would have hit her, hard. He was pleased that this was unnecessary. She even went so far as to open her legs invitingly. He pondered for a moment wondering what he could have conceivably missed in this situation that could result in him getting winded and having to punish her. He decided that she was complying with him in a brave attempt to avoid being hurt or killed. This was even better than he had expected.

A few seconds later he was inside her. At first, he wasn't comfortable as he was expecting her to try something. But she moved with him as though she were enjoying it, but he didn't think she was actually enjoying it being truthful. He was deeply shocked when she came before him. At first, he considered that she was faking it – not that he had had any prior experiences of this of course. But she was very wet; very wet indeed. She started to thrust once again taking the driving seat and soon he was coming too. He felt like both barrels have been completely emptied and she seemed to enjoy being pumped full. Part of him wished he'd been a little more tender and made it last longer. She just lay there beneath him looking up at him in the dark glow of the flashlight.

He withdrew and pulled his pants back on. She remained on the bed naked and leaking slightly. He retrieved the paper and pen and placed it onto the bed next to her. "You know what is coming next don't you?" he asked. "Yes. Write a letter to my father telling him I'm your captive and unless he pays, you'll shag my brains out until I'm dead?" she said in that deep and now sexy voice. Her voice now reminded him a little of Francis De La Tour from the Rising Damp comedies, only a little deeper and much sexier. "No – I'll dictate." he said sharply. Five minutes later he asked her to read the ransom note back to him. As instructed, it was written in her usual handwriting. It read "I am being held captive but am as yet unhurt. I will remain unhurt so long as you get two hundred and fifty thousand pounds in used fives and tens. You have three days to raise the money. On the fourth day you will receive another letter with further instructions. Talk to the police and they will know, and they will hurt me. I believe them. If they don't get the money, then I die. Please do what he says, it's the only way." He included a dark, slightly blurry polaroid instant showing her face and busted nose. That should clinch it.

That was it. Short but not sweet. Her handwriting was typical of a young woman. Neat and curly with circles for dots over i's. He took the letter and the pen and went back up the ladder. He shut the hatch, locked it and returned the throw over the entrance. Now he had work to do.

CHAPTER 18

Bruce was in Marks and Spencer's. He selected a black business suit, single breasted with trousers and a belt. He had plenty shirts, many of which had hardly been worn. He paid on his credit card as he was skint as always. He had to queue for some time as the ladies in front of him discussed the finer points of whatever they were buying. He always chuckled to himself in Marks and Spencer's at the way there were seating areas on each floor where the poor old husbands sat and waited patiently whilst their spouses browsed through the entire range of skirts, shirts and underwear. Given the average age of an M&S shopper he called these seating areas Death Row. It looked to him like a bunch of old men waiting to shrug off this mortal coil; they all looked very much alike, dressed by their wives in M&S shirts, slacks, caps and coats, patiently waiting to meet their maker. The store had escalators probably directly to the top floor where Saint Peter awaited them.

He finally paid for his suit and left the store. He was tempted to go for a quick pint as it was approaching 1pm but he decided not to risk fucking up his new suit before he'd even worn it and went directly home. He hung up the suit and selected a suitable long sleeved white shirt and patterned tie that seemed to match. He left them hanging on his wardrobe door as they were already ironed nicely by his wife – they'd be fine until tomorrow. He'd have to learn to iron his own now. His soon to be ex-wife would put the clothes back into the wardrobe and chastise him like a child if he had tried to iron his own. She took great pride in picking him up on the slightest little things. Bathroom light on, toilet seat up, forgetting to put the bins out. Since she had left, he would learn the hard way which bin went out on which day. It was a full month until he eventually got it right and got to once again enjoy the luxury of empty bins and no overflowing heap of rubbish. He'd tried sneaking some of his crap into next door's bin once, but he had to apologise when she too picked him up on this. "Fucking cow" he had thought to himself. She was very pretty, nevertheless.

He put on the telly and flicked 'til he found Gold. Blackadder was on – he liked Blackadder. Blackadder II was his favourite with Queenie and Nursey. Next thing he knew it was 5pm – he'd nodded off. He went to the cupboard, which was almost bare, and retrieved a tinned steak and kidney pudding and a tin of beans. And tomato ketchup of course. He heated them up and ate them in front of the TV. When he had finished, he put his dishes into the sink, another thing that severely pissed off his ex, and then went to his computer. He went straight to Google and looked up Khan and his company to see what further research he could do prior to his meeting tomorrow. He looked for any references to private customers but found nothing. The more he looked the more he found the wording very generic, lacking any kind of detail and unspecific. They had done several, multi-million-pound construction projects, but he hadn't heard of any of them. Never mind he thought, there are thousands of such places in the UK so no wonder I haven't heard of them. Nor did he recognise the pictures of any of the sites. Strange but not inconceivable.

Once he had learned a little more about their style and back catalogue he went back to the TV. After a while he retrieved what was his last can from the fridge. He opened the beer and drank it. After watching a full Inspector Lewis without falling asleep (that was a first) he flicked through the channels to see what else was on. He didn't mind Lewis although it was a bit slow. He had hated the Inspector Morse series as they were just too slow. His ex had loved these, naturally. If he hated it, she liked it. Was it just to piss him off?

After looking through the channels he decided to have an early night. He would, after all, have to get up quite early tomorrow. He wanted to allow plenty of time so as not to be late. But he didn't sleep well. Once again, his dreams centred around big unknown places with sinister rooms where he could enter but couldn't find a way out. When his alarm went off, he awoke with a headache. He hoped it would have cleared by the time his day proper started.

CHAPTER 19

Annie was again in the dark, who was this stranger? Could it be him – the guy her father knew that she'd briefly met just before they left South Africa? She was worried, very worried but this wasn't concern regarding the stranger's intentions. He wasn't the biggest bastard in this unfolding drama. It was the worry that her father would react in the same way he had every other time someone had demanded, or even asked him politely for money. "You want money, you earn money" he had constantly said to her. He couldn't abide any kind of freeloading or scrounging. She guessed she wasn't the only person onto whom he had inflicted that bit of wanton advice. She had despised her father for a long time; as long as she could remember. Only now did she realise for how long and how much. What the fuck had she done to deserve this? Nothing. It was him. Everything was him. Bastard. She felt herself welling up, but she had learned to control her emotions. Determined not to cry and, even more importantly, determined not to show the other bastard upstairs any vulnerability, she bit back the tears and focused on the pain from her nose and toes and the tears went away. Nose and toes, nose and toes, nose and toes but her thoughts soon drifted back to her father once again.

Whilst he paid the household bills and gave her a modest allowance, she had little more than any of the other school kids from far less privileged families. Kids who shared their homes with loving families and siblings. As she didn't have any friends as such, none of them knew where she lived and they all assumed she was like them, only socially challenged. She must have been targeted by an acquaintance of her father she thought. Nothing this bad could have come from her dreary life. Most likely someone who had asked for money and been denied. Or maybe someone who had worked beneath him for a pittance had a grievance. Still none of this mattered now. She was here and that was that. In her brief periods of light, she had tried to take in her surroundings, so she could find her way around in the dark when alone. The first thing she observed were the shackles on her ankles. They were very sturdy but looked very worn and old. She wondered how many other poor bastards had been shackled in the very same place and what had happened to them? Do you get career ransomers? Upon more detailed inspection the shackles were set into a thick metal ring sunk into the concrete of the floor. This was no ordinary basement. It looked like it had been built for this very purpose – converted from an old damp basement or cellar. Maybe even dug out especially for this purpose. The walls didn't look like the usual cellar walls either, they were finished in something – probably to absorb the sound she guessed. Surely, he couldn't have gone to all this trouble just for her. There must have been others…had there? If there had been others then it was even more imperative that she found a way out of her situation and fast, before her father had a chance to fuck things up for her again. She had to try and free herself somehow. She wrestled with the shackles until she bled. She knew it was absolutely pointless, but she had to do something. Even the strongest strong man couldn't free himself from these. Houdini could be locked in here for eternity - maybe he was under the floor, maybe he had company. She turned her attention to the pin in the floor. She felt her way along the shackles to the corner of the room, the corner diagonally opposite the ladder. A deliberate move to ensure she could never reach the ladder or mount a surprise attack when her captor visited – well planned and smart. In a strange way she now felt like she had a purpose. This was a new feeling for her. Her life had always lacked purpose. Maybe if she cooperated with him, he may give her some of the money. Fifty thousand would give her a fresh start. She wondered about this and soon realised she was being childish and mad; kidnappers never did anything like that unless they were in it together from the start. Her best plan was to be obedient and not upset the man. If she was lucky, he may shag her again. That's what it felt like. More of a rough quickie than being raped. She knew he'd enjoyed it and would be back for more, giving him a reason to keep her alive. Then she was suddenly hit with a thought - he hadn't used a condom. What if he had an STD, or worse HIV? She knew there was nothing she could have done about this and so she shouldn't dwell on it but focus on her more imminent worries like trying to get away from this place. Deep down she knew this was a near-impossible task so long as she remained shackled like a prisoner. Her best bet was to not upset him in any way and ride it out in the hope that her father paid the ransom and she was released. Somehow, she didn't think that was how it would end. Nevertheless, if she could just get out of this cell then she'd have more chance of getting free, so long as she was conscious that is.

Up until now she had eaten little and had tried not to think about needing the toilet. However, she now needed a number two. She had forgotten to look to see if he had provided any toilet paper. She felt around the area of the bucket and was relieved to feel the touch of a soft toilet roll on the floor. It was brand new – small virtues. She separated the first piece and then squatted over the bucket and shut her eyes and tried not to listen to the plopping sounds echoing in the bucket. She thought of a comedian she had heard somewhere on the telly saying that a duck's quack doesn't echo in a bucket. Well this sure did. A camera, he must surely have fitted a camera in here somewhere. Shit. She quickly wiped up and got back onto the bed. Although her body held no secrets for the man upstairs, she still wanted to avoid the indignity of being observed having a number two. That would be unbearable.

CHAPTER 20

DI Cable's desk phone rang. Not an unusual occurrence but, given his current assignment and the lack of progress in recent weeks, it had been a little quieter than usual. This was all about to change. It was the chief of police Bernard Trainor. "Cable, my office now please." Bob wondered what this was all about. Was he about to get another bollocking for the lack of progress on his current assignment? Or had something else cropped up, something more important? No time to wonder, "now" meant within the next thirty seconds so he briskly walked towards Nobrainer Trainor's office.

He knocked on the Chief's door and was immediately admitted. To his surprise he saw a middle-aged man whom he recognised, but not from the police staff. He was Nathan Montgomery, a senior diplomatic aide to the British government. He'd seen the man's face in the paper recently. He always looked very smart, pin-striped suit and nice tie, the works. He was one of those people that carried himself well and always looked very important and impeccably turned out although no one knew what he actually did. Bob on the other hand could wear the finest Italian suit and still look scruffy.

"Take a seat Bob." The chief said. "This is David Montgomery; he is a senior advisor to our government and this morning he received this." He passed an A4 clear plastic bag to Bob. It contained a single sheet of plain A4 paper with what looked like a woman's handwriting. Before Bob had had a chance to read the note Montgomery said "They've taken my daughter and are demanding £250,000 pounds for her release. I cannot and will not let this type of behaviour compromise our country. It has to be stamped out. Under no circumstances can they be seen to be winning or it will escalate."

Bob was taken aback. He expected the father to be worried and pleading for their help for the release of his daughter, who was called Annie. Instead he seemed to be more worried about national disgrace and apprehending the captor and exacting justice. He seemed unusually unconcerned for his daughter's safety. Bob knew how difficult this was and from his training he knew the statistics relating to the successful release of the captive and the rate of capture of the kidnapper. It didn't make pleasant reading. "It isn't that I can't lay my hands on the money you understand, it is much bigger than that. You have to apprehend this man or men and bring them to justice publicly. They have to be an example that ransom will not work in this country and this modern British society. There is no place for this kind of behaviour." Again, no mention of Annie.

Bob had now read the letter twice. "Mr. Montgomery, the letter says you should under no circumstances contact the authorities. What if you were being watched? They may already know you are here speaking to us now...." Montgomery cut him off "Don't you think I took precautions before coming here? I'm not stupid. Nobody knows where I am. I left my mobile phone on my desk in the office as a precaution also." My diary has an appointment in Westminster. Surely they can't get in there to watch me. I went in this morning and left by a different exit to come here." Bob realised he wasn't dealing with the average victim here. His behaviour and knowledge in the circumstances befitted a criminal more than a distraught father. He hoped that Montgomery's daughter had some of the grit and determination her father exuded today.

"Tell us about your daughter, Annie, sir." Bob said. "She is just short of her sixteenth birthday, about to finish school. She is five feet two, blond shoulder length hair and pretty..." then after a brief pause he added "and if he so much as touches her I'll rip his balls off....". "This will do no good." the chief said. Bob watched Montgomery; his demeanour was all wrong. After a brief pause the chief went on to say "Mr. Montgomery has given us some photographs of Annie and the techies will be in her social networking accounts as we speak, that may give us a clue. Her mobile phone was left behind so no way of tracking her. The only communication so far is this letter." "It's definitely her handwriting." Montgomery added. The chief continued "We have to wait for further instructions. We have no choice but to follow these instructions to the letter. We will ensure sufficient presence to apprehend the man or men during the collection and before he realises that the money isn't there." "You see that this happens Bernard." Montgomery said with what could have been seen as a slightly threatening manner. "But Mr. Montgomery, if the money isn't there then he'll never make the exchange and you won't get your daughter back unless we take her and that would be just too risky. You'll have to provide the cash. We'll get it back for you. My team is highly trained in this type of exercise" said No-brainer. Montgomery looked at him saying nothing. It seemed to Bob that the money was more important to him than Annie was. None of this quite added up.

Bob photographed and scanned the letter and then sent it off to forensics to see if there was anything on there. Annie's toothbrush and hairbrush were already with them for DNA comparison. Montgomery had confirmed the writing was indeed Annie's, but they would get that checked out also to be absolutely sure. There was what looked to be a tiny bloodstain on there as well. They also had to consider that Annie may already be dead. Bob knew that this week would be anything but quiet. At least the heat was off on his previous case and he could park it for now. He knew that that would inevitably come back after or during this case. Something to look forward to....

CHAPTER 21

The second interview seemed to go very well. Bruce asked his stock questions and came away feeling positive that his skills could be put to good use here and that there were possibilities for a career beyond this first project. Most of the talk had been about Bruce, his past experiences and in particular the last couple of projects he had worked on. One was overseeing the construction of a new baggage handling section of Terminal 5 at Heathrow. Bruce had worked from the planning stages through to the go live which had gone extremely well. When the project went live had stayed on for eight weeks to help with snagging. He had even said he was confident of a role in the next phase of Heathrow's expansions when the plans were passed. They discussed how the new system differed from previous ones, the new security features, how individual items of baggage could be checked within the system and the procedures for auditing the throughput for future reference; such as checking the movements of terror suspects. This project had taken over three years from start to finish and Bruce had lived and breathed it. To his surprise, his passion was still there as he discussed the finer points of the design. He was aware of the non-disclosure agreements had had had to sign at the start of that project, but he felt sure he hadn't said anything that could cause him any problems. Besides the project was completed now and this was a job interview and he had to show off his past achievements.

The previous project was a little more mundane, an extension to the manufacturing site of a large, global pharmaceutical company. The company in question had acquired another, smaller company and required additional manufacturing capability wishing to put in three new lines. This was an interesting project as, during the construction of the extension, the existing production line had to continue to run 24/7. This had posed many challenges and the project took two years to complete. Longer than if it had been done from scratch but amazingly quickly given the constraints laid on him. Bruce went into great detail about the many standards and requirements for that particular industry and how they had built the extension with the provision to remove the wall separating the old and new as a type of go live over the planned three days go live phase. This was the only down time required and exceeded the company's initial brief of a minimum of seven days. Much of it was done at night. During these three days, they also performed maintenance on the old lines which had to be done at some point offering additional wins for Bruce and his team. A full hour had passed whilst Bruce waxed lyrical about these two projects, their challenges, how he got them both delivered on time and under budget and how he felt his current remuneration fell short of what he considered fair for his achievements to date.

In the room with him were the company CEO and the Programme Director to whom the new role would be reporting. Bruce felt confident he had ticked all the boxes that were required of him. Unfortunately, he had no idea how many other candidates were in the frame for this role. However, he hadn't bumped into anyone else leaving before him or waiting as he left previously. There was no visitors book to casually glance through. Ultimately the company was owned by Russians so for all he knew there may be one or two top Russians in line for this role and he was there to make up the numbers. If that was indeed the case, then Bruce could do diddly squat about it so he let the thought go as he had taught himself to do in the past. After all, why would they sit here for over an hour listening to him if he was just there for effect? They wouldn't even have interviewed him twice if that were indeed the case. Focus on the things within your control and don't dwell on those outside of your control he reminded himself.

By the time he left he had overrun his slot by nearly thirty minutes. None of the team had left – so overall a good sign he hoped. No one else was waiting outside indicating that there was no other interview immediately after his as was often the case. They had given him the additional time willingly and had shown none of the classic tell-tale signs of wanting to be out of there. All he could do now was wait. He reiterated that he was available immediately as they shook hands and he was shown out. As he walked back to his car, he was quietly confident that this wouldn't be his last visit to this office. That said, he'd been in this position before and been disappointed. Take nothing for granted. I need a beer he thought.

CHAPTER 22

She was listening to the quiet rumble of traffic overhead. She was trying to analyse the patterns of sound to indicate busy periods. To her it seemed busy all day long. Her thoughts went away when the trap door made a loud noise once again and light came flooding down; it awakened her from her slumbering thoughts. She must have fallen asleep again at some point. At least she wasn't wasting her energies and she was at least making plans of sort. Nodding off was hardly surprising given there was nothing for her to actually do in this pitch-black hole except worry and sleep and plan. She squinted trying to quickly do another pass of her prison to see what she could see that she hadn't seen before. She spotted a glint over his head, on the ceiling by the trap door and far out of her reach. The glint had a cataract kind of effect – not one glint but several in a circle. This configuration rang a faint bell somewhere in the back of her mind. She knew she'd seen this before but couldn't for the life of her remember where. Tiny dots forming a small-ish circle, pointing at her. Then it dawned on her. It was a CCTC camera, one equipped with infra-red night vision, that is what the circle of dots was. It must be triggered by motion. She assumed he could only watch it whilst he was upstairs, assuming he was alone in this which, so far, seemed to be the case. She wondered if he was recording everything, so he could go back and review it at his leisure, or if he had an app on his phone so he could watch her 24/7 regardless of where he was. If he did then maybe someone else would catch a glimpse and report him to the authorities, or it could be used in evidence. Fat chance. He didn't look much like a techy anyway, more like a manual worker than a brainbox. That said, building this prison had taken some brains, but was it him that had built it? Was there someone else that she hadn't come into contact with yet? Was he just following orders? That was a worrying thought. She didn't believe for one minute that her captor was stupid, just not a complete techy geek. The more she thought about this man the more confused she became.

The more Devizes had thought about Annie the more confused he became. Once again, he approached the bed with a bottle of energy drink and a sandwich. This time he brought biscuits too. Was this a sign that he wasn't actually a sociopath and that he didn't intend to hurt her unless he had to? Was he working alone or was he part of some team or organisation? From what she'd seen so far, she thought it more likely that he was working alone. Her ears had become more adjusted to the low sound levels and she was now quite good at listening to the movements upstairs. She didn't think she'd heard anyone else up there moving around except him, but she couldn't be certain. He had nothing to gain from hurting her – all he wanted was the money. Her biggest problem remained the same in her mind's eye – and it wasn't this man, it was her father. If he refused to pay, or went to the authorities, then what would happen? Her value would diminish to zero, unless she continued to satisfy this man. She could only wait and see what happened over the next couple of days. She considered broaching the subject with her captor but what possible use could it be? If he was a ruthless killer, then if he didn't get what he wanted he'd likely kill her. He wouldn't let her go as she had information about him from her time in the prison cell. She had to keep him onside and hope he wasn't a sociopath or psychopath and try and build a relationship with him. That way he'd be less likely to harm her or kill her. Only she had never really built a relationship with anyone before. The pressure was building up inside her head.

The silence seemed to last a full minute. Before she knew what she was doing she blurted the words out: "What if he doesn't pay up?" She felt tears welling up in her eyes once again but this time she couldn't hold them back. She wanted tears, so the kidnapper would maybe feel a little sorry for her, surely this would build on their relationship. The man just looked at her. This thought obviously took him by surprise. He waited for a few seconds and then said, "Don't worry, he'll pay up." His London accent didn't seem as strong as he said these words. Maybe the accent wasn't genuine. If this was indeed the case, then she'd rattled him with her question. What had she done?

After a few seconds the man then left in the usual way leaving her once again in total darkness, crying. The tears stopped as the trap door shut, and the darkness once again overwhelmed her. She rubbed her eyes to make them appear red. She decided to do this periodically to give the appearance of being a teary girl with no hope. That said, at this point in time she had no hope. Her only hope was to try and get to her captor. What if her father refuses to pay and goes to the authorities, she thought? She knew her father better than anyone alive and she knew that was exactly what he would do. The only saving grace was that he would be careful and take precautions so that no one would know that he'd gone to the police. His position gave him influence so he'd be able to go to the top, he wouldn't have to queue up with the piss heads and druggies at the main desk. He was probably there now discussing tactics with them in his 'know it all', arrogant way, pissing off the detectives like he pissed off everyone else. I'm fucked she thought to herself. I'm fucked. I need a way out of this without his help or money. She took a bite from her sandwich.

Devizes had locked the hatch and gone back to his computer. The tracker he had set up on Montgomery's mobile phone showed him in his office. Strangely he hadn't moved in or out of the office all morning. From his research he knew his office in this building afforded GPS reception as he'd seen movement before. "The bastard has left his phone on his desk." Thought Devizes. He knew what that most likely meant - he had gone somewhere and didn't want to be traced. The police? He thought back to Annie's tears when she asked him what would happen if he didn't pay. She knew. The thought of being incarcerated and raped hadn't broken her, it was the thought of her father refusing to pay the ransom that eventually brought her to tears. Devizes had been sure he'd pay. They always pay. He had deliberately not been greedy with his demands. He knew Montgomery could raise the money easily and quickly. After a few moments he decided to return to Annie whilst she was at a low and see what further use she could be to him. He didn't want to kill her. Part of him considered keeping her there for his pleasure but he knew he wouldn't be sticking around for too long. For now, he had to think quickly.

After a few more minutes he had decided upon a plan and without wasting any more time returned to the cellar. Annie looked surprised to see him again so soon. She almost looked pleased to see him. He could tell that she had only just stopped crying from her red eyes. Even without makeup and having been subjected to her ordeal she was still beautiful. She wasn't as strong and ebullient as when she had first arrived. "What did you mean when you said he wouldn't pay up?" he said getting straight to the point. Annie looked at him for a few seconds. She hadn't had sufficient time to plan a detailed response to this question. After a few seconds pause to feign further grief she replied "You obviously don't know my father, do you? Have you ever actually met him?" she asked. There was a pregnant pause as he considered how best to answer this question. But the delay answered it for him. Before he had time to come up with a suitable reply that didn't give her any insight into him, she spoke again. "If you had met him, or had any sort of dealings with him, you'd know that he is utterly ruthless. He would never submit to anyone's demands, least of all where money is concerned. That's all he cares about. Not my mother and certainly not me. He'll be sat with the police now discussing how to take you out. You've picked the wrong guy to fuck with Mr. whoever you are. He won't pay a penny. Not now not ever. I should know. It'll take more than just me to get anything out of that bastard." Then silence. Her expression grim and devoid of hope.

He could tell from the tone of her voice there was deep bitterness and resentment there and little love lost between her and her father. From what he'd seen he'd go as far as to say she hated her father. From his research, he knew she had few friends and probably no close friends. She wasn't big on social media, didn't party, she didn't even go out. Just went to school and came home. What if Montgomery was a cruel bastard who cared only for money not even for his daughter. He knew he would have to seriously consider resorting to Plan B and use his knowledge of her father's habits to strengthen his case for the cash. If money and indeed his reputation were all he cared about then this route would hit him where it hurt the most but indirectly. "Did you know your father regularly uses rent boys?" Devizes asked. He was looking directly intro Annie's eyes – he knew he'd get his answer not from her mouth but from her eyes. She just stared at him with those red eyes. Devizes thought for a moment then said "I'll get him to pay alright. Even if he won't cough up for your safe release, then he'll sure cough up to protect his reputation since without that he's nobody. No reputation, no more diplomatic work, no more money." Devizes said. He realised from the tone of his voice that he was letting his growing dislike for the man show in his demeanour.

"Let me help you" she said "in return for enough money to get the fuck out of this hateful country and make a new life somewhere else. No one hates him like I do. Make him think I'm dead because of him. Let him stew for the rest of his days.

That'll put a dent into his reputation. Add to it a press hate campaign about his affairs and no one will ever deal with him again." He was taken aback both by her hatred for her father and the apparent hatred of her whole life and desire to escape it. This girl was sharp for sure but surely, she was executing a plan to simply get out of this situation without relying on her father. She had had plenty of time to think up this story whilst sitting there in the dark. But nevertheless, he thought he saw real desire in her expression. Her hatred looked very, very real. He knew from researching her background that she had never taken any acting or drama classes. In fact, he had decided that she had poor social skills. Coupled with the fact that she hadn't tried to escape or even to shout. They always tried screaming and shouting from the off. They only stopped when they realised it was futile. Even the movies got this part right. It was almost like she preferred it here with him in this rotten cell than living her life in her little house under her father's wing. It could be an elaborate act, but he didn't think so. "I take it you have evidence of him with rent boys then?" She said. Her tone was more as his manager than his captive.

She sat there looking at him. Her eyes were no longer as red and they'd adjusted to the light. After a minute or two of thought he said "So how do we fake your death then? It would have to be so tidy there was no evidence to suggest you were alive but lots of reason to believe you were dead. And why the fuck would I entertain such an idea?" he said. Annie replied, "A bomb." You send him your evidence, get him to raise the cash and make the drop. Then when he goes to the place you've arranged for him to collect me, we'll blow the whole place to smithereens. You see the one thing I have studied; not at school but at home, is explosives. I've already been research- ing this idea; blowing my house up with him in it, faking my death and going abroad but I'd never managed to figure out how to get enough money from him to make it happen. I'd only need 50k. We could work together, whoever you are, and nail the bastard. You take the rest. That way I'll disappear and there will never be a witness or supporting evidence to convict you even if they ever do manage to work out your identity as I'll be dead. Most of all I won't want to be found. You could stick with me for the first few days 'til it's all blown over. We both win that way."

It was some speech and surely not a rehearsed one. Devizes' head was spinning. What she said actually made some sense. But how would they explain her being blown up? They'd need a body. And DNA could be used to identify even small body parts. Most of all it didn't fit in with the plan. He could string her along then blow her up too, but she wasn't stupid. And he liked her. he liked the thought of spending a few more days with her.

They sat in silence. He thought for a few minutes then decided to test her. "How about we plant the bomb as you said but as well as faking your death, we blow him up. They'll have bits of him for miles around. Same DNA. They'll assume you went up too – absolutely no reason not to. Will you see him dead in return for your new life Annie Montgomery?" "Fuck yes." She replied without hesitation. Her face was radiant, but with a nasty grin, the same expression he'd seen on other murderers both immediately before and after a killing. He could feel an erection coming on. He undid his belt and started to remove his trousers. By the time he had removed them Annie was also naked. This time it seemed consensual. It was a very long time since Devizes had had consensual sex. And he was surprised to find how much he liked it, even better than usual.

CHAPTER 23

Devizes decided he would go along with Annie but only as a plan B, should things stray from his instructions for planning the drop, such as a refusal to cooperate with him, but he didn't tell Annie that. At the end of the day, all he wanted was the money and he wasn't keen on sharing it. Maybe he should up the ante in the event of having to go to plan B – 500k? He had temporarily provided Annie with a small desk and lamp and a pad and pen. She had made a list of the chemicals and quantities she would need to make the bomb and where to get them from without being easily traced back to him. He then retuned upstairs and went out towards Manchester looking for an internet café or anywhere with a public computer he could use that didn't look like it had CCTV. It didn't take him long to find one. He knew that in the event of his name coming up later in their subsequent enquiry they'd look at his internet browser history. Here he was close to Manchester city centre in a seedy looking internet bar full of students. They were all ages. He'd dressed so he would blend in as far as possible. He took a PC facing the wall, so no one would look over his shoulder. In fifteen minutes, he had both confirmed everything Annie had said about the construction of the bomb and found where he could purchase the stuff he needed. None of it was particularly expensive. The problem was getting the stuff in an untraceable manner. He liked the idea of making bombs, another useful thing for his repertoire. But how could he hide this bomb and deflect the blame?

He briefly considered a gas leak. This was too risky though.

He'd need accurate timing to within seconds. Montgomery would have to be at the exact exchange point, thinking he was going to collect Annie or, if it came to it, the evidence of his activities. To do this he'd need to leak sufficient gas beforehand and ignite it without leaving a trace. He knew a bomb was the only way. A controlled, remotely activated detonation. Annie had indeed gotten this part right.

As he browsed, he came across an article on the BBC web site. Four men had been caught and jailed after planning to make homemade bombs and blow up an army base. It came to him in a flash.

The best way to deflect this explosion was to make it look like a terrorist attack. They happened all the time. He could build it into a terrorist plot but involving several explosions so as not to directly focus on the kidnapping exchange location. The anti-terrorism squad would then take over the case and, assuming he'd planned it properly, all their enquiries into radicalised Muslims and other groups would draw a complete blank. He wouldn't even be on the radar. If he so wished, he could effectively set up a group by claiming responsibility for the bombings in their name. He was liking this plan, but he didn't yet know how far her hatred went. Was it just her father she hated or was it bigger? He could take no risks. He still had to decide whether letting her go after all this was a good idea. She'd know too much. That said, she would be complicit, and she too would face the ordeal of trial. Her father wouldn't help her, so she could well end up serving life. But the thought of killing her was now becoming an issue for him. He liked her. He had never met a woman like her. Even though she was young she had a much more mature outlook. Maybe her unhappy life had hardened her. She wasn't unduly emotional unlike most of the women he'd known, however briefly. In his periods of youth detention, he had been told he had a low EQ. They had to explain this to him. EQ is Emotional Quotient –

nothing to do with intelligence, but having a lack of empathy for others. Not quite a sociopath but nowhere near what they deemed a normal person to be. That was why he believed he could never have a normal relationship with a woman, a normal woman that is. Those he referred to as friends at school were either those he relentlessly bullied or the drug dealers or runners who occasionally asked him to run errands. Maybe he and Annie were more alike than he ever thought. He needed to focus on his plan B as it became more and more apparent that Plan A wasn't as sure-fire as he had thought.

Devizes decided to go along with Annie's plan as his new plan B and make a bomb with which to blow up her father. Whether or not she was to go up with it too he hadn't yet decided. This could be done during the exchange. He hoped he could avoid this and keep her for himself with her being fully implicated, but this didn't fit in with her current plans and these were her only driver at the moment – getting away and starting a new life. But could they share this new life? At least whilst the dust settled on this and she was declared dead. If it turned sour, he'd dispatch her.

He continued to build on his plan B. Making these bombs wasn't half as tricky as he had thought it would be. It opened up new doors and new opportunities to make money and cause havoc in the future. The problem he was pondering over was that a single, isolated terrorist bomb just where the drop was planned would strike the police, assuming they were involved, as highly suspicious. To be deemed a terrorist action, where they were just in the wrong place at the wrong time, required a bigger plan – a bigger terrorist plot. Something so big it couldn't possibly be related to the drop. Something so big that it would take all the coppers off on a wild goose chase for months.

After deep consideration he had come up with a new plan.

A bigger plan, much bigger, in a different league. He had decided that he wouldn't make just the one bomb. He would make five and detonate them remotely at strategic places. He hadn't decided yet upon where these locations would be, apart from the fact that they would be sited so as to disrupt travel. He wanted to create terror and panic and prevent the authorities from getting to the sites quickly so as to allow himself the best escape route. He would flee the country using a boat whilst the rail and road network was gridlocked, and the country gripped in the latest terror threat. He may even take Annie with him. The attacks would dominate the news as well leaving no space for a kidnapping gone wrong. He had used fishing boats before to get across to France. From there he could go on to just about anywhere. And there were several airports within a few hours' drive. In the past he had hitched anonymously and without trace. The primary location from where he would activate the devices would have to be close enough to his destination port so as the confusion caused didn't affect his own journey to the boat or the boat itself. Speed would be of the essence. He would ensure that other targets were more significant than this one thus attracting more of the initial efforts into tracking those behind this series of explosions. They would also happen earlier setting the scene and creating the illusion. He was liking this plan. He felt sure it could offer other financial opportunities – he just had to figure out how, and if he wanted to do this or keep things simple involving no one else. The fewer people involved the less the chance of getting caught. The ransom money would be enough, he knew this. Lots of people had gone down for being greedy and there was no way he was going back to prison – any prison.

After a while, Devizes thoughts drifted back to his previous exploits. When he was sat quietly in the back of a truck, or in a wagon, after hitching a ride, he would often wonder what would happen if, for example, one of the many bridges at Spaghetti junction collapsed. Then no one would be going anywhere for a long while – possibly days. He'd seen bridges collapse on the news from natural disasters or cutting corners in construction and maintenance. Say the highest one, falling onto the traffic below and damaging or destroying lower levels of the junction crushing vehicles and people in its path. This would effectively gridlock the surrounding area making it extremely difficult for the emergency services to access the area. The queues would be miles long in no time. Within minutes there would be traffic backed up across all lanes of the incoming roads.

What if he planned several such targets, one being where Montgomery would collect Annie? All he had to do with hand over Annie, collect the cash, then attack, stun or kill Montgomery, then place him in the chosen spot and detonate the bomb. He could plan all five bombs to go off at a similar time. The whole country would make the assumption it was terrorists. He would get his cash and a whole lot of kicks from completely fucking up all those bastards in cars who had driven past him on those wet days and nights that he walked along the side of the road or loitered in service stations badly needing a ride. If Montgomery hadn't involved the police, then he would simply be missing. If they traced his whereabouts, they'd assume he was just one more innocent victim of the atrocities. He liked this idea. They would soon blame a terror group, under immense pressure to identify who was behind the events, and the public would believe everything they heard on TV or read in the papers as always. No doubt some group or organisation somewhere would claim the credit anyway? Montgomery would be collateral damage – simply in the wrong place at the wrong time. They may or may not identify his remains. His kidnapping ploy would be forgotten, and if he had involved the police then his case would fall down at the bottom of the police's priority list – possibly even erased with the premature demise of those parties involved. His mind was now set. The next chapter of his life was coming into shape. The only piece that still didn't quite fit was down in his make-shift cell. But this was the prettiest piece.

CHAPTER 24

He set about acquiring the materials he needed. Enough to make at least five bombs that were each powerful enough to do some serious damage to a road or bridge. If he picked the right locations, the weakest areas of a given location, then he wouldn't need the device to be quite as large making it easier to build, transport and carry whilst he remained unseen or unnoticed. He would target quite a large area and include at least one London target as that would create the most attention from the media and police whilst he made his exit far away. Montgomery would be elsewhere, and his end would come not as the first event but maybe the second or third. He would plant the devices over a couple of days, so he could return to Annie each evening to feed and water her. He didn't have much time. He would use a simple detonator linked to a mobile phone. Call that number and boom. He would purchase five sim cards – unregistered and untraceable to him and from different shops in different areas. He would need to ensure a good service at the locations, so he purchased five Vodafone and five Three SIM cards. He knew that would reduce the chances of no signal – he could ascertain which offered the best service at each location. It was important to time the bombs precisely so that the one taking out Montgomery was in a timing sequence consistent with the others thus adding to the illusion that the bombings were a single orchestrated terrorist action, him being in the wrong place at the wrong time, whatever he was up to.

Annie's cellar provided sufficient room to manufacture the

devices. They were built into a wheeled suitcase. Annie assisted. He had stolen several of these over the years and kept them in the loft for just such an occasion. He managed to lay his hands on four and proceeded to steal a fifth in his usual, casual, style later that day.

Annie gave him instructions on how to construct the devices and he double checked them at a different internet café in a different area to be sure she wasn't trying any tricks. He chose a predominantly Muslim area this time just in case his browsing was identified. He had done this for every aspect of his project, even down to purchasing the SIM cards. He made a small device first and took it with him onto Saddleworth Moor where he found a very quiet, secluded place within the wilderness. He wondered if Myra Hindley and Ian Brady had walked this very same route in their search for a quiet, secluded area. He set the bomb close to some large rocks and stood well back. Even though his test device was somewhat smaller than his final devices, the explosion was far larger and far more devastating than he had ever expected. At first, he panicked that a passing motorist on the other side of the hill would see the smoke or hear the sound, but no one came. It was a good job as he would have had great trouble explaining what had happened, and he didn't want to have to silence someone in such an unplanned way, even though the location leant itself very well to concealing the body afterwards. But then he'd have a vehicle to dispose of and unnecessary complications. It was unplanned events like that that often lead to the mistake that subsequently lead to capture. He also didn't want to be carted away by some copper only to leave Annie to rot in her cell. He realised he was becoming somewhat attached to her. He both liked this and hated himself for it at the same time. He would need to make doubly sure that this didn't lead him to making any fatal mistakes.

He quickly dug a hole about two feet deep in order to bury all the remains of the bomb that he could find. The bag was in charred pieces. He found what he thought was most of it and buried them and the remains of the bag in the hole, being careful not to touch anything. It had started to rain. Soon most of the remaining signs would have washed away leaving little trace of his trial run. Mind you, the remains of a small bomb were the last thing anyone would expect to find up here. And let's face it, it was so remote that it could be years before anyone passed through this area. He was pleased with his trial and was confident that he could put his plan into action starting tomorrow. The devices currently being constructed were much larger and would be placed in strategic places. Even if a couple of them didn't create the devastation he hoped for, the effect would be the same as far as his plans went.

He'd not been in any trouble in this country for over five years now. A reformed man who had seen the error of his ways and made a modest living renting terraced houses to young families. He would do no more testing. He was confident both from his own experiences and from what Annie and the internet had taught him that the cases he had acquired would be able to house enough materials to wreak sufficient destruction on his targets that his plan would be a success. If he could cause mayhem that lasted 24 hours, that would be enough to ensure his disappearance, though he suspected the mayhem would last much longer than that. Annie had seemed invigorated by the plans for the bomb and for victory over her father. She urged him to select the largest bag for him to ensure he was totally blown apart with no risk of survival. She didn't as yet know what the other bombs were to be used for, so he agreed to her request. He said the other four bombs were part of the plan too but didn't elaborate. She had considered the ramifications of more than one bomb but had thought maybe they were there to cause a distraction and maybe afford a better getaway, or as a failsafe should the first one fail to go off. Just so long as one of them didn't have her name on it.

After consulting an old map, he selected his intended targets. The Hangar Lane gyratory was to be his London target. That was gridlocked most of the time anyway and he hated it with a passion, and he hated the drivers that cut him up every time he tried to navigate it. Both Western Avenue and the North Circular would be badly affected, stopping the flow of traffic in and out of London from the West. All other routes including the M25 and M4 would soon be at gridlock and all London would suffer to some extent. It was also easily accessible without having to travel through the city centre. He took the first completed bag bomb and now he looked into how best to plant it. After consulting several other maps he had collected, he decided that the sewers would be a good place. He'd used sewers before, so he was familiar with navigating them and gaining access.

That evening he went about setting the first target. He planted his bomb in a large sewer drain adjacent to the road. He had to do this in the early hours of the morning due to the amount of people and traffic. He stood there like a tourist for nearly thirty minutes before his opportunity arose. He donned a high vis jacket to look like a workman and lifted the grid and placed the black bag inside. As with the other devices, he used an old-style Nokia phone handset whose battery would last several days. He had tested all five handsets in the past and knew that from this full charge they would last four days minimum. That was more than he needed. He also set up a call bar whereby only one number would cause the handset to ring. The last thing he wanted was a PPI call centre operative triggering his device at peak time in the morning.... the "Our records show that you have been involved in an accident that wasn't your fault....". Maybe he should find out where those calls came from and blow them up as well – do everyone a service.

He walked the half mile back to his car and then drove West

to his second location – the junction of the M4 and the A4 by Heathrow airport. Although quite close to his first location, there was nothing like airport issues to flood the UK press and that of every other country trying to fly into and out of his least favourite airport, especially amidst the animosity towards the plans to extend the airport again. This was an easier spot as he had found a location right beneath the junction, close to one of the supporting pillars. He hoped to collapse the junction effecting closure and lengthy repair times thus ensuring media coverage for days or weeks to come. Things were going well so far.

He then went North up the M25, onto the M40 and all the way up to the Gravely Hill Interchange, otherwise known as Spaghetti Junction. He wanted to damage the uppermost section of road, but this proved to be very difficult to choose a suitable location to adequately conceal the bag so had chosen a concrete pillar holding up the carriageway of the M6 in the hope that it would collapse part of it onto the roads beneath. He wasn't intent on killing the great British public but, that said, the number of casualties didn't really bother him. His plan would revolve, not around minimising collateral damage, but on minimising the chances of Montgomery escaping with his life or his money, and maximise his own chances of effecting an escape under the radar, cash in hand.

The fourth location was to be where Montgomery would meet his maker. It was now 5am as he approached Warrington and his target, the Thelwall Viaduct. He parked his car in Lymm and walked back under the bridge. He had once more chosen the concrete pillar supporting the motorway but here there was an adjacent track accessible by car. He would do his exchange here ensuring that the car was blown up and the bridge tumbled on top of the wreckage. This part would require more planning so as to ensure his goals were fully met. You never know, would they assume he was driving over the bridge when the bomb went off? Not if he had already gone to the police as Annie had suggested. Still whether he had, or he hadn't, over or under, his demise would still be considered accidental as part of the terror plot. That was all that mattered. He could have been meeting a rent boy under the bridge for all they knew. I'm sure someone somewhere must have known something about his proclivities and there was a chance they'd put two and two together and get rent boy. If not, he could fill them in at some point. Still that wasn't so important right now.

He had decided to set six devices, not five as he had previously thought. He had enough materials to make six and he was enjoying his newfound talents. His fifth and sixth locations would have to wait until tomorrow though. He drove home, parked half a mile from the terraced house and called into the late shop for two breakfast sandwiches and a bottle of energy drink. He also added a half bottle of whisky. By the time he got into bed it was early evening. The traffic on his return was terrible as he ended up driving during peak time. He wondered how many of the motorists he had encountered that day would end up blown to bits?

He slept for 2 hours then awoke, his mind on the day ahead. Firstly, he went to Annie, gave her the sandwich and drink and emptied her bucket. He apologised for leaving her alone for so long. She didn't seem too worried. She seemed pleased to see that he hadn't abandoned her but by now she badly needed a shower. He had been considering this during his long drive back. It would give him an opportunity to test her intentions and see if she made any attempt to escape or steal anything to fashion into a weapon. As he had half expected, she asked if she could take a shower and if he could provide her with some clean clothes or wash the ones she had on. He blindfolded her and tied her legs loosely together, so she could shuffle but not run. He then led her naked upstairs to the bathroom. He shut the door and closed the blind before removing her blindfold. She got into the shower. He stood and watched her as she performed her ablutions. Occasionally she looked across at him and he was sure that he'd spotted a slight smile. She would now require some clean clothing. Devizes was prepared for this and had a change of clothing ready for her. He had taken some of her own clothes when he had abducted her, such was the extent of his planning. His time incarcerated meant he had gone over things time and time again, adding details and contingencies.

A pair of jeans, underwear and a couple of tee shirts. Enough to last her through her remaining days he had thought; he hadn't planned for more than three or four days. He had placed the clothes on the top by the sink. "Thanks for the change of clothes." She said as she spotted them. But as he was handing her the towel to dry off, she looked into his eyes and whispered, "Would you like to join me for being such a good boy?" He was somewhat taken aback. He wondered if she had been planning something. But what could she do? Five feet two inches, barely more than a girl, equipped with a bottle of shampoo and shower gel with her legs still partially tied together. Maybe it was a ruse to get the ropes tied to her ankles removed? He had intended to test her, and he would do just that. Without further ado he removed his clothes and warily entered the shower after her. She started off by giving his swelling best friend a good wash with lots of rubbing. He started to wash her delicate curves and her plump breasts. It was the first time he'd had a good look at them in the light. They were exquisite. Shiny with the shower gel and her nipples stuck out like two clothes pegs. She was obviously enjoying his company; he didn't think she would be able to fake this. He took her from behind and she made no kind of attempt to hurt him or to try to escape. He had locked the bathroom door and hidden the key when she first stepped into the shower just in case she tried to escape. He hadn't taken any sort of weapon in there in case she had got hold of it. Besides he shouldn't need any more than his fists to remedy any unplanned alteration. But there wasn't one. He took with him some brown hair colouring because she was worth it. They applied the colouring then rinsed it through. Being a brunette suited her. If they were spotted during the drop he didn't want anyone recognising her in the event of Montgomery going to the police and the thing being made public, not that he expected that to happen for a minute. But you had to plan for every contingency. He left the shower first and quickly dried and dressed. Annie then dried herself and put on the clean clothes he had left for her. When they were both dry and dressed, she waited whilst he blindfolded her once again and took her back to her room. This time he didn't tie her ankles, but he was nonetheless very wary as he guided her back to the cellar. It appeared that she had passed his test. She made no attempt to escape, look at her surroundings or make any noise. She did as he had asked. Or told her, as the case may be.

After they had returned to Annie's room he said, "I'm going to plant the bomb today." "Where will it be?" she asked. He had decided to tell her, as she would, after all, be going with him. "It'll be on a quiet track under a bridge where few people will venture late at night." he answered. "Have you made the bomb big enough to blow his bollocks all the way to London?" she asked with fire in her eyes. Those black eyes had returned. He couldn't decide whether this Annie was more desirable than the Annie from the shower. The deep brown seemed to have been replaced by pools of black nothingness – the eyes of a killer as he had previously observed. "Yes, you have no worries on that score." he said. "Have you thought about what happens to me?" she asked. He had thought of little else between planting his bombs whilst driving up and down the motorway. "Once he's dead I'm working on a way of getting us both out of the country. It'll take a few days, but we'll be long gone and untraceable. It'll mean you spending a lot of time with me. Can I trust you?" he asked. She looked into his eyes saying nothing. After a few seconds he continued "If they knew about your kidnapping, they'll assume you were blown to bits with your father. But before we do that, I need to know categorically that you are not going to try anything. You know I'll kill you if you try anything. If you behave exactly as I tell you, you know you'll get what you've always wanted – it's the only way. So, I'll ask you once again, for the last time, are you sure this is the way you want it?". "I'm sure. I won't try anything. Besides I'm complicit now. When he's dead I'll be virtually penniless, so I'll need the money we agreed on." was her reply. In his mind he hadn't agreed to anything, but he said nothing. Her father had made a point of telling her that she had to earn her own fortune as everything he left would go to his club. Her place was in his name so in effect she only owned the things inside her flat – clothes and a few furnishings. Nothing worth going back for to sell. He wanted to preserve his image even after death at the expense of his daughter's welfare. Devizes believed her. He almost felt sorry for her. But he was looking forward to spending more time with her during their journey. "You need to understand Annie that I won't hesitate to kill you if you put a single foot wrong. And even if you did escape, I've got enough evidence that you planned this kidnap yourself and I'd ensure you ended up in jail, penniless." She nodded. If she caused him any trouble, he'd dispatch her, however much it irked him to do so. He certainly wouldn't be letting her go even if Montgomery paid up with great compliance.

He returned upstairs, locked the hatch and collected his things then walked back to the car. He checked that the two remaining holdalls were still in the boot. Maybe it was a risky manoeuvre leaving them there in the car, but he thought it was better this way than carrying them or taking his car back to the house where each visit made it more conspicuous and memorable to any nosy neighbour. These terraced streets were full of nosy neighbours who didn't work, just sat by the window. None of his closest neighbours were like this – they were out most of the day working. These old terraced houses tended to be popular with young families and older people or couples. Nosy neighbours, quick to offer words of admonishment when the music was loud, or when the bin wasn't put back in, abounded in the back streets of Northern towns like this. He'd never put a bin out in his life. He disposed of his waste in other places.

He drove up the M61 and onto the M6 and eventually onto the M74. He kept to 75 miles per hour as he didn't want to be clocked by a camera van on one of the bridges or stopped and searched by some sweaty sock. He couldn't help but smile at the thought of wreaking some havoc on the Jocks. He had spent time up in Scotland and knew the West coast very well. There had been on-going work on the Erskine bridge which went over the river Clyde then up to Dumbarton and the Highlands. He drove over the bridge and parked on the other side at Bowling where he couldn't see any CCTV. He walked back and along the bridge with the holdall to where the workmen had been working. He donned his high vis jacket and climbed through their barrier and onto the gangway type area which gave access to underneath the bridge. This was where the workers gained access to effect the repairs. He hung the bag beneath the carriageway as far in as he could reach. It was about a quarter of the way in on the Northbound section. He placed it securely on the under hang where it would remain dry and clear of the strong prevailing wind and unnoticeable. He didn't want it to drop into the water below and cause the phone to die. An unexploded bomb would give the police something to go on and he wanted to leave as little evidence as possible. From what he could see there were no ongoing works so no reason to expect workers down here any time soon. Still he didn't want it to be obvious.

He climbed back up after quickly checking there were no runners, cyclists, jumpers or vehicles nearby. He proceeded to walk back along the footpath, stowing his high vis jacket, back to Bowling where he had parked. He had enjoyed the walk and it reminded him of a girl he had known a few years back that had lived in Balloch. He then drove down the A82 towards Glasgow to his final destruction destination – the Clyde Tunnel. It had been built after the war to relieve the traffic heading North of Glasgow and up the West coast. Even then the roads could be very busy and this new route afforded much more bandwidth for the traffic. If he damaged the bridge it would bring untold havoc on Glasgow and all points North and West as the M8 was already beyond capacity. He parked about half a mile from the entrance and put on his high visibility jacket and trousers. Nobody looked twice at a workman around there – they were everywhere. They never removed their jackets when they went to or from work or to the shop for lunch. He had also considered the Kingston bridge as a potential target, but it had proved less easy to gain access and would have made his day even longer. He waited until no cars were coming and ran down the narrow path beside the traffic lane. After a few seconds he came to the point where workmen could get away from the road. He went in and searched for a suitable place to conceal the bag. He didn't honestly have any idea how much explosives would be required to cause enough damage to force the closure of the tunnel but either way the tunnel would indeed be shut for at least a day, or possibly much longer, whilst they sifted for evidence and the like. He suspected that, by the time this device went off, the authorities would close and seal all the sites in order to look for clues to the offending terrorists. They may even suspect further bombs and close off other key places as a precautionary measure if they had the resources.

With the bag hidden out of sight he got out one of the mobile phones and verified that he still had a signal. It was only one bar but it was a signal. That would be enough. The bag was well-hidden, and no one would expect a bomb here after the Erskine bridge attack. Even if the signal was intermittent, he could keep trying until he established contact and triggered the device. The timing of this one wasn't critical to his plans. He packed his things into his pockets and peered out. After the cars had gone, he ran back up the path and out of the tunnel and across to his parked car. This part of the plan was complete. All the bags were now in position. Now all that remained to be done was to orchestrate the drop and lure the target, and his cash, to the drop off point.

It was evening by the time he got back into the house and locked the doors securely ensuring no one got in or out without him knowing. Again, he had collected sandwiches for himself and Annie, plus some pork pies. He also picked up a bottle of red wine and some beers. He didn't know what Annie liked to drink but thought she'd be OK with one or t'other, plus he had some whisky left, but he doubted she was a whisky drinker. That said, she'd surprised him on a number of accounts thus far. He could see that both the cars belonging to his next-door neighbours' houses were gone. By now he had learned their movements. Both occupiers worked nights and had left for their shifts. To the best of his knowledge both were middle aged and single. If Annie made a noise, he was confident that no one would hear unless someone was stood outside his front door. He went down to Annie. "As you've been a good girl, I'm going to let you go upstairs and eat with me." He said. She looked up at him and seemed a little pleased. "I look a mess." she said then suddenly realised how ridiculous that was given the circumstances. She was with her kidnapper not her intended. She smiled and looked down. "What can I call you?" she said. "Dom. Just Dom." he answered. "OK, Dom, take me upstairs." And that's exactly what he did. Right up to the bedroom where they made love in the clean sheets. No shackles or rope so she was free to move her legs wherever she pleased, and she did. He'd taken precautions regarding security just in case she made a run for it. Afterwards they lay side by side for few moments then they both quickly showered together and then went down to the kitchen and ate the sandwiches, pies and shared the red wine. Devizes was careful not to consume too much alcohol as to cloud his senses – she may still be planning something. He still had to be on his guard. After two glasses however, Annie became a little tipsy. He wondered how much drinking experience she had had in her short, unexciting lifetime with few friends. He now knew what he represented to her. Something exciting, something that made her alive, a bit of rough and possibly her first 'boyfriend'. Funny how things turn out. In a world without love, this tainted love could be seen as a shining light. He represented her escape from her old life and her father. She made no attempt whatsoever to try to escape, break a window or even shout. She didn't seem to pay any attention to her surroundings at all. Her eyes and attention were firmly on him. Either it was a good act, or the coming days were going to be a lot more enjoyable than he had ever thought.

He let her sleep in his bed that night. He had already taken the precaution of locking the front and back doors and removing the keys as was his practise, and also locking the bedroom door and hiding the key. He was a very light sleeper; this was something that came with the territory for him. His ability to wake up as though he had never been asleep and get the better of an attacker had saved his life on more than one occasion thus far, although being honest he didn't think was likely to happen to him again any time soon. He was very aware that he was beginning to let his defences down with Annie. He liked her; he liked her a lot. She was different to all the other girls or women he had known. She was more like him than he had ever imagined. Funny how life throws up this kind of thing at you just when you least expect it. Nevertheless, he had to keep in his mind that this may be part of a ruse on her part to get close to him in order to avoid him hurting or killing her. He had to remain sufficiently detached that, in the event of having to act, he could do so quickly and clinically, without any second thoughts. So far, he had always managed to retain this ability.

Before they retired for the evening, they had planned the pick-up. Annie had written another note advising Montgomery that her captor suspected that he had gone to the police. As a precaution he included a couple of photographs showing Montgomery and his acquaintance of the other evening. Not proof in itself, but enough to show Montgomery that he had been watched, followed and that they knew his weaknesses. Enough for a media shitstorm and that was all it needed. Who knew what else they may have by means of evidence or to whom they may send them onto if he didn't comply? The note said that the drop had been set up. If he didn't attend the meeting point at the designated time with five hundred thousand pounds in cash tomorrow at 11.30pm sharp, **without any police,** then Annie would be tortured. He cut one of Annie's fingers slightly and smeared her blood onto the letter. He knew the police would DNA test this letter and find her DNA on both letters from the blood and touch. He also knew that it wouldn't come to this as this letter would never reach the eyes of the police, only Montgomery would ever see this letter. Even though he didn't care about his daughter's well-being, he did care about his own reputation. Dom knew he had him where he wanted him. It wasn't the recovery of his daughter that would force him to pay up but the salvation of his image, his job and his lifestyle. No photographic proof of her being alive was required. He had him by the short and curlies. Why hadn't he just done this to begin with instead or a risky kidnapping? Maybe he'd spent too much time in the planning.

He had put on a disguise and posted the letter with a first-class stamp at a box in Rusholme. He knew it would be de-

livered promptly by the postman at around 9.30am the following morning giving Montgomery adequate time to raise
the additional cash. That way the police wouldn't be present
when he discovered and read it. He had asked Montgomery
to visit a certain public telephone box and call another one
of his untraceable mobile phones to confirm he had received
the letter. Sure enough, at 9.45am the designated phone rang.
He recognised the number as the call box in question. He and
Annie stood side by side as Dom picked up the phone, putting
it on speaker phone. He didn't say anything. After a couple
of seconds Montgomery said "I have the letter, you fucking
bastard. He pronounced it 'Barstard' in his plummy accent.
He had developed this as a young man as part of his diplomatic training. This was where Dom played his trump card.
"Daddy?" Annie said in a weak feeble voice. "Daddy, he's cut
me, and he said he'll kill me tonight if you don't do as he says,
and he has showed me pictures of you, he's got prints in enve-
lopes waiting to be sent to your friends and colleagues. Please
do what he says, I don't want to die." Dom then rubbed his
hand on the phone to make the noises of a disturbance and
Annie screamed. He disconnected the call. The plan was set,
and the wheels were now in motion. He now set about collecting the passports he had ordered for Annie and himself; or
rather James and Charlotte Brooke. He'd picked Brooke, as in
Brooke Bond, James Bond. Tenuous but it tickled his fancy and
his ego. Annie went willingly down into the cellar but free of
shackles. She had passed her first major test. She'd acted her
part and hadn't tried to say anything other than what they'd
planned. He closed and locked the entrance, replaced the run-
ner and, for peace of mind, moved the heavy table on top of
the entrance. As always, he carefully noted its position so he
could check if it had moved when he returned in a couple of
hours, even though moving it would be impossible.

He went out, this time on foot. He walked for just over a
mile to one of the local boozers. Jimmy was sitting at a table

in the corner, facing the door as was his habit. He waved his half empty glass at Devizes as he entered, and Devizes went to the bar, bought two pints and went to sit opposite Jimmy. Jimmy's eyes were small and darted around the room. This was both due to his furtive career choice and his habit. The latter funded by the former. "I trust you have them?" Devizes said curtly. Jimmy took another look around to ensure no one was watching, took a slug of his pint and then produced a small brown envelop from his jacket pocket. "No sweat DoDe." He said casually. Devizes took the envelope and carefully studied its contents. As his back was facing the bar no one would be able to see what he was looking at. The passports looked fine to him. He had used a photo that differed from his regular passport photo and he had taken a picture of Annie after her first shower when she had dried her brown hair and gotten into the new clothes. These would do just fine. Devizes then produced a small brown envelope of his own which Jimmy took eagerly and placed directly into his pocket, knowing him well enough not to have to count its contents. Devizes then finished his pint in one and made his way out. As he left, he looked over his shoulder and saw Jimmy at the bar with a crisp twenty in his hand. No doubt his dealer would be his next stop. He liked dealing with the likes of Jimmy. They asked no questions, spent the money quickly usually in untraceable ways and had too much to lose, and, often as not, didn't enjoy long and happy lives. Devizes then started on his walk back to the house. Everything was now in place.

PART 3

CHAPTER 25

Dom had stored the numbers of all the mobile phone detonators into his own disposable phone as speed dials. Not the one on which he had spoken to Montgomery, that had been disposed of already. This too would be destroyed when it had served his purpose. These phones he only ever dialled out on once after which he destroyed the phone and SIM card separately. They were cheap, and it wasn't worth the risk of reusing them. He was very careful. These old handsets however were ten a penny at many a high street phone shop or secondhand shop. Tottenham Court Road in London was crammed with cheap old phones – strike a deal, pay cash and off you go. Over the past five years he had accumulated quite a few. Some had to be thrown away due to their incompatibility with the newer SIM cards sadly, but he would never run out. He always held on to them for a few weeks before using them thus ensuring any CCTV in the shop showing his purchase would have been wiped over. Annie's room was a great place to store things when it wasn't put to better uses.

He had decided to detonate the Heathrow bomb first at around 10.30pm. Then the Hangar Lane one approximately 30 minutes later at 11pm. If all went well Montgomery was to be dispatched at 11.30pm or thereabouts whilst all the efforts and media were focused on London. He would then take Annie and the cash down the M62 and across to Liverpool where he had made arrangements to join a fishing boat that would take them slowly but safely to Southampton where he had booked two tickets on a cruise liner in the names of Mr. and Mrs.

Montygon - Piers and Kerry. A little dramatic but he liked to tease. He knew that even if they were tracked to here they would never be found if the rest of his plans worked out. He knew they would as he had used a similar cruise liner once before but under a different name. No one suspected bad things could happen on a cruise liner. Especially Doctor Crippen but ironically Dom thought that he had been innocent after all.

Cruise liners were typically full of reasonably well-off, well-to-do, middle class folk, who had planned their trip months or even years before. Everyone on one of these was well to do, had some money, and naturally there were no criminal types, so people thought. Whilst they were effectively captives on board, no one was looking for a young, white, newly married couple on their honeymoon. Her blond locks were now a lustrous dark brown and the colour suited her and blended with her eyes. She also did her eyebrows and used some heavy makeup that made her look older, which wasn't difficult. She would easily pass for twenty-one at any club or casino. Dom would be clean shaven and fashionably attired thus making him look a little younger than his true age, thus drawing less attention relating to their age difference, which on a cruise, shouldn't cause anyone to bat an eyelid.

It would take him approximately 45 minutes to get to the meeting place in the other car. He typically kept two or three older but reliable cars at his disposal during an operation. This operation required just two. One in which to make the drop; a vehicle that would then be blown up. A second in which to effect their getaway – both stolen and untraceable. He had changed the number plates again on both cars. This was the fourth set he had used in the past week. You couldn't be too careful. Montgomery had been told where to park and to walk to the meeting point on foot and, of course, alone. The route was a clearly visible one whereby Devizes could see him approach and also see for a long distance in each direction to check for a tail. He and Annie arrived two hours before the allotted meeting time and parked their car beside the pillar underneath the viaduct where it was less conspicuous to any passing boats, cyclists or joggers. The weather was foul – it had been raining all day. Devizes knew this would work well as it would reduce the number of people out and about and decrease visibility. He no longer thought she'd make a run but he carried a gun and she was too smart to make a run for it especially in a location like this. The windows in the car were blacked out. They had a single suitcase containing their two outfits and passports. He knew the cruise ships were well equipped with all types of shopping therapy and sourcing new clothes would be easy. They could drop their old ones overboard at some point. Annie now changed back into the now filthy clothes that she was wearing when she had been ab-ducted. They hadn't been washed and smelled pretty ripe. She dirtied her hands and face and feet to appear unkempt from days of abduction, not that it would make much difference he thought. She then closed her eyes and rubbed her cut fin-ger onto the pillar reopening the wound. They then smeared traces of blood onto her arm, hand and face. She wore an old baseball cap to hide her clean, newly coloured hair. Montgom-ery would have to rely on her facial features and the sound of her voice for confirmation of her identity, if he needed it. Annie had said she often wore her hair up in a cap if it needed washing.

Annie was to be tied in the car boot where she was clearly visible and unable to make a run for it. Montgomery would be seated on the back seat, Dom in the driver's seat. Once the transaction had taken place Montgomery was to release Annie and leave with her on foot whilst Devizes made his getaway. That was how he would explain the script to Montgomery when they met. Annie had the chloroform ready. Dom had a gun too. He didn't want to shoot Montgomery, or Annie for that matter, but he wasn't too fussy as he doubted that even with a bullet in his head he would be never be found or identified in the ruins of his existence under the rubble when the bomb caused as much devastation as he planned. Much would end up in the Manchester Ship Canal. Not a pleasant body of water. There were many more bodies, both complete bodies, or skeletons, and various body parts; some in black plastic bags, some in holdalls hidden over the years in that body of water. He knew this as he himself had assisted in the disposal of a couple some time back. He wouldn't be surprised if sharks lived down there too.

Dom kept checking his watch. Annie was still in the boot of the car. "Dom what time is it?" she asked. "Showtime!" Dom replied. As the time approached ten thirty pm, he took out his phone and dialled the number of the Heathrow bomb. The phone answered and immediately went dead. He tried calling it again but no ring this time just a message about being unable to connect. It had started. The game was on.

He felt sure that the first bomb had now detonated. He didn't think about the casualties – and there would be some. That area was always busy with cars, bikes, pedestrians and lots of taxis. A few less taxis wouldn't do any harm he thought. He wouldn't be shedding any tears. He switched on the radio in the car and tuned to Radio 5 live. Nothing about a bomb was heard. He casually listened to the sport banter and when he next checked his watch it was approaching eleven pm. Both he and Annie had been watching for movement in case either Montgomery turned up early, possibly with company, or if the police were already there. He had discounted the latter. He felt confident Montgomery would come alone, unable to risk public humiliation, but you couldn't be too careful. He was a little disappointed not to have heard anything about Heathrow on the radio. He dialled in the second number for Hangar Lane and listened. The phone answered, and it too was immediately cut off.

The radio carried on broadcasting football banter and cricket banter when the presenter suddenly said, "And now we go to London for a newsflash." The radio went silent for a second and then he heard "This is... "the radio crackled and as the presenter introduced himself. It sounded like Jonathan something. But it didn't matter. "It appears there has been a major incident in the area of Heathrow airport. A bomb has exploded and resulted in the surrounding roads being blocked off. The police are setting up a major incident unit at present and it is unknown as yet whether there are any casualties. We will bring more details of this tragic event throughout the evening as we get more information.". He knew the presenter would be in for a long night. Ironically this could be the making of him – a vehicle to propel him to stardom. He may even be presenting the 9 o'clock news in a few months. Dom didn't care. Where he would soon be, he wouldn't get the 9 o'clock news anymore. Even if he did, he wouldn't watch it.

Ten minutes later Jonathan whatsit came back with the news that a second device had gone off nearby. Several people had been injured and four killed when a car had been blown in the air and landed on another vehicle. A minibus carrying French tourists had also been wrecked – this brought a smile to Dom's face. The police suspected a terrorist plot, but the emergency services were having trouble getting to the scenes of the incidents due to the traffic. Even at this time the roads around London were still busy. Traffic was backed up along the A4, M25 and in the City. Was it another 7/11 type campaign? Speculation continued. All the football banter had now ceased, and it was now pure speculation about who was behind this, which organisation, how had they done it, how many people were injured, had the police sealed off the areas? Would there be any more devices in London tonight? Buses and trains were being cancelled and security at Heathrow was high. They had people calling in saying they had heard the bombs, or they were stuck in traffic close to the scene. They had reports of black men seen running in the areas of both sites. The police were working on identifying these men. All the attention was on London – it was an affront to London the capital city. All about London, typical of this bloody country. Dom couldn't wait to get away. The police were apparently also looking at terrorist alerts and recent intelligence but denied having any prior notice of such an event. The conversation, in the lack of new information, went on to what if there were warning but the authorities hadn't let on. Dom loved it when a plan came together. This was a real shit storm, with so much more to come.

It was now 11.20. By now he should be able to see Montgomery approaching along the path, but the rain was heavier. He hadn't planned for rain. He knew Montgomery wouldn't keep a fast pace and had accounted for this in his timings. A few minutes later than planned he appeared in the distance, soaked to the skin, walking swiftly, with a slight limp, down towards them carrying a holdall as instructed. The holdall appeared to be heavy. Dom got out of the car, gun in hand and opened the rear door, signalling to Montgomery to get in. It took over a minute for him to get there. Montgomery stopped briefly, glanced at Annie then looked into the car and upon seeing no one else in there, reluctantly got in. He briefly glanced at Annie in the boot through the back window, but his eyes didn't linger on her for long, but on Dom. Dom got back into the driving seat and looked at Montgomery in the rear-view mirror, gun in hand. In his best New York accent, he said "You didn't call the cops, now did you?". "No, not this time. I am at home resting whilst they work on the first letter." he said, admitting that he had called them in the first instance. Just then Annie whined in the boot. Montgomery turned around and saw her bound and gagged in the boot of the car behind him. A normal father would have been beside himself and asking her was she alright? What had the bastard done to her? Had he touched her? etc. etc. But Montgomery just looked down on her with an expression befitting a father who had found his daughter drunk in the gutter having soiled herself. Being gagged she wouldn't have been able to answer any of his questions anyway. Without saying anything he turned back to make eye contact with Dom in the mirror. "Have you brought the cash Mr. Montgomery? Because if you haven't, you'll both die here, tonight." Dom said in his New York drawl. "I have the cash." He replied. "I need the negatives of the photos. Without these the deal is off.". "I don't think you are in any position to make any demands Mr. Montgomery." Dom said in his New York accent. He paused for a few seconds then said "All the prints are here. There are no digital copies. Negatives are a thing of the past Mr. Montgomery. Now hand me the bag."

Montgomery pondered for a brief moment then leant forward and passed the bag between the drivers and passenger seat towards Dom and Dom felt the driver's seat move slightly. Instinctively he leant forward just as the blade penetrated the front of the seat – the bastard had brought a knife and tried to stab him in the back – a contingency Dom hadn't thought about. Luckily for him it had failed. Just as Montgomery leant back Annie put her hands in front of his mouth pressing as hard as she could with the chloroform-filled cloth. Now this really did take Montgomery by surprise. First his fingers and toes went numb. Then his vision went black and lastly hearing faded to silence. He made a "Uh" type of muffled sound then fell unconscious. She held the cloth to his face for a full 15 seconds afterwards. Far more than required to knock him out. From her face she was hoping to kill him there and then, her eyes deep pools of black. Dom left her to it. After all it made no difference to him or his plans.

The car was now silent. Annie's breathing was heavy. Dom had a slight cut to the left side of his back where the blade had penetrated the seat and nicked him. It stung a little but wasn't bleeding too badly. Dom got out of the car and opened the back door. He took the knife that had fallen into the foot well and put it into his pocket. Annie retreated to the back of the boot and Dom opened the boot to let her out. "Did he hurt you?" she said to Dom. "No." he replied. She stood under the boot and together they changed their clothing. They put their dirty clothing into a black bag which Dom put back into the boot after applying a little accelerant. Annie remarked that the cut on Dom's back was nothing more than a scratch and nothing to worry about. He took the bomb from the boot and placed it in the nearside foot well beside the unconscious Montgomery. He then sprayed a little more accelerant inside the car. "Squirt him to be sure" Annie said with her black eyes burning into the sleeping man. Dom did so and then closed the doors and locked them using the spare set of keys that he had brought with him. He kept the spare keys for disposal later, where they would not be found. He had left the main keys in the ignition as though Montgomery, or the mystery man, had driven there himself and was just in the wrong place at the wrong time.

They walked arm in arm back down the path and back to Lymm where their other car was waiting for them just where Dom had left it earlier. This particular car was a Ford Mondeo. It had been stolen to order and made untraceable, or so he was told. He had paid over the odds for this car from a contact he had used on previous occasions. It was a shame that it was only going to be used for this one journey. Dom drove and Annie sat in the passenger seat with her lustrous brown hair now on show and glinting in the lights of the other passing cars. She seemed exhilarated about the night's actions. She was in no way fazed by the fact that she had aided and abetted in the murder of a man tonight, her own father. Not to mention assisting in the bombing of countless others. Annie's old clothes had taken the brunt of her share of the mess. She had applied a plaster to her finger. They drove directly to Liverpool. As they headed towards Liverpool he drove quickly and erratically often turning down side streets for no reason. The car still didn't look conspicuous. Despite the fact that he was sure that the police hadn't accompanied his quarry, he had to be sure that they hadn't been followed. They parked down a side alley, one renown for muggings and cars being burned out. The car park across the way was one that didn't have cameras or require you to pay by text message. He'd tried to avoid all the cameras known to him en route just in case they traced the untraceable car. There would be no record of who dumped this car or from whence it came. They took their suitcase out of the car leaving it empty. Again, the keys would be disposed of later in the sea. Dom took the petrol can he had brought and sprinkled it onto the seats inside the car and onto the bodywork outside. The heavy rain would prevent people seeing anything, but it wouldn't slow the impending inferno that was to engulf the stolen car destroying any fibres or DNA. It was just another stolen car, joy riders having their fun. Dom had thought of everything.

The car went up like a torch. They were close to the river when they heard the explosion. BANG! They saw other pedestrians, mainly people pissed and pissed wet through, turning and looking at the source of the noise. It wasn't really anything so out of the ordinary, they looked then continued on their way. No one went running, no police sirens ensued. People largely ignored it. They were on the boat before they saw a single blue light. They didn't even know if it was there to check out their work or that of some other tradesman of that area. An area awash with skilled tradesmen. They had called for a kebab on the way and taken it onto the boat. Whilst it didn't have much room, and wasn't designed for passengers, this particular one had a single cabin, that could loosely be described as a bedroom or berth. A death was probably more appropriate. It smelled like there were bodies rotting and hidden corpses in the boxes and paraphernalia that also resided there; it reminded him of prison. As Dom had paid a good fee for this five-star transport and accommodation, they had cleared the room sufficiently to fit an old double bed, AM FM radio and a table plus a few of bottles of red wine. This would be their home for the next day or two for the short journey to South-ampton. They had made good time, taking just over an hour. The first thing Dom did was take off his wet coat then turn on the radio. He tuned to Radio 2. It was after Midnight and six-ties songs were being played. The show was just finishing. He was hoping for a newsflash, but the programs went on as though nothing had happened. His portable AM/FM radio only offered the traditional stations. He scanned AM for 909 but the signal was weak, so he continued to listen to Radio 2. At around 12.20 the program was interrupted by a newsflash. "A major incident has been reported close to Heathrow airport tonight and a further incident in West London. The police need to speak to anyone who saw anything or took any photo-graphs or video of these events. It is the belief that these inci-dents may be connected. A senior police source was quoted as saying that they did not expect any further events and that the citizens of London should stay at home and not to worry.". "Damn right." Thought Dom. He suggested they go upon deck for some air before they settled in so he and Annie put their coats on and went on deck. It was now 11.30 and Dom took the trigger phone he had christened as his big red button. The boat was now heading out down the Mersey. As he stood out-side the kebab house earlier, waiting for Annie to collect their meals, Dom had dialled the third mobile number – the num-ber that would send what remained of Montgomery into ob-livion and hopefully take down part of the bridge. He had dialled the number and a split second later he was sure his eyes detected a faint flash in the sky towards the East. Warring-ton would be what, less than twenty miles as the crow files, maybe nearer fifteen. Had he seen the bomb with his own eyes? No one else seemed to notice. Maybe it was just wishful thinking, or a spot of lightening. Either way her father was gone, and it was him that was in bits not her. She was now like a caterpillar turned into a butterfly, like the weight of the world had been lifted. He liked it, but he also felt a little concern in the back of his mind. She'd helped to kill her own father for money. What was this girl he'd become too fond of?

The boat was a small trawler and a working fishing boat. From the deck, whilst looking at the lights of Liverpool, Dom dialled the number that was for Spaghetti Junction. He waited a few moments in contemplation then dialled the fifth number that was to wreak havoc upon bonnie Scotland. He then dialled both numbers again – both coming back with no connection. As they headed back to their quarters, he could hear the sound of the radio. They sat back on the bed and listened. Annie had been so focused on her own situation that she hadn't been taking much notice of the radio. "And now we are hearing that there has been a third explosion in the Warrington area….." At this her ears pricked up. "The Thelwall viaduct has been seriously damaged. We believe one of the carriageways has collapsed into the Manchester Ship Canal and we have unconfirmed reports of several dead including passing motorists and a lorry. Eyewitnesses claim to have seen the remains of a taxi below also. "Bonus", thought Dom. Annie looked at Dom. "Why so many?" she asked. Dom looked at her and smiled. "One isolated bombing would have attracted a lot of attention from the police and the media. One bombing in the midst of several other more significant bombings will naturally be assumed to be another terrorist attack by ISIS or Al Qaeda or some other bunch of radically extremist idiots, thus taking attention away from dear old dead daddy." was Dom's reply. "Have you planned any more Dom?" she asked, a sparkle in her now brown eyes. "Yes, two more have been detonated whilst we were up top, and one is about to happen very, very soon." He said with a wry smile. "Can I press the button?" she said, her eyes lighting up. The reason he hadn't told her about the other bombings was that he half expected her to turn all moral on him and bleat about innocent deaths and families and kids, but he had been wrong. She wanted to pull the trigger. Dom gave her the phone and told her to press 5 and hold it down. This activated speed dial 5. She listened at the earpiece. The phone answered automatically and then the line went dead. "Is that it? She asked. "Ring it again now" Dom said and she duly obeyed. "This time it won't connect." After a few seconds she said, "I'm taking number six!", like a child at Alton Towers or something. "OK he said, but we have twenty-five minutes to fill between now and then......"

At exactly twelve thirty Annie pressed speed dial number six. This time the line didn't ring. After a pause there was a continuous tone. "It's not ringing." Annie said with a puzzled look on her face. "Shit – maybe it hasn't gone off." Dom replied. Dom tried it himself with the same result. He double checked that the speed dial was the correct number – it was. He tried again – same. They switched the radio back on. Within a few minutes there was talk of the Erskine bridge being damaged but not seriously – just the inside carriageway and cycle path. It was of course shut for a safety assessment and the repairs could take days. All traffic would have to be diverted through the Clyde tunnel. But still no mention of the Clyde tunnel bomb. All talk had now changed to that of a nationwide attack against Britain, not just an attack on London or England.... Where would be next? "It was a nation of scared people just like during the Blitz" the reporter had said. If it had failed to go off, then what next? Did they need to retrieve the bomb in the bag before anyone found it? He had hidden it well. He took out one of his smartphones and looked on the BBC Scotland web site, Scotland Transerv and Google to look for planned road works in the tunnel. It didn't matter that he was using his own phone, after all half of Britain would be doing likewise. He couldn't find anything. He wouldn't worry about this for now. He had gone to great lengths to not leave any fingerprints or DNA on the bag. It would probably have fibres from the

Mondeo but that was blown to fuck – and stolen so he doubted they'd trace it to that particular vehicle let alone back to him. None of the materials in the bomb or the phone and detonator could be traced to him. He had sourced them from all over the North West over a long period of time. Maybe it was the shit weather in Scotland that had affected the mobile signal. He'd try again throughout the night. Still there were lots of reports of terrorist cells in the North West. There was a high Asian population there and many went down South for the good life. If the bag was found it wasn't the end of the world. All their enquiries would be aimed at bringing terrorists to justice.

They listened to the radio for another hour, still buzzing from the night's events and the successful completion of their plan. The journey South would be punctuated by brief periods of fishing, so they wouldn't get to Southampton until the next evening. It was now the early hours of Monday morning but neither of them was ready for sleep yet. Annie held fast to Dom's hand. He wondered how many morning commuters would get into their car and head for London or Birmingham or Glasgow blissfully ignorant of the fact that they would likely spend the vast proportion of their day stationary and listening to the radio. Maybe he'd go upon deck and try his hand at fishing. Then again there were more interesting things to do down here. They applied themselves to more interesting things for an hour or so and then they fell asleep with the radio on.

CHAPTER 26

Bob tried calling Montgomery again. He was now getting very concerned for both his safety, the safety of his daughter and the safety of his cash. Initially he had been cooperating fully. The first letter had been proven to have been written by his daughter and contained her DNA. No other DNA was found and the paper on which it was written was proving to be very difficult to trace due to its age and unknown origins. It was plain, no markings and was apparently several years old. Annie's prints and DNA were all over it but sadly no one else's apart from Montgomery himself. This would make it very difficult to trace and he didn't hold out much hope that investigations in this area would come up with anything significant. No one stocked this type of paper any longer, hadn't for years. The envelope was covered in fingerprints and DNA from postal staff etc. They would try and eliminate each individual set of prints, but he knew this would be fruitless. If the letter was clean, they wouldn't have left any evidence on the envelope either. They would also test it for saliva where it had been sealed and under the stamp itself. Whoever was behind this it had been carefully planned; or they had just gotten lucky, probably a bit of both. Still it was a lot more interesting than his previous week's assignments. He relished working on a proper case for a while.

The thing that concerned him most of all was, whilst they had been trying to contact Montgomery, the deadline for the second letter had come and gone. Rarely did the family member being blackmailed go to the police initially then go solo but that is exactly what he was so concerned about in this case. He was surprised as Montgomery had shown so little concern for his daughter in their previous meetings. The thing that he couldn't fathom was the way that Montgomery was so unemotional when it came to his daughter's safety and any risk to her life. He seemed more concerned about himself than her. Most unlike any parents he had met, even the unfortunate druggies, and especially well to do parents in a situation like this one. He had dispatched a uniform to Montgomery's place, but he wasn't in and his car was missing. He had traffic looking for the car. He had tried to get a location from Montgomery's mobile phone, but he had just heard that that appeared to be switched off. All the talk in the station was about the bastards who had taken to blowing up the country and wreaking havoc to the poor working man and woman trying to get to and from their place of work. Speculation was rife. No coppers had been reported as affected yet which was a small mercy. Apparently counter terrorism hadn't got a clue that anything like this was going to happen, or so they said. The targets seemed to be chosen deliberately to disable the road network and bring the country to a standstill. Anyone wanting to get in or out of London from the West would have great difficulty. The routes North to South were now limited to the M1 which was typically stationary at this time anyway. With the number of cars on the road, when one of the major junctions or roads was affected, it only took a few minutes for the traffic to back up in all directions. Soon all the side roads and alternative routes became clogged and it was gridlock. Birmingham was at a standstill. The whole of spaghetti junction was closed. Inspectors were in there assessing the structural damage along with health and safety. Apparently, bits of road had fallen onto the lower roads damaging those also. It could be weeks until it was back to normal. This attack was against the British nation itself. First, they had to ascertain that there were no threats left there in the form of further devices. The bomb squad had spent half the night going over every inch of the first site and had just given the all clear half an hour ago. They had collected some evidence, small fragments of what they believed to be the device and that would be analysed to see what information it could yield. CCTV footage of the surrounding areas, lots of it, was being collected and some poor bastards would spend the next few days glued to a TV set looking for the man or men, so far unknown, who did this with absolutely nothing to go on except they suspected terrorism, giving them a not entirely unbiased view of the colour of the perpetrator's skin. Bob's money was on radical Muslims as was most everyone else's. Sad times. Bastards. Maybe Brexit would make things a little better. He doubted it.

CHAPTER 27

The assumption was that this was a targeted attack on British soil and the perpetrators would claim responsibility in the name of whatever organisation or country they were fighting for in due course. It was all about getting attention to their cause and their chosen name. Only so far no one had done so. But within a couple of hours three such organisations had claimed responsibility. This would require careful due diligence to ascertain the validity of these claims. The sooner they could finger someone the better. One central team was being put together to deal with the attack as a whole. The evidence gathered from each site would be given to the team, so they could analyse each in isolation and look for connections in the bigger picture of events. They assumed the group had built or acquired the explosive devices and placed them there. For all they knew there was a separate coordinated team for each event which would make tracing them very difficult. The explosions were quite close together again indicating several individuals involved in the planning and execution.

As for identifying the victims all they had were body parts plus one or two unfortunate motorists who weren't blown up but couldn't avoid the damaged road and crashed or fell to their deaths. So far 13 people were known to be dead. Witnesses had so far come up with nothing significant apart from the sightings of black men running away but these too needed corroborating. Had these events taken place at 8 or 9 am then the toll would be much higher. This too was the subject of much discussion and conjecture. Why pick a quiet time? To facilitate their getaway. The whole thing was planned carefully so there had to be a reason for this blaring exception to terrorism principles. Why not maximise the devastation in terms of the number of people affected? Maybe they had plans for further events at busier times? These could be a way of blocking the roads as a precursor for something else. He hoped not.

The Glasgow police and Dunbartonshire police were looking into the Erskine bridge event. So far, they had nothing. All traffic up the west coast had to be diverted via the Great Western Road or the Clyde Tunnel. All routes were currently very busy indeed. Given the close timings of the events, roughly 30 minutes apart, the authorities all agreed that the event was now over, and the perpetrators were probably lying low or long gone. All UK airports had heightened security. Everyone passing through security was being randomly checked for explosive residue and this was taking a huge toll on the security resulting in long queues. A full search would have taken much longer. The police had issued a statement warning commuters to stay at home if possible. Anyone who had the ability to work from home should do so today and await further advice as the day wore on just in case further devices exploded. Drive only if you have to and be prepared for severe delays and take food, drink and warm clothing in case you end up spending the night in the car. Most of the station night shift were still there as the dayshift, like Bob, who normally arrived between 8 and 9 but had been there since 6am. It was going to be a long day. One or two smelled of alcohol from the previous evening. Nothing new there then Bob thought.

By 9am no breakthrough had been made. It could take days to identify all the bodies. A hotline had been set up to report missing persons, but it had been flooded. Crank calls hampered the progress but each one had to be followed up in order to be eliminated. Some of the night shift had left, others said they were prepared to stay on – all overtime greatly received. He knew there wasn't the budget to pay for all the overtime that would be needed and delivered. All holiday had been cancelled for the coming week. Bob hadn't taken any holiday for six months and had nothing planned. One of the team was due to fly out to Tenerife on holiday later in the week. He'd been on the phone to explain to his seriously pissed off missus what the score was. "If we make progress towards catching the bastards then things might change but for now love you're on your own." His wife's voice was clearly audible – a high pitched sound, loud but indistinguishable. Bob got the gist of what she was saying even without being able to pick out the words clearly. So many coppers' marriages ended because the partner considered themselves second priority.

Five events across the UK but what made these locations particularly relevant? And what the fuck had happened to Montgomery, Bob wondered. He suspected Montgomery had received the second letter with an explicit threat to not only his daughter's life but also his own, hence his change of heart. Maybe they had found out about him involving the police or just expected this? They could have tailed him or tracked his phone, but that wasn't easy. Without the police, it would inevitably end up badly – it usually did. He'd been missing for over twelve hours – maybe it already had. But now they had bigger fish to fry. There would be no one looking for him any time soon.

CHAPTER 28

Bruce wasn't wrong. Two days later he was again awoken early by the postman seeking a signature. The letter looked very similar to the first letter he had received. He opened it with anticipation; skipping the introductions and going straight down to the first paragraph which read "we are pleased to offer you the position of Project manager blah blah blah". He'd got the job! Bruce was elated, not only because he had grown to want the position above all others, not that there were any others at the moment, but because he needed something quickly in order to be able to keep paying his bills. Maybe this evening he would go out and celebrate. All he needed now was a pretty young girl on his arm and his life will be complete. Dream on. His wife was staying at her mother's. He'd seen it all before. To be honest he wasn't even sure if he wanted her back anyway. Now he'd gotten this job it would be the last straw for her and a new start for him.

He got showered and dressed and went down for his breakfast. Bruce wasn't a big breakfast person but occasionally he liked a bowl of porridge with a little sugar sprinkled on it. He preferred the sugar option to the salt option. He picked up the letter once again. The letterhead said his starting date would be the following Monday. Now he had secured himself a position he could spend the next couple of days relaxing and not having to worry about where his next pay packet was coming from. He decided to make the most of these two days off as they may his last holiday for a while. Projects like this were full on and his role couldn't be parked for a week or two to accommodate holidays. His holidays fell between projects and this one was to be his last few free days for months.

Even after getting answers to all the questions he been able to ask the team at the new company he nevertheless still had a nagging feeling in the back of his mind about the new role; more specifically about the project and the layout of the rooms. He wasn't going to let this dampen his mood though. It might be nothing whatsoever to do with his upcoming project. He was being paid to do a job and it wasn't really his concern what the purpose of the building was, only the construction thereof. He had achieved his objective of finding a new role within a month and was due to start very soon – that's all that mattered. Over the next month or two he would still keep his eyes open on other potential roles cropping up just in case he concluded that this wasn't the right role for him after all. However, the remuneration that he had agreed may make it difficult for him to switch roles because he knew he'd be incredibly lucky to get anything that paid as well as this.

Now it was time to plan his evening celebration. He went to his computer opening up his browser and went straight into Facebook. After checking his latest updates, he then set about sending messages to half a dozen of his friends telling them that his new role was in the bag and, although not sharing too much information about the role itself, he suggested a little get together to celebrate the fact that he was once more employed. It was to be tomorrow night, Friday. It wasn't long before he had some replies.

CHAPTER 29

Dom and Annie decided to go for a walk at around 7:30 AM. There seemed to be a lot of noise coming from up on deck. Dom assumed this would just be the morning's fishing activities but nevertheless he needed to know for sure. He got out of bed, switched on the radio then went for a slash. When he had finished, he got back into bed and listened to the news broadcast. All they were talking about were the bombing events in the previous evening, mainly in London. It appeared that the Heathrow bomb had been the most devastating and had caused the most problems in terms of traffic and access to the airport causing pandemonium to many international and domestic flights. Many of the airlines, including British Airways, had advised passengers to stay at home and change their flights if it all possible to other airports. This had appeared to make very little difference to the number of people trying to get to the airport however. He wondered how many people were actually in a situation where they could change their flights to a week or two weeks out. He couldn't imagine himself being in that position; he flew for holidays or business and neither of these could be easily moved. Many of the affected were holidaymakers; families with children setting off on that one yearly well-earned family break. Dom didn't feel sorry for these people however as they were just collateral damage. He didn't have the capacity to feel sorry for random people whom he had never met and never would. He often wondered about people who worried about the extinction of animals in countries where they have never visited. Why would anyone give so many pounds a month from their hard-earned wages to save an animal they'd never seen – he wondered if indeed that's where the money was going anyway. He was far too streetwise to fall for anything like that.

Talk on the radio then moved on to the Hanger Lane events and then briefly to the Thelwall viaduct event. There was a small amount of talk about the Erskine bridge events but, due to it being in Scotland and having been the least effective of all the explosions, it received the least coverage. In Scotland that would be all they would talk about, he thought. There was still no comment whatsoever about the Clyde Tunnel bomb. He was forced to accept that this particular device appeared not to have gone off. This caused him some concern. He didn't like it when any part of his plans, however small, didn't go exactly to his script. Dom retrieved the phone from his pocket and speed dialled number six once again. His thinking was that maybe there had been a cellular outage yesterday, not entirely unknown in Scotland. He put the receiver to his ear and listened. The phone didn't ring, and he got the same continuous tone. Fucking Scottish cellular network – shit as always thought Dom. He had tested it when he was up there, and the phone had indeed had a signal, all be it just the one bar. He hadn't bargained for a cellular outage or changing in conditions reducing the one bar to zero. The detonator had failed to trigger the bomb and it was still sat where he had left it inside the bag. At least if the phone was retrieved and the history revealed the number he had used to dial from to test it, it couldn't be traced to him. Maybe in time they could trace the whereabouts of the phone. Reluctantly he knew he'd have to dump the phone in the water from above deck very soon.

He was most concerned that someone, probably a worker, may find the bag or hear the phone ringing if the detonator failed. He pondered this for a while. He should have set it to silent – but he never expected ringing to be a problem. How likely was it that someone would have cause to go to the spot where he had placed the bag? Even if they did go there, would they see the bag? Given the amount of traffic going through the tunnel at the moment they wouldn't dare do any roadworks on it until the bridge was fully open again. After pondering the situation, he decided that was sure the phone was set to silent after all – they all were. How long would the battery last for? Another day? Possibly longer. If indeed somebody did see it would they leave it or look at it? Would they recognise it as a bomb? They may think it belonged to another worker and just leave it there for a few days. He knew what he would do in those circumstances. This meant that at some point he may have to consider returning to collect it. He needed to weigh up the risks involved in both collecting it and leaving it. He was still concerned that, should the authorities eventually retrieve this bomb and, subject it to further analysis, that maybe some fibre or fingerprint or something might be detected that eventually lead to his downfall. He knew he had taken all the reasonable and practical necessary precautions and there was nothing else that he could have done. After all he never expected the bag to be seen or retrieved – it should have been ashes and fragments of charred remains. He pondered the situation but for now he had other things that demanded his attention. Time was on his side and if he did decide to retrieve the bag then it wouldn't be for a couple of days or so at the very least.

He and Annie got dressed and went up and onto the deck. The crew of the ship were indeed fishing. They were reeling in their nets, which contained all sorts of fish and crustaceans. Dom wasn't very good at identifying fish, but he thought that most of the contents of the net looked like mackerel. He didn't really like to eat fish either. It wasn't just the taste it was all the messing about with the bones. Life is too short to mess about with things like that. Give him a curry or a kebab any day. Or a fry up of course. Now he was hungry. He checked to where he could see no nets and threw the phone into the sea.

With a small splash it disappeared beneath the choppy waves.

He and Annie remained on deck, mainly in silence, for around 15 minutes. They watched the fishermen and imbibed the sea air but by then Annie was becoming chilled. She said she needed warming up. They returned to their cabin to plan their next move. Dom explained that he had got the two new passports in their new names and that they have to practice using their new names before they got onto the cruise ship. They were newlyweds and Annie was aged 20. He didn't think there would be a problem passing her off as aged twenty. She looked much older than her 16 years. She didn't act like a 16-year-old either. Although he now was apparently trusting Annie, Dom never fully trusted anyone, ever. He learned that lesson at a very early age. His father could never be trusted to deliver on any of the promises he made to Dom. His mother could never be trusted to deliver any of her promises either because alcohol or drugs often distracted her for hours or days on end. It wasn't that they didn't love him, they did in their own way. But they were also both addicts each in their own way. She was dependent on drugs and alcohol; he was dependent on gambling and the occasional prostitute when he had winnings to spend. Young Dominic fell below all these on both their priority lists. He understood this and grew up living with it simply as the norm. He knew of nothing else. No doubt an analyst would say that this was where his lack of trust was rooted from. He couldn't disagree. But not trusting anyone was the least of his problems and any analyst would be very quick to spot this. In fact, they'd have a job for life. Now all they could do was wait and make plans for their arrival at Southampton and subsequent stage of their journey. And what to do with the Clyde Tunnel bomb.

CHAPTER 30

Bruce got dressed for his night out, smart but casual, suitable for pubs. He didn't plan on going to a nightclub. Besides, he would probably be completely pissed well before that, knowing what his mates were like. Bruce could drink but a couple of his friends could drink most people under the table. They were already ready to get the next round when Bruce was only halfway through his. He knew the wise thing to do was skip the round but that never seemed to happen. They had met at 7:30pm in the Bridge. This was quite an old pub and Bruce had frequented it since he was a teenager. It had changed hands a couple of times and been refurbished. He spent many a happy night in here, most of which had been with some of the friends that were coming out this evening. In recent months, there have been threats to close the pub apparently because the Brewery didn't think it was making enough money to cover its costs. None of the locals can get their heads around this as the pub is always busy; particularly when they showed football matches or any other sporting events. It was one of the few pubs they could go to to watch a big sporting events and get served at the bar in under 15 minutes. The staff are well trained, and they knew the locals who constituted their best customers well and by name. If you were just getting a drink for yourself and they spotted you there in the queue they will craftily pour your drink amongst the round of other drinks they were serving to someone else, and then put it on the bar for you. Sometimes visitors noticed what was happening, but they rarely complained as it didn't really slow down their own order of drinks. This was a practice that used to be common place but these days it seemed to Bruce that bar staff didn't consider it a career, it was merely something to do in order to earn a few quid to cover their short-term money worries or education or schooling or whatever. But then again what did he know? He'd seen a lot of staff come and go in this pub over the years. Where they used to stick around for years it was now months. Days if they got caught on CCTV with their hand in the till. Things weren't as easy as they used to be.

After the usual chitchat about what are you doing now; it's been a long time since we last did this; we should do it more often; talk moved onto the recent bombings; who was to blame and if they would ever be caught. As more beer was consumed this line of conversation moved on toward World War three, Potential reasons for it and if and when it would happen. Cheery stuff for a bar, but then again most of them wouldn't even remember it by tomorrow morning. And that said, it was better than talking religion and less likely to result in a scrap. Everything boiled down to religion. Dom being an atheist, he considered himself above all this. He couldn't understand how religion motivated people to do bad things to others or to wear certain clothes. As the night progressed, they because more drunk and their conversations became louder and more animated. Talk had turned to the recent batch of barmaids and who was hottest – Bruce knew that he'd have a sore head in the morning when he woke up alone in his bed.

CHAPTER 31

Annie lay on their makeshift bed listening to the continued fishing related noises and voices above. A lot had happened in the past few days. She thought she was destined to a life of subservience to her father, him controlling every aspect of her life. In such a short time she had gone from dominated to dominatrix – and all this with Dom who had kidnapped her. Dom thought he was the dominant one in this, the leader but she knew better. If she could change her life around so quickly and so effectively, she could do anything. She considered dialling the number, her special number, but what good would it do? When she set the wheels in motion, she didn't have a plan for how it would work. She still didn't. She knew it would put a spanner into Dom's plans but only a small one that didn't affect the outcome. At the time she thought she may be able to use it to her advantage against her captor. But things had changed. She no longer wanted Dom to be caught. She wanted him for herself. She had gone from having very little to being with a man she liked who now was a man of means. They were on a journey. If she wanted him caught bang to rights, then she would be her own judge and jury. For now, she would enjoy herself and see how things panned out. There was a lot of money to be had. A lot more than a measly 50k.

The news came on again. Dom listened intently for any reference to the Clyde tunnel, but in his hollow heart he knew there wouldn't be one. It would be packed with diverted motorists right now. The fact that it was still open didn't affect the outcome of his plan one bit. But it did leave a large loose end; one for which he would have to mitigate any associated risk. With it being so busy there wouldn't be any further road works for a while, so it would probably be safe where it was. But at some point, the battery would run out and eventually someone would find it and they'd realise it was related to these incidents. They'd spare nothing in getting anything from that bag and its contents and this worried Dom. Even plans as detailed as his could go wrong. He cursed his luck.

The ship was now moving side to side much more than previously. They were further out to sea and the sea was rougher. Dom didn't feel sick, but he was acutely aware that if he did the wrong thing, like read, he may become nauseous. Annie didn't seem to have noticed. She was lying on the bed on her back staring at the ceiling. What could they do to pass an hour or so? He had a good idea.

Later that afternoon they both went up on deck once again. They could see the coast of Wales in the distance. Neither of them had the faintest idea whereabouts they were but both agreed it must be South Wales. They went below and set about planning the next phase of their journey. Dom was still mulling over how to tie up his Scottish loose end.

CHAPTER 32

Bruce awoke with a thumping head. He had no idea what time he had gotten to bed or indeed how he had gotten home, or from where! That was a great night he thought to himself as he fumbled through his bedside drawer looking for the paracetamols. It had been a while since he had let his hair down. His job meant that he went for periods of weeks with his head down, often being too tired or simply not having time for anything social. This was the cause of his relationship breakdowns ultimately. He put his work before everything else. But it was his job, it's what he knew, what he did. And although he didn't admit it, even to himself, he liked it. He liked the buzz of the site, the juggling of priorities, the risks and the getting things done according to his plan. He was good at getting things done. His CV was impressive, detailing the roles he had played in several large construction projects, a couple of them high profile. He took their requirements and their suppliers and contractors and turned them into a team working towards a series of common goals. To be successful in his role, he needed to ensure that everyone else, the cogs in the machine, were also successful in their roles. He was constantly monitoring things, speaking to the foremen about progress, snags, problems, manpower and availability of resources and equipment. Timing was crucial, especially where they required to hire expensive equipment or people in for a given time period. Any slippage would cost money and he had to keep to his budget. No slippage and no creeping of costs – these were his main concerns. This was why they had hired him, his skills, knowledge, experience and track record of on time on budget projects. And so he had convinced himself. He was lying on his back looking up at the ceiling lamp which was still slowly revolving around his head.

Time for a shower he thought, but another ten minutes won't do any harm. However, when he opened his eyes some minutes later the ceiling lamp had gained speed and he felt the rush of nausea coming over him. He quickly tried to get out of bed but became entangled in the sheets falling onto the bedroom floor with a jolt. The jolting of his head advanced the nausea and he threw up on the bedroom carpet. The smell hit him hard and he retched again. This time he made it to the bathroom and stared down the pan. Never again. He would be stuck here for a while – at least there was no one there with him to nag him.

CHAPTER 33

Back in the nick, Bob had spent the whole of the last day, and most of the evening, working on the terrorist attacks. By now they'd had several calls claiming responsibility, but none looked viable to the team. They needed to know why an activist group would perpetrate these well organised, deadly effective crimes. After all it was possibly the most effective attack of its sort in terms of crippling the country's commuters. But was this the main idea of the attacks? Or was it simply to kill and maim? Were they trying to paralyse the British infrastructure? Was it some kind of revenge for something that had happened abroad off the media radar? They had very little to go on. Counter terrorism and the powers that be had come up with nothing. This was different to any other terrorist attacks and this was playing on Bob's mind. He tried to get into the mindset of the type of people who would design and orchestrate this particular series of attacks. It didn't match the usual terrorist profile. Or did it? Every attack was different. Each time they thought of new ways to kill and get their publicity, abhorrent ways that killed and maimed innocent citizens going about their daily affairs. In that way, this was just another terrorist attack he thought. But different……

They had several teams assigned to going through the hours and hours of CCTV footage from the vicinity of all five bomb areas. Some of the media was from streets, shops and social media. Others were from fixed roadside cameras. It was an unenviable task. Hours of footage and little idea what to look for. Still everyone in that nick had done this in the past, some more than others. Initially they were looking for pairs of males, probably dark skinned, looking suspicious or carrying boxes or bags that could have contained the bombs. At present they didn't really know much about the bombs or indeed enough to know how big they were likely to have been. Were they looking for people on foot carrying them, or vehicles? They had forensics looking into the makeup of the bombs from the small fragment and residues they had collected at or near the scenes. They would undoubtedly find something by way of a lead, but it would take time. From the knowledge of the composition of the bomb and the size of the impact they could work out the original size of the bomb. This would narrow down whether they were looking for one person, several or one or more driving a vehicle. But they needed to start scanning the media now and they wouldn't know the size of the bomb for days. The chief inspector was under a lot of pressure to provide information to the media to prove they were in control and some way towards identifying the guilty parties and preventing any further attacks. At this point they had close to nothing. But he was skilled at turning nothing into leaps which in turn heaped even more pressure onto his team. But fast-tracking cut out much of the legwork, the days scanning footage, and without this basic training and understanding it wasn't possible to truly understand the amount of work needed to fulfil your promises. This was one thing that really got Bob down. No matter how hard they worked, how clever they were or how many extra hours they put in, the next time they needed even more.

He had been researching other recent attacks, the various perpetrators or radical groups responsible and in particular ones where no one claimed responsibility. This would help to build a profile of possible suspects. The US homeland security was on the case too, worried about further attacks on American soil. But many of the recent attacks were orchestrated by a small number of radicalised individuals. The modus operandi often as simple as getting into a car and aiming it at people. Anyone could do that. But making five bombs and detonating them at strategic locations within a small period of time was much, much more. Surely if an organisation had gotten this far, they'd want their name on the front of every newspaper in the western world. But still they had no credible names to blame.

CHAPTER 34

Vincenzo took a deep breath as the final gates opened. He exhaled as he proceeded to walk casually out of the gates. This was the furthest he'd travelled for five years. His initial sentence of 15 years had been reduced to five for good behaviour and a few favours from his loyal underlings. That's the thing about organised crime. Being in prison doesn't put a complete stop on your activities. So long as your family remain loyal you can still control things from afar. Being inside hadn't slowed him one bit. But it had made him even more determined to get even and never return inside. Communicating with the outside wasn't too difficult. Sometimes coded messages were required but this was tried and proven. You didn't need fancy drones or high tech, just loyalty and a few quid. It always worked best.

Vincenzo's family were spread far and wide. His little brother Marco was there to greet him; their parents were long since dead. His father had died at the hands of Vincenzo, relinquishing his position to his eldest son. A legacy that Vincenzo had built upon. None of his family knew who had done the dispatching, they naturally assumed a rival gang had done the hit - he had had many enemies as did they all. The extended family was spread far and wide and in all walks of life. When he felt threatened, he ordered a hit. On occasion, he hadn't been against doing his own hits, but it was getting more and more risky as forensic techniques improved. DNA, blood spatter, residue, fibres. Too risky for everyday business. He only took that risk when things were personal. Not many had eluded him. But one name stood out. It had appeared that he had been beaten to his goal by someone else in the same prison leaving his quarry dead before Vincenzo could do this himself. However, another inmate had apparently been discharged but never heard of since. If it wasn't for the fact that this particular man worked for Vincenzo, he wouldn't have suspected a thing. It was possible there had been a swap – both men were white, similar height and hair colour. He didn't believe for a minute that his man had done a bunk. His tentacles extended beyond the borders and he had made his own enquiries and determined that it was possible, even likely, that his quarry wasn't dead after all but had got out of prison posing as another man – the one who was indeed dead. Vincenzo was both vexed and pleased – pleased that he would get the chance to dispatch this man, slowly, with his own hands. Once he had celebrated his own release, caught up with the family matters and made a few houses calls he would look at calling in a few favours he had with the police, customs and other services. He wanted to know what had become of this man, where he had gone, what he was doing. And when he found him, he would kill him, slowly and personally. He always got his man and without the use of a horse. There was no rush. It would wait until the time was right. This man had killed one of his best assets in that prison. He had no doubt that Devizes had no idea who this man was, just that he was similar build and skin tone to himself. Once covered with shit and grime they could be difficult to tell apart. The prison was big enough to hide in and no one made friends in there. It was just possible he had killed his man, assumed his identity and walked out at the end of his man's sentence. Clever, but not clever enough. His guard would be down, his arrogance increased. His time was nearing.

Marco was a fine cook. He had prepared a five-course traditional Italian meal. He had closed the restaurant for the night to accommodate the family in privacy. The menu read as follows: -

Antipasto.
Primo.
Secondo di pesce.
Contorno.
Secondo di carne.
Dessert/Dolce.

Olives, cheese and asparagus, followed by stuffed ravioli. Then the fish course – sole in lemon butter sauce, followed by rocket and cherry tomato salad in balsamic vinegar all accompanying the finest fillet of beef and wild mushrooms with a traditional garlic sauce. All washed down with a range of fine wines and a fine dessert. Vincenzo had never liked coffee flavoured desserts so the obvious was never eaten in his presence.

Talk was kept away from business and focused around how the kids were growing up, who was planning their holidays and how fine the food was. After a couple of hours, when the food was finished, and everyone was sated, the wives and children went home leaving the men to talk business. This was how it always was, into the small hours and sometimes till dawn. No one, not even the children, questioned this - it was just how things were. Surely every good Italian family did likewise. Never did they ask the nature of the business, it was always better not to know and by asking you would reap the consequences of a beating - initially verbally then physically. But you couldn't tell what you didn't know and that was how things were. Vincenzo hadn't experienced a meal like this for a long time. He didn't plan any more such sabbaticals in the near future or ever. Anyone who threatened his freedom would disappear. Everyone in the room knew this. But one more than most for he had reason to be afraid.

CHAPTER 35

Bruce awoke once again with a throbbing head. He had recovered from the previous day's hangover from hell. For once his throbbing head wasn't the result of alcohol excesses but from what he believed to be stress. Over the past week he had been thinking a lot about his new role. The more he thought about it the more convenient it had seemed that he had fit the bill so well, as though the job had been designed specifically to secure his services and his alone. But surely no one would do that – and why? He wondered if they would call any of the references he's supplied. After they'd agreed to take a call from his new company, he'd asked them to call him if they indeed got the call. He knew that not all companies actually called references.

After showering he donned his new suit. He didn't wear a tie – a tie was just unnecessary in his line of work. A suit was optional and required regular visits to the dry cleaner. He still had his other suit and he planned on using this one for the foreseeable future, trying to keep it clean. If the job panned out and he seemed secure for a few months or more, he may consider investing in a second new suit. For now, his old one would suffice when this one needed cleaning. By then he'd have made his first impressions and the project would be underway and he'd have made some wedge.

He'd had advanced copies of the plans delivered to him and over the past few days he had studied them to familiarise himself with the layout of the building to be constructed. The foundations were already in and work had started on the basic ground level outline. The first day was to be spent with the general manager and with meeting and briefing his team. Day two would be on site. That would be his working environment for nine out of every ten working days. The tenth day being back in the office for the bi-weekly project review. He knew he had to hit the ground running and be ahead of plan for the first few meetings in order to build credibility. Every project had one or two setbacks at some point – hopefully due to unforeseen circumstances that couldn't be blamed on the project manager, often suppliers letting them down. He'd cross those bridges when he came to them as he always did. Time had been built into the plan for contingency. He wanted to complete the project ahead of time – mainly by using as little as possible of this contingency element. The early completion bonus was well worth the additional effort.

He looked at himself in the mirror admiring his professional look, a far cry from what greeted him in the mirror the previous day. I'm ready for anything he thought to himself. He gathered his things and headed out the door and into a new chapter in his life.

CHAPTER 36

Bob had worked 18 hours straight as part of the team investing the atrocities in London, Manchester, Birmingham and Scotland. But it didn't quite have his full attention. Bob hated loose ends and when he started working on something, he liked to finish it – with no loose ends. With Montgomery still missing, along with his abducted daughter Annie, Bob knew that, whilst he couldn't save any of the people who had been killed by the bombs, it may still be possible to save Annie. He hated the thought that a young girl was incarcerated with no one looking to help her escape whatever was being done to her. By now, having had no contact whatsoever from Montgomery regarding the drop, he knew something had happened that had meant no more cop involvement. This meant one of two things: either the drop had been made and Montgomery had got his daughter back safe and sound, or the kidnapper had stepped things up with a personal threat to Montgomery or another family member, or he had taken the money and killed the both of them disposing of their bodies. If the former were the case, then surely, he'd have heard from Montgomery saying he'd got his daughter back. But Bob knew this just never happened, unless it was drugs related and that clearly wasn't the case here. No news meant bad news; the only kind of news Bob had known for a while now.

Whilst he had been told to put all his attention into the bombings, he knew that when Montgomery's disappearance became known, sooner or later the media would get involved and the case would take a whole new turn, leaving Bob in the shit again and under even more pressure. This job could be a real drag. He wanted to save lives not clean up after the villains but that meant more proactive work and less reactive work. Right now, it was all reactive. He was due to go off shift within the hour. He'd spend a little time at home reviewing where this kidnapping case was and make a few calls to see if anyone had any sightings or internet or phone activity from either Montgomery or his daughter. If it proved, as he knew it would, that they had both disappeared, then he would broach the subject with his boss tomorrow, highlighting the possible embarrassment of a senior figure being blackmailed then possibly killed under their noses whilst they had taken their eye off the ball, albeit for a much bigger ball. It was all balls.

The following morning, he was in the office for 8am. Four hours sleep had helped him but not enough. On his desk was a post-it note with a message to call DI Ramsden regarding a possible victim's identity; the remains of what appeared to be a car had been spotted under rubble beneath the Thelwall viaduct. The area was still unsafe, so it would be a day or two before it was secured, and the health and safety lot gave the OK to do any further investigation. The bridge needed support work as it was feared that more parts of the carriageway could fall.

"DI Cable here, you left me a message." The phone line was crackly and the voice at the other end was a little quiet. Luckily it was still early and the background noise level in the office wasn't too bad. By 10 am it would be like a football pitch once again. "The car in question is about 500 meters from the bridge parked up. Looks like it has been there some time, probably from before the attacks. "

Ramsden was 39, quite a bit younger that Cable, and he sounded like he'd had more sleep the previous night as well. "Is there any sign of any bodies in the vicinity of the car, or survivors matching the description of Montgomery or his daughter – you saw that on the system I take it?" said Cable. Ramsden replied "Yes my team has the description of them both. So far, no people rescued or any of the witnesses we have spoken to match either description. We can't get close to the rubble under the bridge yet to see if there may be any remains there. But, if you don't mind me asking, why would they be there anyway? The car doesn't appear to have fallen there but to have been parked beneath the bridge. Are they involved with the bombings?" Ramsden asked in a matter of fact sort of way that policemen do. Policemen who have become hardened to death. And in his case a little stupid. "Thanks again" said Cable and hung up. Ramsden had said that he or one of his team would call the minute they were granted access to the remains under the bridge and the rubble on the small chance that either of the Montgomerys had been victims of the blast. A very long shot but everything had to be reviewed.

Why was there a car so close to the site of one of the bombs? Was it coincidence? Was it him that had driven it there? Or was it a bomber? None of this gave up any clues as to the whereabouts of the pair. Bob would have to sit tight for a few days before he heard anything back from Ramsden, if he had anything to offer him, that was. He checked google maps and couldn't find anything else of significance within walking distance of the car. He didn't imagine Montgomery to be much of a walker, especially in the fine tailored suits he wore. He wouldn't want to get his shoes dirty, that's for sure.

Looking out of the window he saw the Chief Super's car had arrived whilst he'd been on the phone. Now was his chance to strike whilst the potential queue of people needing to speak with him wasn't round the block. He went upstairs and knocked on his office door. "Enter" Chief Superintendent Bernard Tailor bellowed. He was a police veteran having worked his way up the ranks from bobby on the beat, not a fast-tracked graduate like so many of his peers nowadays. Bob didn't like the bloke much, but he knew he was just about the best around. Tailor was pushing 63 years old, so he would be retiring soon. He wouldn't want any embarrassing failures to blot his copy book with his retirement and benefits so close to his fingertips, hence Bob thought he may take an interest in what he had to tell him about Montgomery and his daughter to avoid any potential embarrassment further down the line. The Diplomatic angle would add weight to his argument that continued effort should be put into this case despite the bombings, so as to avoid pressure from Westminster or the spooks. Taylor listened to what Bob had to say. "As soon as you get confirmation of the contents of the car and we know whether either of them died in the bombing let me know and we'll make a decision then. Naturally if either shows up in the meantime let me know immediately." he boomed. He remined him of the boss in 'The IT Crowd' who also had a similar vocal style comprising military booming. "In the meantime, focus on the bombings, Cable." That was the best outcome Bob could have hoped for. He went back to his desk knowing he'd be there for the next twelve hours. Bob knew it would be a sight longer 'til he could look forward to retirement.

CHAPTER 37

It was now Bruce's third day on site. The foundations were in and work was underway on the basement. The plans had incorporated storage areas and space for electrical and plumbing service areas and the large, secure room set in the middle. On the plans it was referred to as secure storage facility. Bruce wondered what would be stored there. The design was very similar to what would usually be referred to as a panic room or strong room. It had its own air and water supply and drainage. Solar panels which would be fitted into the roof would charge batteries to give the room a small, independent electrical power supply so even if the building were cut off or damaged, the panic room should be safe to live in for a few days, or even weeks or months if sufficient food and water provisions were stored down there. They could keep tins and frozen food for years if they wanted as long as the sun shone to power the freezer. The design had the room in the centre along with other storage areas and piping. To someone unfamiliar with the plans, walking around the basement area, the secure storage facility wouldn't be obvious to them – apart from the doorway. The finishing of the door was too detailed to be on these plans – he'd have to wait and see how it looked in the coming weeks as the building progressed. All the main suppliers were on-board, contracts negotiated, and Bruce had a preliminary project plan for the next 19 months to cover the full construction of the building. He had been led to believe that the buyer had signed the purchase agreement and had had an input in the design of the building. He wondered if the buyer had specified the secure storage facility. He must have done so. He would have to see if there were any earlier plans. If this was the case, he could see what the basement had originally comprised. For now, he focussed on the current stage of the project. The basement walls and floor would be in place by the end of the month, the fitting of the piping and wiring etc. could be undertaken in parallel with the rest of the building. As such the basement would be worked on for several weeks to come as the building rose on the skyline. He was enjoying this new challenge and had quickly fitted into the project. Life was good again.

CHAPTER 38

Annie didn't sleep well that night. Her head was in turmoil. On the one hand, she had been taken by force – abducted and possibly raped by Dom and, whilst he hadn't hurt her, his motive had been purely for money. That was the sort of guy he was. On the other hand, she quite liked him. In all her favourite movies she always seemed to like the bad boys. But where was this going? She was now complicit in multiple murders – she could end up in front of a packed courtroom – her future dependent on people she had never met. And she didn't feel guilty. She would have to convince them of her complete innocence in anything related to the bombings. Would Dom corroborate this? How would she explain her running away with him? There could be witnesses to say she appeared to go willingly. She had been careful not to show any feelings toward him in public where anyone could brand them a pair. But for how long could she keep this up? She had never officially met him before the kidnapping, so they couldn't show they knew each other all along and planned this whole thing. She was worried that as soon as Dom thought she was a risk to him, he could send her to the bottom of the sea. He seemed to be completely emotionally disconnected from any of the victims of the bombs. He had his money, but he could have gotten this a lot easier and without the carnage. Why had he wanted to damage the UK like this? Did he have a grudge - a score to settle? Was he getting his own back on the government? Had they really pissed him off so badly about something? She turned on the radio, this time listening to the detail to see if there was anything that could lead her towards the reasons for Dom's sledgehammer approach to obtaining money. Her plans for now were to get closer to Dom and appear to be close to him to anyone who saw them. This would give her time to think.

Dom looked out at the water. There was something quite peaceful about being on a boat in calm weather. It seemed to sooth him – the sound of the water passing by the boat, the sound of the gulls chattering to each other, the rumble of the engines below. It helped him think; to plan his next move. This whole adventure had been done to a plan – but the plan so carefully put together over all those months had quickly changed, evolved into something so much bigger, adapting to circumstances; and Dom's needs. He needed times like these to go over what had occurred, where and if he had made any mistakes and how to put them right. Apart from the remaining bomb, Dom couldn't see how anything could relate back to him. Even if they found Montgomery's car or body, they couldn't tie anything back to him. But Annie being missing would attract significant attention. But by the time the interest in the bombings had subsided, the trail would be well and truly cold. The government was good at burying news that they didn't want people to hear. By all accounts Annie didn't have many friends or much of a social life. She wouldn't be missed like most girls her age would be. He hadn't seen anything in the media about the Montgomerys. He didn't know how much Montgomery senior would be missed. He didn't really know what he did over and above being an ambassador. He was sure the police would be far too busy chasing down potential terrorist links to be worried about a missing teenager and her father who was stupid enough to go it alone despite the police advice. For all they know he could have paid off the ransom and buggered off with his daughter to start a new life.

He focussed his attention on what to do about the remaining bomb. Thanks to the success of his other locations he wouldn't easily be able to travel up to Glasgow. The roads were in turmoil and flights and trains were fully booked. The previous evening, whilst Annie slept, he had been researching other means of travel. They were heading towards Southampton. The easiest way to get to Glasgow was by air. Flybe did Southampton to Glasgow – he could get there, hire a car or pull in a favour, or even steal a car, retrieve and dispose of the bomb, and be back for dinner. But travelling by air involved documents, CCTV, security, and posed a risk – even if he could get a seat. If his name had come up in any of this, they'd be looking for him. Facial recognition could possibly be the undoing of him when he was so close to the end. But only if they were actually looking for him. He thought the chances of this were extremely slim to zero. After due consideration he thought that, if they were after him in connection with the kidnapping or the bombings, he'd be Europe's number one criminal. Making a flight would prove to him that they were nowhere near. This massaged his ego. After due consideration, he decided that taking the flight himself was indeed a valid option. He had his new identity, but he didn't want to risk using it to fly thus leaving a trail behind. He couldn't trust anyone else to do his bidding – they'd look in the bag for certain. But not until they got out from the tunnel entrance and back to their car. One option would be to get someone else to recover the bag at a given time. Dom could call the cell and detonate the bomb, blowing up the person, their car and everything within a 25-metre radius. This could go two ways. Either they'd suspect he was involved somehow and had had an accident, or they would think it another bomb deliberately planted. But he'd be nowhere near Scotland.

So he needed to either detonate the bomb or recover and dispose of it. If he detonated it so long after the others, they would either assume that it was the start of another spate of bombs or that this one had somehow gone off late prompting further investigation. The final option could be that this was unconnected to the other attacks. But a similar device detonated so soon after the others would surely make it very difficult to pass as a random, unconnected attack. He could use this portion as an opportunity to dispose of a previous acquaintance with whom he had loose ends to tie up – permanently. After thinking on this for a few minutes his line of thought changed somewhat to any options open to him to swing the finger of blame towards someone else. If that someone else collected the bomb and was then subsequently blown up, the authorities would soon trace the car, its owner and determine the identity of the person pretty quickly assuming they were the bomber, or part of the group responsible. CCTV would show the vehicle's route to the bomb site. It wouldn't be too difficult to add further confusion by getting someone who could be considered a potential terrorist to get the bag. Someone fitting the stereotype bomber.

Should he leave it there to go unnoticed for days, possibly weeks? Should he retrieve it and dispose of it somewhere? Or should he detonate it? It was a bomb after all.

CHAPTER 39

Paolo was getting nervous. He knew only too well what Vincenzo and his so-called family could and would do to anyone they thought was a traitor to them. But he was now stuck between a rock and a hard place. Both sides posed threats to his own family. Soon he would have to make a choice, one that would shape the rest of his and his family's lives – however short that may turn out to be.

He hadn't slept well for a few days. Violence, mutilation and killing didn't keep him awake at night – this had become a way of life, just business. But it was as though he was immune. He was on the side that was delivering not receiving. All of a sudden, he had a new perspective. He could see things from both sides, and this didn't sit well when he thought about the things he had done or facilitated; all of which had resulted in carnage to families all over the country and beyond. None of these had managed to evade Vincenzo's justice. No one had ever run out on Vincenzo and lived to tell the tale. Nobody had ever turned against him and lived long enough to attend a trial, most not even long enough to reach the police station to make a statement. If he was to take this path, he would need certain, cast iron guarantees for him and his family. He didn't have an extended family as such. Both he and his wife were only children and three of their parents were now dead. Paola's mother was still alive, but she was in the final stages of dementia, aged 92. If Vincenzo decided to put a hit out on her he would be a doing them all a favour. Vincenzo had made it his business to get to know the families of his associates. Just the mention of a name would remind his team of miscreants what would happen if they put a foot wrong.

Two years ago, one of the younger guys working for him had made an error resulting in the police taking an interest in his affairs. Whilst most of the cops knew Vincenzo and were either in his pocket or too scared or clever to follow anything up, there was one detective who was straight as a dye. Most of his colleagues warned him that he'd get into trouble. This younger guy, Pedro, everyone called him – whether that was his real name Paolo didn't know - had found himself facing a few years in jail and had spoken to this particular detective about brokering a deal for a reduced sentence and new identity for himself when he got out. Within the first week of being under the highest police protection he was no longer a threat. Pedro was *deadro*. And whilst Paolo wasn't a good man, he loved his family. Good old Italian family values instilled in him from childhood. But he never talked about his childhood. When he had to do a job for Vincenzo thoughts of his childhood would help him psyche himself up and the anger would return and make the job easier. All the things life throws at you can come in useful at some point. Except death, or what immediately precedes it.

CHAPTER 40

The waiting was getting to Bob. He called his contact from Warrington and they advised him that it was still not possible to get to the rubble to sift it for evidence. The team of engineers were working on securing the structure ready for repairs to commence. It would be another couple of days 'til the area was safe. Bob was hoping that the car, or something inside the car, may give him a new lead on why it was under the bridge at the exact moment the bomb went off and whether Montgomery, or a bomber, was inside the car at the time. If it was Montgomery, and it was indeed a very long shot, he also needed to know if the money was inside the car.

The car appeared to offer no clues. It was clean as a whistle. No paperwork or other evidence to indicate anything at all. No other cars had been observed or reported there indicating a meeting, but it was still possible that he was there in order to meet the kidnapper and either exchange the money for Annie or to take further instructions.

They were still looking into if and how Montgomery had got hold of the 250k. It was also possible that this amount had been increased. Montgomery was still missing as was his daughter – he hadn't shown up anywhere close by – he could have left the car there as instructed by the kidnapper, in transit to a meeting place nearby but if that were the case surely Montgomery would have surfaced by now. The Diplomatic office were very concerned about his whereabouts. They'd been briefed on the kidnap of his daughter and they were of the opinion that he was dead as he hadn't spoken to anyone or fulfilled any work commitments since the reported disappearance of his daughter. Bob had no idea what Montgomery was currently working on and of course no one would tell him. Could that in some way be related to his car being where it was? That question especially intrigued him more and more.

He went back to his other lines of enquiry regarding the bombings. So far, they had no forensic evidence to give them any definite lines of enquiry, but he was confident that evidence would be found that would help them determine how the bombs were made, with what and maybe even from where the components had been purchased if the bombers weren't too clever. Once they had some of these facts, they would have definite lines of enquiry and dedicated teams of officers working on them. It would be a start. But for now, they didn't know who had set the bombs, what they were made of, why they were set off or what the logic was regarding the locations. None of it made any sense – yet. Some aspects seemed very professional, others a little amateurish. Still this was often the case when dealing with radical groups – limited budgets and limited knowledge; this usually led to them being caught. The suicide bomb angle had been discounted early on. Suicide bombers left bits and pieces of evidence, but none had been found. Given the nature of the destruction it was probable that the bombs used here would be too big to easily conceal on a person without attracting attention. Most suicide bombers would be observed either by people or CCTV. They were about to die so they didn't care about leaving evidence. Their motives were different to most other criminals. Their gain wasn't to be in this life, but the next – if there was one. So far no one had come forward saying they had seen anyone resembling a suicide bomber and no CCTV footage existed showing anyone especially suspicious at or around the time of the detonations. Bob suspected that the devices could have been triggered by a timer or remote trigger. Of the five bombs, there would surely by pieces of the mechanism discovered that would answer this and many other questions, another thing they would have to wait for. In the coming hours and days, the picture would become clearer. But for now, everything was merely speculation.

The previous evening he'd left work and gone directly to the pub with a few of the other lads. All he'd wanted to do was talk about rubbish – general stuff not related to work. The rest of the lads were all wrapped up in bombs, terrorism, hatred, revenge mixed with a hint of ignorance and racism for good measure. Bob didn't like this kind of talk. He wanted facts, information, structured thinking, logical analysis leading to new lines of enquiry. He'd had a couple of pints then gone home for a microwave dinner. Every now and then, when either he had time on his hands at the weekend or he had friends coming around, he'd make a curry. He was renowned for his curries. He had a big pot specially for making curry. If you were gonna make a meal for one you may as well make a big pot. He'd eat it for dinner a couple of nights then box and freeze the rest. It was better than microwave meals from the supermarket, cheaper and tastier. The longer it spent in the freezer, the tastier and hotter it seemed to become - he never really understood why. He probably had curries in his freezer that were months old. Frozen inside a Tupperware box they all looked the same. It didn't really matter which type, choosing a frozen one added a twist of intrigue! Would it be madras, vindaloo, keema or a mixture of everything left at the end of an evening?

On the rare occasions he had friends around for dinner he would cook up a batch of curry and produce three or four different dishes. First, he'd make the base sauce or gravy - choosing his spices, mainly seeds, and roast them in the pot for a couple of minutes. Sometimes he roasted garlic as well. He'd then add oil and chopped onions, ginger, garlic, fresh and dried chillies. He also liked to add a finely chopped half stalk of celery even though he hated celery. It seemed to add a bit of flavour to the dish in a similar way as adding a couple of pieces of dark chocolate did – which he added later on. Once the onions were browned, he added a couple of tins of chopped tomatoes and simmered for half an hour. He then blitzed the contents of the pot with his hand-held blender, or dildo as he liked to call it. The soupy end product was to be his base sauce or gravy and could be used to create any number of dishes. He then split this into three or four separate saucepans each to be used to produce a different Indian curry with varying amounts of other spices, chillies, garlic, chopped vegetables and meat; usually chicken, sometimes minced meat for keema, or lamb, dependant on the tastes of his guests.

His cooking had driven his wife mad. The cooker top was usually awash in bits of vegetables, overflowed liquid from the pot being too full or spillage. He also took over the whole kitchen and rarely remembered to don his chef's apron until it was too late. His wife usually went out with her friends leaving him instructions to clean the kitchen, do the dishes and light a couple of scented candles afterwards. Now she'd gone out and was unlikely to return. Except to collect her stuff.

He opened the freezer to find he only had three boxes of curry left. He picked the nearest one, prized the lid off, cracking it in the process and inserted the frozen meal into the microwave to defrost. He put some basmati rice into a pan along with cardamom seeds and powdered turmeric and dried chillies and left it to soak for a few minutes whilst the kettle boiled. Ten minutes later his meal was ready to eat. He put the rice and curry into a Balti dish and then he went into the living room. He switched the telly on and sat down to enjoy his meal along with a program he'd recorded earlier in the week. He chose an animal program. Anything to get away from work or current affairs. A different type of animal.

Just as he was tucking into his curry, mouth burning, his mobile rang. "Shit" he thought, now it'll go cold and he didn't like to talk whilst eating. He reluctantly set his dish down and picked up his phone.

"Cable." Bob answered with his familiar one-word response only this time a little short as he expressed his displeasure at being disturbed whilst eating his favourite meal. "Bob it's me. I left shortly after you and made a few calls and did some digging around that Montgomery guy you were asking me about. It appears he isn't as squeaky clean as he makes out." At this Bob forgot about his curry, listening intently at what DI Jordan had to say. "In his diplomatic role he has travelled all over the world. It appears that, whilst he was in South Africa, he got into some sort of trouble. I'm not quite sure of the details yet but whatever they were he upped sticks and moved back to the UK within a week, taking Annie with him. He's remained in the UK ever since. There's so much shit goes down in South Africa that we may never get to the bottom of it unless we can question Montgomery himself." Bob thought for a moment then replied "Well it's looking like we may never get a chance at that line of enquiry, No one's seen him for days, not since he reported the kidnapping. For all we know he could be dead. He's either dead or gone to ground, either way he won't be talking to us right now, if at all.". Jordan thought about this for a few seconds then replied "Well we can't get his phone records due to his diplomatic status.". "Fuck." was Bob's only reply. The line went quiet for a few moments then DI Jordan signed off with "I'll let you know if I hear anything else. Bye for now.". "Cheers." replied Bob, but at least he had another small potential piece of the jigsaw.

Bob went back to his curry. It was still hot but a little easier to shovel down than before. Where was Montgomery? What had happened to Annie? Did they make the drop? Who was or were the kidnappers and had they gotten away with the cash?

ROBERT H PAGE

He knew from experience that disappearing diplomats didn't go to ground for long. They either showed up somewhere or they became priority uno as they always knew stuff. From sheer professional interest, he hoped for the latter. Montgomery had been missing too long. Bob smelt something bad going on. All he needed was time to follow his nose.

CHAPTER 41

Dom still hadn't decided whether to make his day trip to Scotland or not. He had been trying to think of someone who he could finger for the bombings – someone who he could get to collect the bag, then fall apart. Literally. But it was risky. If the police thought that this person was retrieving a bomb that hadn't gone off then it could open new lines of enquiry – and they'd be on the right lines. He knew that sooner or later they would find pieces of cell phone and that would lead them to the discovery that the bombs were triggered remotely. That in turn would lead them to the possibility that it wasn't a group responsible but possibly an individual. He needed them to pursue the group responsibility angle for as long as possible – at least until they were far from English soil, either cruising or thereafter. He decided that if he were to finger someone then the timing would be best when the police had found bits of cell phones. He knew this may never make the public news, so he would have to make a guesstimate of how many days it would take them to find pieces and draw their conclusions. If he were lucky and they never did find pieces, then all the better. The big question was who would he get to collect the bag and take the blame. He had tested all the cell phones' battery life, and each had lasted 4 days minimum. Assuming it was just a network outage or degraded phone signal, he still had time to remotely detonate the bomb, but in a couple of days the battery would likely have run out and the option of remote detonation would have gone away. This would mean one big loose end – the possibility of the bomb being discovered. Also, if it didn't go off, he'd have to have a plan B for retrieving and disposing of the bomb. If for any reason, it was disturbed then it was unlikely it would go off. He had to decide today whether to do the job himself tomorrow when they docked at Southampton, or whether to go with the other option, but this relied heavily on finding the right person to do the job and take the blame. He'd have to speak to them, come up with a ruse for the bag, such as stolen goods to fence or the like, and get them to agree to collect the bag at a set time without looking inside it – a big ask. Who could he use? Who did he want to both see dead and ultimately get blamed? Someone fitting the stereotype bomber profile. He'd surely be spotted on CCTV. Dom was drowsy and he must have nodded off for a few moments.

He awoke with a start. He must have been going through his acquaintances in Scotland in his head during his dream, searching for a name, and now it was there right in front of him – Abdullah – Abs to his friends and cohorts. Abs had started off as a small-time crook burgling houses in the more affluent areas of Glasgow. His father had come over in the 60's and opened a curry house in the city centre. Abs had worked there after leaving school, but it wasn't enough for him. He liked fast cars and faster girls, and this meant he needed money. He liked money the most. He would do anything to make more cash whether or not he needed it, whilst working in the restaurant for his father and keeping up a pretence of family values and hard work. He had gotten better at burgling – gone upmarket so to speak, making good use of his free time when the restaurant was closed, and his victims were hard at work in the city. His knowledge had extended to burglar alarms and home security. This allowed him to burgle more lucrative properties. It was a few years since Dom had last been in Scotland. On that occasion, he had met Abs via another acquaintance. He didn't know him well at all, but he knew he was reasonably smart and could be trusted to do a simple job exactly as per the instructions he would be given. He also couldn't afford any shame on his family, so he was very, very careful in his activities, planning everything and being extra careful who he dealt with when fencing his loot. Dom's acquaintance, through whom he had met Abs, was Abs' planner. He worked as a security system installer. He knew the good places to visit. He told Abs of the addresses and best times to visit and in return took a cut of the fenced earnings from Abs. They were a good team. They came from completely difference backgrounds and had no other connections to each other. Should one go down for something the other could sleep at night. Dom knew that if he called Abs and told him of the stolen loot he knew was stashed in the entrance to the tunnel, wrapped up in some story or other about the person who nicked it being unable to collect it due to death or imprisonment or such like, or that it was disguised as a bomb or something, that Abs would see the opportunity of a quick cash pay-out as irresistible, plus he'd be careful and wouldn't blab. On the one occasion Dom had previously done business with Abs, he had helped himself to more than his fair share. Dom knew this, but due to other pressing things, like the need to get out of Scotland pronto, he had chosen not to follow it up, but had made Abs aware of the fact and that one day he would be asking for a favour in return – in return for not killing him, that is. He hadn't forgotten however. Abs had thought he had gotten one over Dom the last time, only this time he would be sure that it wouldn't happen again. He was the best candidate Dom could think of. All he had to do now was choose whether to action this plan or to do the job himself.

He had to get this decision right and make right on his months of planning. If he did the job himself, he would need to dispose of the device somewhere – and he wouldn't have much time to do it as he would be doing a day flyer. There was a big risk of being seen on CCTV. The more he thought about it the more he liked the option where he didn't have to go back to Scotland at all. He went online looking at flight availability. He would have to book online, and this meant using a credit card and leaving a trail. He could also go to the airport and pay cash. However, if things went to plan, no one would be looking at anyone flying North from Southampton. A day trip there was a typical day in the life of a businessman. It was doable. He had his new identity – credit cards, passport and cash. Both options had risk – that was the trouble with loose ends. They meant unnecessary risks. Luckily, he'd had a couple of days to work on this one. The next thing to consider was what to do with Annie whilst he was away. Could she be trusted? If he took her with him there was the huge risk that she'd be recognised. Unlikely as it may be, given her change of hair colour and the current focus on potential terrorists, this wasn't ideal either. He decided to get up and go up top and stare out at the sea and see what other inspiration he could muster.

CHAPTER 42

It came to Dom as he watched a seagull glide over the water surface and casually catch a fish. Whether the said fish was already dead and floating or whether it had been a demonstration of the bird's eyesight and agility he would never know. In the end it didn't matter – the bird got its fish and he would get his metaphorical fish to add to his already full net. He went below for a different disposable phone, one he hadn't used before, and looked up Abdul's number and dialled it into the disposable phone. After two rings the phone was answered, and he heard Abdul at the other end. The conversation lasted barely a minute. It went along the lines of "I have a job for you, it's good money for doing very little and you owe me one, remember? Under no circumstances look in the bag, do exactly as you're told", and a ploy about getting rid of the bag in a quarry which would actually work as plan B should the bomb not go off. The bag contained documents of no material value to Abs. The important part was to call him as soon as he had retrieved the bag and was at the entrance to the tunnel. He needed the bomb to go off somewhere that would be deemed a target, as per his original plan. If the bomb still wouldn't detonate then Abdul could go and get rid of it, job done. But plan A was far more preferable.

It took Abdul only 20 minutes to finish his whisky and get from the pub in Clydebank to the Clyde tunnel. He parked in a layby and walked the three or four hundred yards across to the tunnel entrance. He was wearing his high vis jacket just like every other council worker on the streets of Glasgow. This was his idea, he was no fool. Everyone looked the same in a high vis jacket – highly visible but invisible at the same time. He was the only one around. It was 10pm. This was a good time as the traffic wasn't quite as heavy as it had been earlier, reducing the chances of Abdul being seen. Abdul called Dom to say he was parked and heading towards the tunnel. Dom knew it would only take him 5 minutes to get to the bag and another couple to get to the tunnel entrance where there should be a good signal. Once again, he took his detonator phone and dialled phone number 6. For the first 5 minutes he got the dead tone. Annie looked on with a strange expression on her face. She insisted he put the phone on speaker, so she could hear. She seemed to be taking great pleasure in the anticipation of hearing the death of someone she'd never even met. Dom knew that when the phone eventually rang, and he expected it to, given his thorough testing of the battery life of the handset, one of two things would happen. Either the call would be answered and immediately go dead as had the previous ones, or it would continue to ring, being on silent. Hopefully Abdul wouldn't detect the phone vibrating, Dom wasn't sure if the phone was set to vibrate or not, he hadn't gone so far as to check that. Another lesson learned for next time. Abdul was to call Dom after getting the bag and returning to the tunnel entrance to confirm his pickup. At least it would give Dom the knowledge that the detonator phone would work there and if it didn't it wasn't due to cell coverage. If he got as far as speaking to Abdul, which he hoped he wouldn't, he would speed dial 6 and hear him get blown up, or at the very least the line disconnecting. If it failed, he would again tell Abs to take the bag straight back to his car and dump it exactly as instructed. Ideally, he wanted to detonate the bomb as soon as possible thus taking some of the tunnel entrance with it and indicating a further terrorist attack hopefully attributable to Abs, whom they would assume was a terrorist, having put the pieces of the jigsaw, and Abdul, back together. He was hoping the authorities, upon finding Abdul's body, would go public.

He had planned for this unlikely event.

For a further twenty minutes he redialled and each time the phone went dead immediately. And then things changed.

CHAPTER 43

The phone answered and then it immediately quiet and then disonnected. Dom immediately called the number again – but it was dead. He continued trying for a further ten minutes. Whilst he tried, they listened to the radio hoping to hear about another bomb. Annie said, "Either he's in bits or the battery went dead." Dom thought about this then answered, "The chances of the battery going dead at that precise moment are miniscule." Dom wondered if Abs had managed to damage the detonator whilst examining the contents of the bag, which he wouldn't have put past him despite the threats. "What happens if he has the bag and doesn't get rid of it then?" Annie asked. "The only link he has to us is that phone and the number of the disposable we used to call it from. That one will be at the bottom of the sea so no one will ever find it and the sea would clean it of any DNA. Whatever happens we're in the clear. We thought of everything." Dom didn't sound quite as confident as his words implied.

They sat in silence listening to the talk on the radio. No newsflash. They'd also got Radio Clyde on the laptop via the radio player site as they thought it would be the first station to report the incident. They knew that something had happened – they felt sure that the bag had been moved to where there was a mobile signal, after all it had answered as per plan, as had the other five phones. Dare they risk ringing Abdul's own phone again? One way or another they needed to know the outcome before they disembarked later that morning. He should have waited for Abs to call him at the tunnel entrance, but he hadn't entirely rusted him to call and not look in the bag first. Dom really needed to tie up all loose ends before they went off on their cruise of a lifetime. Had he just created more loose ends? He decided to wait until midnight then call Abdul's local pub in the city centre and ask for him by name. Abdul was a creature of habit. If he had retrieved the bag and the bomb had failed to detonate the chances were he would have disposed of it as instructed, or looked at the contents, realised it was a bomb and, thinking he was being set up as Dom's revenge, he would now have disposed of it anyway – ensuring there was no link back to him, and then returned to the boozer to recover. If he wasn't there by closing time, then he'd have to think of something else.

At ten to twelve Radio Clyde went to a news bulletin. "Reports are coming in of a major explosion at the Clyde tunnel. It is, as yet, unknown as to whether this explosion is related to those throughout the UK earlier this week, including the bomb by the Erskine bridge which is still closed and will be for some time. We are just hoping that there aren't more of these explosions to follow in a second wave. We will bring more news as it comes in. The next news bulletin will be at midnight." Annie's face had a smile on it. She looked over at Dom, with a satisfied look. "I guess we did it" she said. "Let's see what they have to say later – I want to know exactly where it went off." Dom replied. He then went up to deck taking both burner phones with him, removed the SIM cards, and threw the lot into the sea at one-minute intervals to spread them out a bit – just in case.

When he returned to the cabin the BBC news still hadn't broadcast any further news bulletins. Even by the time Radio Clyde was offering its midnight conjectures, the BBC still remained quiet. It reminded Dom of the odd times he'd been looking at the BBC Football web pages for a score. The site always seemed to be 10 minutes behind the real time and all the other sports web sites. Maybe the BBC was in a time warp 15 minutes behind GMT. "Police and forensics are on the scene now. The explosion occurred at the North end of the tunnel by the South Street junction. It was a large bomb of similar proportions to those earlier this week leading us to believe that there may be some connection between them and the possibility that they were all perpetrated by the same group. Two eyewitnesses have reported seeing a black man dressed as a worker a few seconds before the explosion – they passed him whilst walking in the other direction. They both suffered cuts and bruises and are on their way to hospital but nothing serious. The police say any information they can provide will be vital to tracking down the perpetrators, for whom so far, the police have had little or no clue as to their identity. This sighting represents a significant step forward. The whole country is now on heightened alert in case this is the start of a second wave of bombings."

English language never was a strongpoint of most of the Scots he'd met. The presenter was definitely Scottish but had had the corners of his accent rubbed off. Halfway between Andy Murray and Alan Partridge. "Looks like we're off on our honeymoon tomorrow" Dom said to Annie. Annie just smiled at him. She was taking pleasure in all this mayhem, death and destruction. She wasn't bothered about the possibility of Abdul having been next to a mother and pram when it went off – not that that was likely given the location, but she hadn't even considered it. She seemed unaware, or unbothered by the risks they were taking. And he thought he was a sociopath. Maybe they were better matched than he thought. But what could come from the union of two sociopaths? Was she still faking it a bit to somehow escape? Dom thought he could see through her. Could she see through Dom? Given that he'd gone from killing her to bedding her to almost eloping with her, was it really him who was calling the shots? Course it was. Would their relationship be a constant fight for control? Dom was still in control; she was following his instructions to the letter. But Annie wasn't frightened of joining in and taking the lead sometimes. In his experience of women, he would have expected a female him to be by far the scarier of the two. But he liked her. Why was that? Was it because she could see through him too? Or was she just putting on an act? Maybe that was it. No one Dom had known previously could see through him like Annie could. Mind you, none of his previous relationships, if that is what you'd call them, had been with a kidnap victim. This would surely give her an initial diagnosis of his character.

She had never once tried to escape him, overpower him or even resist him. She probably knew that Dom had had her when he had first taken her whilst she was still unconscious, but she hadn't made a big issue of this. Was this a control game? Maybe she was so desperate to find someone who could understand her and accept her for what she was that she'd settle for anyone, even him. All her life she'd been controlled, she was used to it, expected it – it was all she'd ever known. Them working as a team - it was a definite possibility; Bonny and Clyde syndrome. He shouldn't forget that she was only 16 after all and still at school in theory. She appeared to be besotted with him, all good girls liked a bad boy, especially an older one. But how long would it last? She was a lot younger than him.

Safe in the knowledge that the last bomb had finally gone off, loose ends eradicated, and false perpetrators identified, Dom and Annie turned off the radio and the PC and went to bed. Dom turned off the light and lay contemplating whilst Annie decided she wanted a little action. Soon Dom couldn't resist her, and they made love. They slept well that night, safe in the knowledge that things were once again going according to plan. Tomorrow would see the next phase of their plan unfold.

PART 4

CHAPTER 44

"And where did you get that scar from, Vincenzo?" This question always came up the first time he got naked with a girl. The scar ran from his right nipple down to his belly button. "I got in a fight in prison" was always his reply. "You should see the other guy" was usually next, but this time he didn't fill in the second part. She looked at him, studying the scar. It was a little ragged. "Who the fuck stitched it? Stevie Wonder?" she asked. "Prison doctor. Never did like me. Not sure if it was my colour, nationality of the fact that I knew his daughter." Was Vincenzo's reply. That one liner was new... he'd remember it for future use. It wasn't strictly true; he didn't even know if the doc had a daughter – they were very careful not to share any personal stuff with inmates and he himself rarely told the truth to anyone outside of his family. "Who done it?" she asked after a pause. "Some English guy in there. He got out the following night, whilst I was still in the med centre. I never did get my own back on him". His whole demeanour had now changed, she'd unknowingly pressed the destruct button. "But when I catch that SOB, I'm gonna cut him from ear to ear and nose to dick." "Now you're scaring me." She said – "I'm through". "Fuck you – piss off, I'm done with you anyways" Vincenzo shouted as she grabbed her coat, slipped into her boots and headed for the door.

Vincenzo sat for a while thinking of the guy who had cut him. "When I find him, I'm gonna make him suffer good." he thought to himself. He had already put feelers out to his contacts back in South Africa but so far no one had come back with anything firm. They had now worked out how he had switched identities with the other guy, who was about to be released. No one knew how he had escaped thereafter, where he had gone and if or how he had gotten out of the country. He knew Devizes would head back to the UK at some point, he wouldn't be able to resist, rats back to the cellar and all that. Vincenzo wasn't the only one with revenge on his mind. Dominic had the same idea and that was what motivated him to get out in the first place. And then it hit him. Devizes was incarcerated due to the fact that something had happened with a transaction he was working on with a guy there in South Africa. The guy had contacts, good ones as something had transpired resulting in Devizes ending up in a jail he was never planned to leave. Devizes had mentioned to him once how he had been shafted by this guy Montgomery, a diplomat. The name should be relatively easy to look up. Instead of chasing leads in South Africa, he'd find out who this Montgomery guy was. Devizes would surely, at some point, approach him for money or kill him or something worse. If Montgomery was still alive and well then maybe Devizes is still in South Africa or didn't make it out alive. Everyone had enemies in prison, South Africa especially. Money always helped but Devizes didn't have a lot of that, unlike Vincenzo. Vincenzo bought his freedom and escape, that and by killing a couple of key witnesses. Either way he was out and enjoying life in Miami. But now, with little else to think about, the burning desire for revenge was beginning to eat away at him. He needed to know what had happened to Devizes, so he could put it to bed – one way or another. Devizes would need good contacts and money to effect an escape from South Africa under the authority's radar and it would take time. But he had time plenty. His mind returned to the hooker who had just left his apartment. She looked a little like Debbie Harry.

"Vincenzo, it's good to hear your voice after all this time. I'm glad they saw fit to release you. Now what is this all about?"

said Thomas Eldridge. Eldridge was a solicitor in London. He was very rich and influential and he was in the pocket of just about every mafia there was. He'd worked for several high-profile people – not directly, but in doing their bidding legally and above board. The law always held that flexibility that, in the right hands, it could be exploited to make murder legal and being a victim punishable by a prison sentence that lead to an untimely accident in jail. "I'm looking for someone. He was inside with me. He escaped, and I need to find him. He has something of mine." Vincenzo tried to sound calm and reasonable. He wasn't good at keeping his temper. He had Italian blood coursing through his veins. He knew its benefits and shortcomings. "What did he take? If I know it'll help me track him down." replied Eldridge. "Just find him. I believe he'll be looking to speak with a diplomat called Montgomery, now based in London. Use him as a starting point. I'm planning a trip to the UK in a week or so. I need to know where he is for when I get here. You won't let me down will you Eldridge?". "You don't need to threaten me, Vincenzo, I've got worse cases on my back and I have friends." After a brief pause he continued "I'll start working on it tomorrow morning. I'm sure I'll have something for you by this time next week on one or both men. Have you got someone covering the South Africa angle?"

Vincenzo hung up the phone. He wasn't in the mood to talk. He had fire in his heart, and he needed to burn something. Having money, or spending money more like, didn't give him everything he needed. Money can't buy you love. It can't buy a lot of things, but it could help to get revenge. Vincenzo looked down at the scar on his chest. Every time he looked at it the burning fires of revenge were stoked a little more by the memories of burning pain. Every time a whore remarked on it more fuel was pushed onto that fire. Soon someone would get burned. He had a blue touch paper ready to attach to Devizes when he showed up. He knew Devizes was probably too clever to get himself killed in South Africa. If he could get out of there, alone, then he sure could work his way cross country, to a city and out of the country by sea or even plane. He felt sure Devizes would be in London soon if not already and on the tail of Montgomery.

He had heard of the bombings in London and the UK. Something smelled funny about these bombings. It appeared that no group had claimed responsibility. He knew that any terrorist group making that much mayhem would surely admit to it and shout it from every rooftop, even if a few got caught or killed in the process. Something wasn't right. And it could hamper his travel plans.

In the brief time he'd spent in the company of, or watching and following Devizes in prison, mainly in a bid to harm him where no one would see, he had never once spoken about anything personal to him, why he was in there, why he was so angry or even what he planned on getting out. His mention of Montgomery had only happened once, and he got the impression this was a slip. Dom hadn't spoken to him after that but had appeared to be watching him, studying him.

Most jail breaks require more than one person to effect an escape. He must have had help – but from whom? He thought of who had the necessary resources to assist someone to get out of jail over there. Whoever it was they'd be doing it for money. But by only working for one inmate wanting out, they'd be limiting their return on investment. It would make more sense to break two, three or more out, and get payment from each. Maybe Devizes was clever enough to get out alone and with no one else's assistance. If so, he was a more formidable opponent that Vincenzo had thought, or a lucky bastard. Either way, he was a dead man walking.

CHAPTER 45

Bruce was well ensconced into his new job. He now knew most of the workmen by name. He knew who was good, who wasn't so good, who was open and honest and who was likely hiding something. The basement structure was well underway, and work had started on the ground floor. The walls were shooting up around. He was now too wrapped up in the project to be unduly concerned about the basement room. Working away had its advantages. Whilst he didn't really enjoy kipping down in a B&B or cheap hotel, his rate for this job meant that he could afford a half decent one – and he'd treated himself so a nice room – fit to take a lady back to – a lady that wouldn't require payment, if he could find one, that was. It even had a mini bar. Each evening after work most of the crew would go out and have a few drinks in a pub. They were mostly from out of town like Bruce, so didn't have family commitments in the evening or even friends to visit. They just had each other, work and whatever bars would let them in and take their money. Not every bar welcomed workers from the building trade. If some of them had made an effort to clean up then they'd likely be welcome in more places, so most nights they ended up in the seedier bars. Some went home to their families at weekends, but the building work went on around the clock. Time was money. So many worked straight through only going home once a fortnight or once a month. Some didn't even own a place to live – choosing to be transients going where the work was, living in whatever accommodation was on offer. It meant fewer outgoings – except to the bars, pubs, clubs and strip joints. More money to blow. Bruce tended to mix with the more senior staff wherever the opportunity arose – the foremen, project office workers or other managers. Many of these weren't full time but came in for a few days every now and then to work on a particular stage of the project. He hadn't yet met all those involved but he knew quite a few. Today was Thursday, and he was with four others – two foremen, one project manager and the accountant. They each had a beer. It was karaoke night. The other three loved it but Bruce had never liked karaoke. He'd seen it in the States where the singers could actually sing and did it for prize money in competitions. In London or the UK, the singers seemed to do it to alleviate pain of some sort whilst inflicting more on others. Like they had a giant clamp on their balls or knife in their back. He had never once seen anyone do karaoke in a place like this that could carry a tune. He preferred a live band. Some of the bands around the circuit were good, covering many of his favourite songs. He didn't like tribute acts though. He preferred to see the real thing.

Tonight, he was about to listen to the two foremen duetting on Oasis's 'Don't Look Back in Anger'. Oasis were bad enough to begin with! He downed his pint and went to the bar for another round. It was his round again. He knew he was approaching his limit – limit up to which he could survive the next morning that was. If he imbibed further after this round, he'd have a thick head tomorrow. But he'd bought the first round and this last one – he felt he should stick around it was only fair. After all it was only eleven thirty.
But soon it was one am. Most of the bars had closed. Some of the guys had decided to move on to a lap dancing bar where they could continue to drink. Bruce, by this time, was slurring his words and a little unsteady on his feet, so had decided to call it a night. He headed off to his nice little hotel room alone. Maybe one night he'd manage to find a nice girl to take back with him. For now, he might as well have booked the B&B. He went in though reception and went up the stairs to

his room. He entered his key card – it took several attempts before he oriented the card properly and the red LED turned green granting him access. The first thing he badly needed was the toilet. He'd resisted urinating down an alley somewhere as the hotel wasn't too far away. Once he'd relieved himself, he lay down on the bed for a minute. Just a minute....

CHAPTER 46

Dom woke early – not as early as the fishermen above, but before seven. They were packing up their things in readiness for docking at Southampton. He went into the shower and a few minutes later Annie joined him. The sound of the shower must have woken her. They washed each other and made soapy love in there. Finally, they wiped each other, dressed and packed their few things, including the radio, PC and the last couple of disposable phones, into the bag they had brought aboard with the money in it and, along with their new passports and documentation, went up to the deck. They were due in Southampton in under an hour. The weather was overcast and blowy. The captain saw Dom and went over to him. "You got all your stuff?" he asked. "I don't want anything left behind down there. You were never here." Dom just looked at him for a few seconds then said, "What time are we docking?". "A little over an hour or so I think. This weather shouldn't slow us down too much." As long as they were off the boat by 11 o'clock they would have time to go and buy a big suitcase and some new clothes. No one turned up for a cruise empty handed. That would indeed look suspicious. They watched as the land drew closer and the captain navigated past the other vessels and buoys and sand banks to the docks where many other similar fishing boats were moored, each unloading their catches. Everything looked normal. Their boat was not out of place. It looked very similar to the other boats. This part of his plan had worked very well. As the fishermen started to unload their crates of fish, crabs and lobster, Annie and Dom got off the boat and walked down the pier towards shore. No one said anything. The captain watched them depart, glad to see the back of them. Dom surveyed everyone around in turn just to be on the safe side. The captain never knew who his frequent passengers were, all he knew was that they were running from something and were usually bad people. But he needed the money. Fishing wasn't a lucrative game anymore and he had bills to pay.

They crossed the street and after walking for a few minutes came to a bus stop. They waited for a couple more minutes and then a fairly empty bus arrived. They got on, paid the fares to the town centre and sat at the back. After a short ride they disembarked and walked into the town where there were many shops, restaurants and bars. Dom accompanied Annie into a couple of ladies' clothes shops where Annie chose half a dozen outfits aimed at reasonably nice weather, plus a trouser suit for when it got a bit chillier. She finished off with a couple of pairs of tight-fitting jeans and a dress. She didn't dawdle or take hours like every other woman Dom had known. She was decisive and quick to choose. She knew what suited her, all her choices looked great to Dom. They also helped her to look 20 years old, not someone still of school age. He was impressed. Then they went across the road to a gent's shop where Annie chose half a dozen pairs of shorts and tee shirts for Dom to wear on board. He also picked up a cheap suit, tie, and a couple of pairs of jeans. She also got a raft of makeup products – they needed to ensure she looked at least twenty, plus a few products for him that she had recommended. They were now laden with shopping bags blending in very nicely with the many other couples shopping there. Next, they visited a chemist to pick up toiletries and a washbag each. Lastly, they found a place selling bags. They chose a reasonably large black suitcase. Nothing that stood out, but Annie added a pink ribbon to the handle, so they wouldn't mislay it. The case was quite sturdy and could carry some weight. Dom wasn't entirely sure what else they'd be carrying this time next week. Dom dragged the new case along behind him on four wheels whilst holding bags of shopping. He placed the money bag inside. He hoped the wheels would last the week out.

After shopping for a few more bits and pieces of cosmetic jewellery to finish off Annie's appearance, they found a café and sat outside. The weather had brightened up – blue clouds were everywhere with no black ones to be found; the sea breeze had apparently carried them away. It had also brought with it a few wasps. Annie ordered a ham sandwich and a latte; Dom ordered a ham and cheese sandwich with piccalilli and a cappuccino. He was well travelled enough to know that it was late in the day for a cappuccino but ever since some Italian dick in jail had told him it was rude to every Italian to drink it after eleven am it was his drink of choice in the afternoons. He took tea in the mornings. They finished their sandwiches and finished off with a slice of Victoria sponge. Annie then proceeded to unpack their new purchases from the shopping bags and pack them into the suitcase. They kept the bags in case they came in handy during the cruise. They were all set. Dom had the passports and tickets in his new jacket pocket. It was now mid-afternoon and time they headed off to the port and on to their next boat, somewhat larger than the last one and somewhat more crowded. And more luxurious.

They took the bus back to the port and disembarked where they could see their cruise ship docked. It was being loaded with all manner of crates and people. Even pets. They stood in line and after fifteen minutes or so were aboard and looking for cabin 103. When they eventually found it, after walking more distance on the ship than they had in town, they unlocked the door to the cabin and entered. It was a standard sized cabin with a double bed, smallish bathroom with a shower and toilet and a reasonably sized wardrobe. Annie proceeded to unpack their clothes and hang them up whilst Dom took their toiletries and set out their respective stalls in the bathroom. No doubt Annie would move it all around later that evening. For now, he went ahead and took half the space for himself and his newly found man products.

Once they were fully installed in their new temporary home Dom produced the cheap wedding ring he had purchased and asked Annie to wear it. It was a necessity and part of their cover. She said, "I do" and slipped the ring onto her slim finger. Dom said he needed a drink so they left their cabin, making mental notes so they could find the room again later, and headed for the nearest bar. Annie wanted to go on deck and take a look at the pools and other facilities, childlike for the first time whilst they'd been together.

They took a lift and proceeded to walk on the deck. There were still people queueing to get on board despite the late hour. It was due to sail in thirty minutes. They took a seat at one of the bars by the larger of the two pools. A waiter came along and asked them what their poison was. Dom ordered a large beer and Annie asked for a gin and orange. The waiter didn't hesitate when taking Annie's order. He didn't suspect she was underage. The makeup and carefully selected clothes and jewellery had apparently worked. She looked like a girl next door in her early twenties, only much prettier. Dom looked like a Jack the Lad from the adjacent estate made good. The drinks soon arrived, and they relaxed. "After we've drunk these I'm going for a swim" Annie said. She didn't ask permission. She just told him what she was going to do. Dom liked this assertiveness. "Sure thing fiancée of mine." he replied. He downed the last third of a pint and they headed back to their cabin to get changed. Annie put on her new bikini and flip flops and Dom donned swimming shorts, Crocs and a tee shirt. Annie didn't like the Crocs, but Dom had insisted. They looked like a regular young couple, Dom being the older of the two by a few years. Annie had never been on a ship like this before.

She'd never really spent any vacation time away from her

father. Vacations with him tended to be diplomatic visits to here and there where she spent time alone in their hotel suite whilst her father went off with his buddies drinking and smoking cigars and purchasing rent boys, no doubt. As they got back onto the deck they went back into the bar for one more, at Dom's request. They saw an older couple sidling towards them. They sat down on the adjacent table. "Get us a drink, Marion." the man said. "Give over, there's waitresses here Jim." she replied. They looked like they'd been saving for a long time for this cruise. They looked kind of out of place in their Benidorm attire and Jim's big cigar. He wasn't so much smoking it as sporting it, for effect. Annie wondered if they'd won the lottery or maybe it was a special anniversary. Maybe he was related to Jimmy Saville? She wondered how old they were – mid-sixties? Late fifties? She didn't really care. Dom stared off at the pool admiring some of the swimmers and sun bathers beside the pool and studying the blokes, especially single ones to see if any smelled like copper. He thought it was a bit chilly for sunbathing, but they were probably sun addicts. There was a sun tanning service onboard as well – why bother? he thought. Annie ordered two more drinks. As it was all inclusive it looked like Annie intended getting her money's worth despite the fact that she hadn't paid for it in the first place. She wondered where Dom had gotten the money from to pay for this. He can't have known he'd need two tickets. How had he pulled it off? Surely, he'd paid a long time ago. But he can't have, or he would have only booked one place. He must have used the new credit card with a view to paying it off with some of the money her father had provided. So, she was paying for it with her inheritance after all. She didn't care. It was about time she had a good time with some of his money. With her newly acquired knowledge and skills she could soon get more. This made her think about her father's estate. When they finally found the body or declared him dead, she would be the sole beneficiary. How was she going to collect the cash? She couldn't just turn up after being abducted. "Dom, when they find out he's croaked it, how do I get my inheritance, what I deserve?" she asked. "Keep your voice down, he said, anything like that we discuss in the cabin." Annie thought about this for a few moments then said, "Drink up husband, we need to talk." Dom finished his pint once again and they headed back towards the lifts. Dom was pleased he hadn't had to go swimming but wasn't looking forward to having to explain anything to her.

"See you later, young 'uns" Jim said as they passed. Annie gave them a wave. She hoped they wouldn't bump into Marion and Jim again. Dom had a sudden desire to throw them both overboard.

They found their way back to the cabin after only making one wrong turn. Dom had insisted it was left, Annie thought it was right but didn't say anything. She was pleased when they discovered he'd gone wrong. Once back in the cabin she said "So?". Dom looked at her. "You can't just go back. Besides if they don't find his body, which is a possibility, they won't declare him dead for years – like Lord Lucan. You'll have to be patient.". "We need to think up a story, I'm not missing out on what I'm due. I've earned that money after being treated like that by that bastard." she said. Dom hadn't really considered Annie's inheritance as a factor in his plan. He hadn't considered Annie a factor in his plan at all after getting the money off Montgomery. He wondered what other things would turn up that he hadn't planned for. Annie had a point though. She was due money – probably a lot of money. How could she turn up unscathed to collect it? More loot for him to claim one way or another. He was pondering the subject when Annie said, "Leave it with me - I'll think of something." Dom didn't want Annie adding her two pennyworths into the mix. Planning was his area. "So, are we swimming or not?" Dom asked. At that point they felt the ship start to move. They were underway. So far so good. Who would think of looking for bombers on a cruise ship?

The only way for Dom to remain in control of Annie and out of prison was to plan everything to the last detail himself and try and keep at least one step ahead of her. She was more formidable than most of the criminals he regularly dealt with. This was the first time Dom had considered that bringing Annie along was possibly a mistake. It appeared she considered herself as his equal partner in this. They were indeed engaged but not married just yet. This would require some thought. He liked to think whilst looking out to sea or drinking. In this case both. They freshened up and headed back to deck. It was approaching dinner time and they were both hungry. They hadn't eaten a proper hot meal for a while, and never together. They were both quietly looking forward to a dinner date to celebrate their marriage.

The ship offered a number of restaurants. Annie spotted an Asian restaurant and headed towards it. Dom followed. They briefly looked at the menu which was a fusion of Indian and Thai food. This ticked both their boxes, so they went in and sat in a quiet corner. The food was a buffet service. The waiter came and took their drinks order and explained the process of getting their food. They waited for their bottles of Cobra beer to arrive. They poured them into their glasses, took a glug, stood up and headed towards the food. There was a small queue. As it was the first day of the cruise everything was new to some but familiar to others. Some had obviously travelled this way before, possibly on this very ship, and knew the score, not to mention the menu. Dom headed towards the starter area selecting a couple of poppadums and a bowl of mango chutney and lime pickle. Annie choose prawn crackers and sweet chilli sauce. They returned to their table, passing a couple seated close by. They were an older couple, mid-fifties. She looked a little older than him, with a dried wrinkly skin borne from too much time in the sun, maybe even too many fags. They sat down and simultaneously started to crunch.

Dom quickly finished his poppadums and took a couple of the prawn crackers too. Annie smiled at him as he partook in her starter. He mopped up the leftover sweet chilli sauce but compared to his lime pickle it tasted more like sugary ketchup. Before they had time to stand up, a waiter came and took their plates away. They then returned for a selection of starters. Dom chose a mixed kebab starter whilst Annie chose a chicken tikka. Once again, they returned to their table and quickly ate their starters. "Want to wait a while before we go for mains?" Dom asked Annie. "Let's order more drinks then grab more food. I haven't eaten like this in weeks.". Annie was clearly having a nice time. Their drinks soon arrived, and Annie took Dom's hand and lead him back to the food area, to where a range of Indian and Thai dishes awaited them. As they passed the older couple, she heard the woman say "Ah, young love." to her husband. "I don't remember." was his reply.

Dom went for the hottest dish he could see – chicken vinda-loo. He took some egg rice and a keema naan. Annie chose kung po chilli chicken, noodles and a couple of spring rolls. Dom wondered if she was going to eat the lot – she didn't look big enough to finish off a plateful like that. But fifteen minutes later her plate was clean. Dom was mopping his plate clean with the last pieces of his naan bread and feeling quite stuffed. More Cobras arrived. This was Annie's fourth drink – Dom had had five. She didn't seem any worse for wear. Maybe she could take her drink well. He'd expected her to not eat much, let alone spicy Asian food, and to drink orange juice, not beer. She was some girl. Was this her or was she playing to Dom? He wasn't entirely sure, but she had seemed perfectly at home eating and drinking. Most sixteen-year-old girls would have some ill effects after downing four strong lagers, even with a big meal. They had chatted about the ship, about some of the people they'd spotted, in particular a lesbian couple seated closer to the food. They were both getting their money's worth – they were on their second plate of curry. As both

Annie and Dom were too full for a sweet, plus neither of them fancied a banana or pineapple fritter or a really rich Indian desert, they decided to go back on deck and find an ice-cream and, of course, more drink. Most of the people seemed to be either eating or getting ready to eat, so the deck was quiet apart from the restaurant areas. They went towards the front of the ship and sat down in a bar. Again, a waiter arrived promptly to take their orders. "Beer please" said Dom in his practised middle England accent. "Glass of bubbly please" Annie said. "You celebrating something special Madam?" the waiter enquired. "We've just got married" Annie replied pushing her ring finger in his direction. "Very nice indeed Madam, you're a lucky man indeed sir if I may say so." he said looking at Dom. Dom smiled. "I'm afraid the champagne doesn't come as part of the all-inclusive but given your happy news we'd be happy to offer you both a glass of bubbly – on the house as we say! I look forward to seeing you both here again for many years to come." Annie beamed at him. "Why thank you very much indeed." she said.

The waiter toddled off back to the bar to fix their drinks. He returned with two large glasses of bubbly and a beer. "A toast" said Annie… "to us, the happy couple." Some of the other guests were looking in their direction. "To us" he said, and they toasted their marriage. He hoped they wouldn't be the talk of the older cruisers – that's the last thing he wanted. Still he was sure they weren't the only newlyweds on the ship. Not to mention the ruby and diamond wedding celebrations that would surely transpire over the coming days.

After another beer they decided to go for a walk around the ship before retiring for the night. Dom wanted to make sure he knew the layout, just in case. Annie had opened up to him during the course of the evening, chattering like an excited schoolgirl about the ship, the people, the pools, the shops… just like an ordinary girl with her boyfriend. Maybe it was the effects of the alcohol. It was as though they'd known each other for months. Acting like newlyweds wouldn't be as difficult as he had imagined. She chattered on and he listened. As he listened, he thought about what courses of action lay open to them with respect to Annie's inheritance. It could be an interesting and tempting option for a plan B or C should their fortunes change. But it would rely solely on Annie. But it seemed just too risky. Inconceivable even.

CHAPTER 47

Bruce awoke with a start. At first, he didn't know where he was. He looked up at the ceiling – it was very bright, and the curtains were open. The ceiling was rotating clockwise slowly. After recognising his hotel room and recalling his exploits last night his thoughts turned to the time. He consulted his watch – 8.30. Shit – he would be late for work. The guys would make fun of him. Still it was Friday and he was looking forward to a relaxing weekend. He quickly showered and dressed. He was on site before 9am. He passed one of the foremen with whom he had been drinking the previous evening – Dave. Dave smiled at him as he went by, and casually looked at his watch and raised an eyebrow with a smirk. Bruce didn't rise to him, just nodded and went on past. He went to the first floor checking on some of the ongoing activities. All seemed well so he went down to the basement to see how the finishing was coming on. Most of the wiring was in, as was the plumbing. As he moved around, he saw some new faces in the basement area. The other foreman from last night, also called Dave, but who preferred to be called David, was answering their questions. Dom went up to David and stood patiently whilst he answered a question about redundant power entering the building. David was explaining that power came into the building from two opposite directions and from two different suppliers. That way they had contingency against either company going bust, which was highly unlikely given they were major players, or unforeseen things like roadworks severing a power cable, or extreme weather etc. When David had finished the answer to the satisfaction of the two new faces he turned to Bruce and said "Bruce – meet Tim and Gavin – they are from Specialist Securities Ltd. who are fitting out the remainder of the basement." Bruce took this to mean the central area referred to on the plans as the secure storage facility. He had been unaware of their visit. Tim and Gavin looked at Bruce. They weren't particularly jolly or welcoming. Bruce introduced himself. "I'm Bruce and I'm the project manager for this project. I oversee all aspects of the project and manage all the suppliers. Any problems come directly to me." David added "I'm just briefing the guys on the ins and outs of the basement, wiring, power, plumbing etc. They will be working independently, mainly inside the SSF getting it ready for use." Bruce considered this answer. He had overall responsibility for the project but had not previously been made aware of this new work to be done within the SSF as David had called it. As overall PM he should have seen the relevant detailed plans and been involved in the decision as to whether a third party was required to do whatever it was that needed doing in there. He didn't know what needed to be done, or who the hell this company was that was doing it. As he considered how to broach this subject Tim spoke up "I appreciate you have been a little in the dark with respect to this facet of the facility, but this is normal practice. Many of the wealthy owners of companies who are in the fortunate position of being able to afford to build a bespoke office block come residence choose to use our services to build in a SSF where they can safely store their valuables or confidential business documents. Whilst it isn't commonplace it isn't particularly uncommon either, especially in the wealthier parts of inner cities. Most of the buildings in Manhattan built from 1990 onwards have something similar. Despite his experience, Bruce had never come across such a requirement. Of all the building projects he'd worked on, none had had a facility like this. Still, maybe the owners he'd previously worked for hadn't been as wealthy as this one, whoever they were. He decided to keep this to himself. "No problem, I understand completely" he replied. "We knew you would. You came highly recommended, so we hear" chipped in Gavin. Somehow, they didn't look like fitters. They were too smartly dressed and didn't have workmen's hands or mannerisms and they didn't speak like workmen either. They reminded Bruce more of homeland security – but not very homely. Still it made no odds to him. He'd done his part provisioning the infrastructure and services for the SSF, let them get on with it. "If you need my assistance for anything please don't hesitate to come find me or call me – any time day or night." Bruce replied and gave them a card with his mobile number on. Tim and Gavin nodded. David then went on to say, "As for the climate control, both heating and cooling systems are fitted, and these work independently to the rest of the building...." Bruce nodded and went on with his business leaving David to brief the SSF team.

Bruce's spidey senses were definitely tingling. He'd suspected from the off that there was something funny with the basement design. For what reasons did they need all these facilities for that one room. The room was highly secure, independent and could be used to store almost anything including people – like a hideaway or panic room. Or a prison. He decided to make no big deal at the moment but to watch what Tim and Gavin were up to and to learn more about what was going in that room, and its potential uses, as the work continued. They were scheduled to be working there for three weeks. That was a long time for one room. A very long time indeed. They could fit an entire floor out in the same time.

CHAPTER 48

Dom could hear the shower. He looked at his watch – seven fifteen. What kind of a getting up time was that when you're on a cruise! It was nearer going to bedtime than getting up time! He could see her outline through the shower door. Steam was coming back into the room. He got up and opened the curtain over the port hole. Open sea, calm weather and blue skies. He suspected it would be chillier outside than it looked! He went into his wardrobe and pulled out a pair of swimming shorts and a tee shirt. He waited for Annie to step out of the shower. She grabbed a towel and, upon spotting Dom up and about, she went over to him, naked but holding the towel. "Dry me off, would you?" she asked. Dom obliged, and one thing lead to another. Forty minutes later Dom finally made it to the shower. When he emerged, Annie was dressed in her new bikini. "Won't you be a little chilly in that number?" Dom said. "OK then, I'll take my cardigan." She replied. He noticed she had put the ring back on. She seemed to like wearing the ring. She was applying her makeup. She was a very beautiful young woman. In the past couple of days, as she had seemed to become increasingly happy with her lot, she had become even more beautiful. Her demeanour was changing from a sullen teenager to a happy young woman. When her makeup was complete, they ventured on deck. It was fairly quiet at this early hour. First on their list was breakfast, they both had a good appetite now. After selecting a place to eat, they both went for a full English – bacon, fried eggs, tomatoes, mushrooms and a sausage. Red sauce naturally. After a couple of coffees each they decided to check out the pool area. They'd take a couple of loungers and let their breakfasts go down for a while. "We should find the bookstore and buy ourselves a couple of books each." Annie remarked. "Good idea." replied Dom, but he found it difficult to concentrate whilst reading in a public place. He was a people watcher. Partly out of interest, and an eye for a pretty girl, and also because, with his track record, he always had to be on the lookout for someone that was on the lookout for him. He was pretty sure that, on this ship, no one knew who either of them was. He should relax. "You pick me a couple of books then." He said. "Well what sort of book do you read? Shakespeare?" Dom smiled. "No, not fucking Shakespeare!" they both laughed. "Maybe a Steven King or a Dean Koontz – something grizzly!". She nodded and headed back to find the bookstore. He wondered what she would choose for herself – Mills and Boon? Fifty Shades of Grey? Agatha Christie? The Railway Children? He realised then that he knew very little about her. She, like himself, didn't give anything away and he hadn't really bothered to try and get to know her. But now he trusted her enough to let her go off to the bookstore alone and without a second thought. How things had changed over a few short days. He decided he should try and make the most of their time together over the coming days to get to know each other better. Whether he chose to keep her or get rid of her, he would be in a much better position if he knew more about her, her past, and above all else, what made her tick. Being with Annie was fun and as a couple they had the potential to get away with murder. A most unlikely criminal pairing.

He carefully watched each person or couple that came on deck. It was mainly couples, aged forty upwards. There were a few younger couples but in the main middle aged. He guessed that not many younger folks could afford a cruise – or wanted to go on one. The next stop was Lisbon, then on to Gibraltar, Malaga, Casablanca and Madeira amongst other places. With the exception of Malaga, Dom hadn't visited any of these places before. He thought they should take a tour of the places wherever the ship docked. In his experience, each place had something to offer a career criminal. Everywhere had something. Maybe one of these places would make an ideal place to spend a few months and lie low whilst spending the remainder of Montgomery's money. He knew that the money wouldn't last forever – especially the way they were spending it at the moment. Annie seemed to be quite bright, if they did choose to settle somewhere for a while, she could get a job at a bar or as a rep or something. He would find opportunities to put his skills to use.

Annie returned with a carrier bag which looked like it had half a dozen books. They must have been cheap as he had only given her twenty pounds. "There you go." She said with a smile on her face. Dom opened the bag. "Wuthering Heights?" he said. "Is that for me?". "No silly, that's mine. I always wanted to read it." He delved deeper into the bag and pulled out Beast House Volumes I, II and III. He checked out the back page. It was about a monster brought to an American town that had apparently bred and eaten locals for many years. "I like this one – good choice." he said to Annie. Her face beamed. He wondered if he'd ever get as far as the second book in this grizzly trilogy. As instructed, Annie had also bought a newspaper – the Independent. Dom picked up the newspaper and scoured it for anything related to their recent activities. It was no longer dominating the headlines completely. As well as significant conjecture about the bombings, the other headlines were back to the same old PM/US President stories of backtracking, corruption and cutbacks. Page 5 was the first page that attracted his interest. He read the full two-page article. It appeared to be an unbiased article about the five bombs, the sixth hadn't made it to press yet, the possible motives and some of the victims. "I was driving up to Stoke from Coventry and as I was approaching Spaghetti Junction, I saw a bright flash and then heard an almighty boom. I saw some of the cars ahead appeared to be swerving so I slowed own, put on my hazards and to my surprise I saw part of the carriageway drop away taking a couple of cars with it. I immediately stopped hoping to God that I wouldn't drop down. Some of the cars tried reversing but in panic they just ran into other cars. It was carnage. All the traffic behind ground to a halt apart from one idiot in a Porsche who carried on trying to swerve around the damage only to take flight. People started getting out of their cars and soon there were a few groups of people discussing whether they should go and help – but there was nothing we could do. We couldn't get down there and it seemed too dangerous to go any nearer, so we just waited. Some turned their cars around in an attempt to get well away and soon the whole place was jammed solid. After 5 minutes or so we heard sirens down at ground level. Then some traffic officers came along the hard shoulder on foot. They put up barriers and told us to wait where we were, in our vehicles with the engines off until they came back with more instructions. Two hours we waited. Then it took another three or four hours to get the cars backed up to the previous exit and off. By then it was so late I just went home." said Geoff from Coventry. Later on, he read that the two cars that had initially fallen had both been driven by businessmen with no passengers. They'd dropped off the side and crashed onto the ground below. There was no mention of the Porsche. Both drivers were in a serious condition at the City hospital, lucky to be alive by all accounts. It was a miracle they weren't dead. There were no photographs of the wreckage as reporters couldn't get close enough, with the large area that was cordoned off. The media had to settle for aerial pictures taken by helicopter. The aerial photographs showed the junction with what looked like a bite mark from the lower carriageway. It reminded him of a cake that a dog had managed to get hold of. The dog would still be hungry - he wondered how much bigger the device needed to have been in order to take the whole bridge down with all its overlying bridges. Still, it didn't matter, his device had served its purpose. He was, of course, more interested in the news relating to the Thelwall Viaduct bomb where dear old Daddy was probably still residing, or reposing, or decomposing. Annie hadn't mentioned him and seemed to bear no indications of feeling any kind of loss for him. Even stranger, she hadn't asked or appeared to be interested in whether or not his body had been found. This was the sort of thing that was troubling Dom. He didn't as yet know whether it should be making him nervous of his new-found travelling companion and partner in unholy matrimony. He was the one who had, on numerous occasions, been told by friends, foes, psychiatrists and law enforcement, that he had sociopathic tendencies. Still, this facet of his character meant that, should he decide that she was no longer of use to him, she could still go for an extended swim with the fishes. And on this cruise, there would be some seriously big fishes around. A cruise liner like this would have a massive turning circle and be unable to slow down or speed up quickly in the event of a man, or woman, overboard. That's if anyone saw them go over and raised the alarm. It was more akin to a coach than a Porsche. If someone happened to fall overboard and was seen doing so and the alarm was raised, by the time the liner had managed to get back to that position, the poor unfortunate would likely be drowned or consumed. Just finding the person would be very difficult as the swell would tend to hide them from view. Unless it was dead calm – but Dom knew no one would have such an accident in dead calm. It was far more likely that someone would fall overboard in rough conditions or on a midnight romantic walk when there was no one around and all the biddies were tucked up in bed. He always had a plan B. Maybe this one should be called plan sea.

CHAPTER 49

"Bob Cable's phone" PC William Burroughs said whilst stretching across his own desk to reach Bob's phone, which had now been ringing for some twenty seconds, driving him mad. He had spent the past two days, and most of the nights, with his small team viewing the CCTV footage he had acquired from the Highways Agency and any businesses in the surrounding area of the Thelwall Viaduct. There was a lot of footage – the area was huge, and they had no idea in which direction Montgomery, the kidnapper, Annie or any of them had come from or departed to. Bob had given him a description of Montgomery's vehicle and registration plate so they could see if it was under the bridge or parked nearby. No motorway cameras or road-based cameras with number plate recognition had flagged his car. Assuming this was the place for the drop, which was a big assumption, Burroughs had been counting on that as a starting point, giving an idea of the direction of travel. He had, in his own mind, chosen what would have been his preferred route under the circumstances, and it didn't involve the M6. He knew the M6 was littered with cameras, average speed cameras and police cars and traffic officers, all eager to grab your number plate in return for penalty points. He himself had six points – all for speeding slightly above the limit and caught on camera. He despised the cameras. Even though he was on police business on both occasions he wasn't treated differently to any other driver. He knew it would be impossible to get all that far without being clocked by at least a few cameras.

"I need to speak to Bob – I have some information that he will find very useful.". "Who shall I say is calling?" Burroughs replied. "Tell him it's Jack." was the curt response. Burroughs was busy and didn't have time to waste so he put the receiver down, muttered the words "ignorant git" and walked over to the kitchen where Bob was pouring himself a large black coffee. "Some ignorant git called Jack on the phone for you gov.". Bob picked up his coffee and returned to his desk, spilling a little as he put the mug down on his desk. This was the call he'd been waiting for.

"Jack, what have you got for me?" Jack was never a man that sounded excited, or pleased with himself, he was always a miserable twat. In all his dealings with Jack, Bob had never found anything about him that made him want to have a drink with him or even talk to him any longer than necessary. Strange, as he'd take a drink with almost anyone in the nick. "Montgomery requested time off, it was straight after he contacted you. Whatever he intended doing, he had done a little planning beforehand. He never took time off work.". "It that it?" Bob replied. "He was due back on Monday. Until then no one seemed concerned about his whereabouts. I think you should contact his office and explain the situation. I'm sure that'll get you more time to work on this Bob – and I know you well enough to know that's what this is all about. Sod the bomber shit, when you have your teeth in something you never put it down. "Thanks Jack, if you find anything else please let me know. And give me a call to see if he's turned up, will you?". "Sure thing, but we both know he won't." Jack replied curtly. "Thanks again." Bob said and put the phone down. It seemed that Montgomery's office was unconcerned about his sudden time off. Surely a guy in his position had commitments that couldn't be easily rearranged to accommodate a week off at little notice? He knew something wasn't quite right about Montgomery. He decided to rattle some cages, but first he needed something firm on which to justify his rattlings. "Bill, found any trace of Montgomery's car on that CCTV mountain you have there?". Bill looked at Bob across the desk. "You see how much I've got to go through – single handed. I've been at it for 36 hours already and I reckon it'll take me another week solid to go through this lot. I'd appreciate some help here gov.". "Wouldn't we all." was Bob's response. Bill tutted and went back to his screen. As well as his PC he had a video recorder and TV on his desk. It amazed him how many businesses still relied on video tapes and hadn't gone digital. He had fitted an IP web cam at home. His camera, which cost him twenty-five quid off eBay, was surveying the front of his house and his car. He could view it on his phone or laptop from anywhere. It could even notify him if it detected movement. Next time those kids off the estate went near his car he'd have something concrete to get them with. Even the police were victims of crime and could share in the knowledge that so many crimes went unpunished. And even unlooked into. Bill was more interested in the bombings; Bob was more interested in the diplomat whose daughter had been abducted. But he remained vigilant with his CCTV. He didn't want to miss anything that could later be used in evidence against him.

Bob was still mulling over Montgomery. He was desperate to know if Montgomery, and possibly his daughter, and even more remotely, the kidnapper, had been crushed under the viaduct in a somewhat inconceivable, coincidental calamity and whether there were any other cars under there. If, as he suspected, this was the location Montgomery had arranged to meet the kidnapper for the exchange, lady luck had definitely not been looking down on him. If she was looking down on Bob now, maybe there would be something useful recovered. As if by magic, Bob's phone buzzed – it was a text message from forensics. "Car recovered and body parts – tiny body parts – it could be Montgomery, but we won't know until we get DNA check done." Bob picked up his desk phone and dialled in the number of the mobile from which the text had been sent. It was answered on the first ring. The call was quite brief lasting no more than two minutes. His main questions were, had the tissue samples been sent for DNA testing and when were they due back? "We're rushing them through now sir, priority uno." was the reply he received. The day dragged a little until a little after three when his phone rang again.

This call was briefer than the last. They had a DNA match against some of the tissues recovered to Montgomery. Not a full match but enough to be fairly sure that it was him. Bob knew it was him – it had been his hunch all along.
So, what had Bob learned? Montgomery was in a car when the bomb went off causing him and the car to be blown up and then crushed beneath the debris. Well, some of him was in the car. Some was beside the car and some bits were missing, possibly carried off by hungry animals for their dinner. Bob imagined rats feasting on selected cuts. Forensics thought that the bomb must have been very close to Montgomery's car to do so much immediate damage. It appeared that the windows had been blown out before the debris fell onto the car and it had been badly burned, as had the carrion. The car was a real mess. Given that part of the carriageway above Montgomery's car had collapsed it was likely that the bomber had placed the device by one of the concrete pillars that held up the carriageway above. These were large structures and would equally well serve as a good place to park where your vehicle would be obscured to any possible witnesses.

Had he stumbled upon the location of the bomb? Was this just a huge coincidence? The reasons for choosing a particular location to meet a kidnapper under this particular bridge were pretty similar to those for hiding a bomb beneath it. He needed to know where the device had been placed. He knew it was possibly just a coincidence that Montgomery was at that particular place at the wrong time, but he didn't like coincidences. Could it be possible that the bombing and Montgomery kidnapping were somehow linked? He knew if he took this to his super that he'd get laughed out of the office. It was plain to see that Bob wanted to focus on the Montgomery case rather than the bombings. Murder was his thing, not bombings. None of the team had much experience with bombings but that made no odds at all. The area was being carefully sifted and any pieces of the car or its occupant would be collected and carefully inspected. It wouldn't be long before they could give him an indication of where the bomb was sited, and where Montgomery was when it went off. Cause of death seemed pretty obvious to Bob but they were nothing if not thorough. It was amazing what they could discover from burned pieces of flesh.

Bob learned nothing else that day and left the office at nine pm, stopping by the pub for a couple before going home to his frozen curry. Lamb madras. He put the kettle on and put some basmati rice into a pan along with various seeds and turmeric. He put his curry on defrost then poured the boiling water over the rice and lit the ring beneath. He set the timer to 9 minutes, just enough time to defrost the curry, heat it up and switch on the telly. Prime Suspect, 1973. Nice, but he preferred the lighter entertainment of Dave when there was something good on. He opened a bottle of Cobra and took a long swig of the cool beer and settled down in his chair to eat his TV dinner.

CHAPTER 50

"How is my new residence coming along?" Rimmer knew that his latest project would take months to build but he kept even his closest, longest service men on their toes at all times. They knew what would happen if they failed him, they'd seen it with their own eyes. They were remunerated well and enjoyed the protection of working for the one of the largest criminal masterminds in London. Their life was infinitely better than when they had been selected and taken from their respective gutters some years previously. Rimmer wanted this project completed as soon as possible as he had big plans. For his plans to be fulfilled he didn't need the whole of the building to be completed. After all, much of the building was a cover for the heart beneath.

Even at school, when he bothered turning up, Rimmer had been a bully. By the age of twelve he was already only a couple of inches shy of six feet. Not the tallest in his year but nevertheless he was known by both students and staff as the one to watch out for, and under no circumstances to cross. It wasn't just him, of course, it was his family. The governors had tried their best to block his transfer to this school, not just because of his past record at previous schools, but because of who he was. They all now knew that they were stuck with this unsavoury character and would have to make the most of it. A couple of the teachers left within six months of Rimmer starting there. One by his own accord, one who was encouraged. The family had plans for Rimmer, even at his tender age. By the time he became a teenager he would have already committed two murders. Now at forty-two he was king of the hill. Succession and premature death paved the way to where he was standing now, basking in the midday sun of Johannesburg. His bags were packed, and his private jet would soon be heading to his favourite airfield, then on to his soon to be new abode. He would have a floor to himself and he would allow Vincenzo a floor to himself also. He'd told Vincenzo that he could have the top floor, but he would, of course, take that floor himself.

CHAPTER 51

Bob's arse had been on fire ever since he woke up that morning. He was now sat at his desk trying to get comfortable on his old, well-worn office chair. The lamb madras was a hot one, must have been in the freezer for eons. He thought about venturing to the gents before he let one rip but decided that he'd have worn the soles off his shoes by lunch time if he did that, so he sat there and tried to make it quietly, whilst avoiding any possibility of following through. Easier said than done, especially at his age. At nine o'clock he called his contact at forensics to see what they had gleaned from the bits and pieces they'd recovered from under the bridge. He was disappointed to hear that, despite working through the night in the lab, they hadn't found anything more conclusive as yet – no further remains indicating any other blown up bodies under the bridge. They were still searching the area during daylight, but the weather wasn't helping. It had once again rained heavily the previous evening and however hard they tried to prevent any evidence washing into the canal, it was near impossible given the amount of rain coming down. No traces of any other parties had been recovered indicating that the kidnapper and Annie were both still unaccounted for. It's possible that, even if they were under there somewhere, that they'd remain unaccounted for – that was a loose end that was unthinkable.

Bob considered all the possible scenarios. Had the kidnapper been there at the time of the bomb? Had he seen Montgomery either being blown up or turned up at the scene to see he was already dead? Or heard the explosion and got the fuck out of there ASAP – that's what Bob thought he'd have done in his shoes. So far, no money had been recovered from the site but, given the nature of the scene, that wasn't surprising either. Had the kidnapper taken the money off Montgomery before the bomb had detonated? No traces of cash had been recovered but they could have simply burned away. He needed answers to these questions, but would he ever get definitive ones? It was still nothing more than conjecture. There had been no reported sightings of Montgomery's daughter that could be corroborated. He knew the chances that she was still being held alive were slim to none at all. If the kidnapper had indeed seen Montgomery get killed in front of him and had no way to recover the money what would he do with Annie? He knew the answer to this question already. Nevertheless, he wanted to be sure that she wasn't slowly dying without sufficient attempts to find her, that would be unbearable and a PR disaster for the boss. But there was no pressure from her family to find her. Her father was gone, he was all she had. Poor bitch. There were no relatives or friends sat in reception asking every cop coming in and out what was happening to find her. There was no media pressure as they were all focussing on the bombings, ignorant of this by comparison small crime. It was lucky that Bob liked a challenge. Most of his colleagues wouldn't have given her a second thought and just followed orders.

Bob looked up and saw Bill returning to his desk. "I think I may have something for you gov." he said. Bob needed a break, this case was getting to him more than he realised.

CHAPTER 52

Annie selected a summery dress and she and Dom went up on deck for breakfast. Lisbon was their destination today and they should be there before noon. The newlyweds would go ashore and spend some time checking out the town. Annie had suggested that this was a good place to pick up a more convincing wedding ring. Dom just wanted a change of scenery, so he could think clearly and refine his plans. He was reluctant to spend any of the cash on the ship in case the serial numbers blew their cover, despite the fact that he was almost certain that the notes he now had were untraceable. Nevertheless, they needed more Euros. After their breakfast, they returned to their cabin and changed into something more appropriate for walking around the town and followed the hordes of elderly tourists off the ship and towards the shops and restaurants. They managed to walk past many of them and headed towards the town, as they walked quicker than them. First on his shopping list was a couple of British newspapers. They had the Daily Express and The Independent. By then it was after one and they chose a tapas place overlooking the sea. They ordered food and drinks, and each took a paper and proceeded to read everything about the bombings. By the time their food came they had both read through the salient parts of the stories. Nothing whatsoever of interest or to cause them concern. Nothing about Montgomery or Annie's abduction either. It looked like that had been kept quiet or completely overshadowed by the bombings. For now, they could continue to enjoy their honeymoon. Dom ordered a couple more drinks. The sun was shining, and they were enjoying each other's company. Both making plans.

They left the restaurant with a couple of hours left before they needed to head back to the liner. They decided to head back now, have a swim then get showered and dressed for dinner. The pool wasn't as full as usual. There were several pools of course, but they preferred the largest of them as it offered a better chance to swim. They were both fit and good swimmers. On the far side of the pool was an elderly couple. Once again, they fit the bill for cruisers; mid-sixties, well dressed, brown wrinkled skin from too many cruises and beaches, beer bellies and bingo wings from all the rich food and drink and probably a good few bottles of bubbly to boot. She had a nice swimsuit which would have looked great on Annie, if it were 6 sizes smaller. He had a polo top and shorts. Annie sat at the edge of the pool dangling her feet in the water whilst Dom ordered them a couple of beers.

The seagulls flew all around the ship, sometimes diving to steal food from people. Some idiots put food out for them. He was beginning to understand the attraction of cruises. A daily routine with no worries, not a care in the world. Everything you needed all there 24 hours and free. Bars, restaurants, shops, entertainment, music and sun. They stayed by the pool until the sun started to set and it got a little chilly. Then they went back to their evening routine of cabin, shower, dress for dinner then eat.

CHAPTER 53

Bob was standing beside Bill looking at the footage from a CCTV camera that Bill had indicated could possibly contain Montgomery's car. The footage was dark and of poor quality, but it showed a car of the same make, similar in size and colour to Montgomery's heading along Warrington road. The road ran parallel to the water and the vehicle was heading from Latchford docks towards the bridge. It was by no means conclusive but useful in building up a picture of Montgomery's movements. "Good work." Bob said, adding "For now we'll assume this is him. If we assume he came in from the West, prioritise any CCTV on the way in that could follow this route.". "OK, but there aren't many cameras over that way that work. If he knew their locations, he could have bypassed them.". With that, Bill went back to his desk to continue his laborious work that was the essence of police work but never appeared in the movies. Bill was the guy that did all the leg-work and got none of the credit.

Bob had come to the inevitable conclusion that Montgomery had gone solo. Maybe they should have tracked him and considered that possibility from the onset but that was just not how it happened. They didn't have the resources, or the legal right. Somehow the abductor or abductors had known that the police were involved, and they had threatened Montgomery. How had they known? Did they even know – had they tried their hand to test him like a game of poker? Montgomery must have disregarded everything they'd told him for whatever reason and gone solo, complied with the kidnappers' demands and gone to make a drop. Whether he had actually made the drop, was making the drop at the time of the explosion, or just happened to be under the bridge with a mistress or something they may well never find out. What he knew for sure was that Montgomery hadn't been seen since the explosion. Neither had his daughter Annie. All these events had to be connected. It was too big of a coincidence. The only logical connection was that he was planning to meet the abductors under the bridge. It would have been a good place, out of sight and leaving Montgomery exposed. They would have found a vantage point offering them a good view of the surroundings so as to check for him having brought company. Bob was convinced he had been alone at this point. Maybe Montgomery had arrived early.

If he had made the exchange, he would have gotten out of there sharpish. He must have been waiting to make the drop when the bomb went off. That meant that the abductors and Annie couldn't be too far away and if that were indeed the case then the exchange was to be made somewhere under the bridge or close by. "Bill, forget what I said earlier, I want to focus on the possible abductors' vehicle. Assume that Montgomery was going there to meet the abductors and possibly to make an exchange of cash for his daughter. Focus on any vehicles that could be the abductors with Annie inside." Bob said across the desk to Bill. Bill thought for a few seconds, frowning then replied "How the hell will I know it's them? We don't know how many of them there are and in all probability the daughter would be tied up in the boot." Bob thought for a minute then said, "I know it's not gonna be easy, but look at every vehicle you see and make a note of any that could conceivably be them." Bill glared at Bob, then tutted and turned away muttering "OK, but don't expect anything quick. It'll take me a week to go through this lot again! And any fucking one could be them.". Bill was obviously very pissed off indeed. Bob felt a little bad, after all, Bill had already gone through most of the footage once already looking for Montgomery's car. "Teamwork. I'll get the coffees." Bob said, then went off to the coffee machine for two coffees. Bill just sat there, summoning up the dregs of his enthusiasm to start back at the beginning of the footage looking for God knows what. As Bob put Bill's coffee onto his desk Bob's phone rang. He put his drink down quickly, spilling a little onto his desk and adding another stain to his vast collection, and picked up the phone. "Cable." he said. Bill was still glaring across the desks as Bob's expression lightened up a bit. Bob was nodding and saying things like "oh" and "right" and "interesting" and "are you sure?". When he put the receiver down Bill was still looking his way. Bob saw this and said "Forensics under the Thelwall Viaduct have found body parts near the remains of a car and they think it's possible that the car housed the bomb. They'll catalogue the remains, bring them in and run DNA checks to see if it's anyone on the database. At this stage they can't say for certain it's just the one corpse or several, the bits are too small.". Bill decided not to have a kebab that evening after all.

CHAPTER 54

Rimmer watched as the jet landed on the short runway. Strictly speaking, and according to aviation guidelines, this runway was too short for such a jet to use. But no one had ever raised this point. The pilot didn't ask too many questions – he just took the money. He knew the aircraft well and had no problems taking off and landing there and he used every inch of the runway. So long as there were no unforeseen issues, he wouldn't have a problem. Rimmer took his case and coat and headed out of the waiting room and onto the tarmac as the plane taxied to a stop. A few seconds later the doors were open, and the steps were in place. Rimmer never travelled alone. He always took with him two associates, or bodyguards. These were two of his most trusted members of staff. They followed him everywhere but asked no questions. They did as they were told and had risked their lives to protect his, taking punches, bullets and killing to meet his needs. The thing he particularly liked about these two was that, whether he was dealing with a man, a woman or even someone's child, they still went about their business in the same professional manner. Never questioning him. Rimmer could have handled this by himself in most cases but he couldn't afford any risks to tie him to any of his business dealings. His team were willing to serve years in jail to protect him if it came to that. They also knew that it was unlikely anyone would ever testify against them were they to find themselves in that predicament. They both loved their job and they made a formidable team.

Rimmer went up the stairs first ahead of his two-man team and took his seat at the rear of the plane away from the windows. His two minders sat in front of him. Rimmer opened his case and took out the latest set of plans that had been sent over to him the previous day. He would use the next few hours to review them and make any alterations he saw fit. Once complete this would afford him many more business opportunities and aid with the removal of any obstacles that came between him and his plans in the future.

CHAPTER 55

"Let's try the Chinese restaurant this evening." Annie said as she sat in front of the mirror applying her makeup. Dom had just come out of the shower and was drying his feet. He always took particular care to dry his feet and especially between his toes to avoid those nasty infections that you can get there that had plagued him as a child. He was always careful to avoid anything that may limit his movement, lest he needed to fight for his life or make a getaway. And that was more likely to be getting away from a woman than a bad guy. He knew he'd let himself become too fond of Annie and that his guard was down way too much of the time. She'd had plenty of chances to make a run for it, or raise an alarm but she hadn't done anything. On the ship her options were far more limited than on dry land. But as she had no means of getting hold of any cash, if she did try and escape, she wouldn't get very far. She could have called the British police but by now she was in too deep and she knew she faced the possibility of going down for life for her role in the bombings, let alone the murder of her father.

She seemed more alive now than ever. She was like him in so many ways – maybe that was why they appeared to get along so well. Despite spending so much of the previous week together, and under what many might find extremely difficult circumstances, they hadn't fallen out or come to blows or even argued about anything. And now, to all intents and purposes, they were on holiday – honeymoon, and fulfilling their parts nicely. They looked the part and did their best to avoid speaking to too many people or making any holiday friends who may remember them at some point in the future when their faces appeared on TV or in the newspaper; something else he needed to avoid.

"Sure, Chinese it is." he replied. When she was done, they left the cabin and headed for the Chinese restaurant. By now they knew their way around the ship well enough to not get lost or to have to ask directions every time. With only one wrong turn they found the restaurant and waited to be seated. The place was quite full and the noise level of the pleasant chatting was high. "Table for two, sir?" said the waiter – a Chinese man with a New York accent. "Yes please." Dom replied. "Follow me madam." said the waiter and he led them, Annie first, to the far side of the restaurant to the last remaining table for two. There were a few tables for four and one larger table nearby that had a reserved sign on it. "What can I get you to drink?" he said as they settled down.". "Two Tsing Tao's please." Dom replied. Annie looked at him but didn't say anything. The waiter went away to fix the beers. "It's a nice Chinese beer, you'll like it." Dom said as he looked into Annie's enquiring brown eyes.

She didn't like someone else making her decisions, she'd had enough of that and didn't plan on putting up with much more of it. But she bottled her anger and simply replied "OK, if I don't like it you can have mine and I'll order something else." She said this with a strange look on her face that Dom construed to be rebellious. "You'll like it, darling." Dom replied fulfilling his role as newlywed. The drinks soon arrived and within five minutes they had both ordered another one along with a starter and a main. For some reason it had irked Annie that he had chosen a drink that, despite never having tried it before, she really liked. They crunched prawn crackers as they waited for their starters to arrive. They weren't in a rush and the waiter had explained that the food here was cooked freshly to order so there would be a short delay between courses. This didn't bother either of them and probably none of the other diners either, given the popularity of the place. On the table next to them was a couple in their thirties with London accents. Dom could hear them discussing the bombings. The man thought it was the work of Muslims which just fed his racist views. The woman was saying that he couldn't possibly know that, to which the man replied words to the effect of "so who else could it be then given no one has claimed responsibility; and they have the body of the guy in Glasgow and he wasn't white".

So, the media were reporting that Abdul's body had been found – that was good, very good. The police could have chosen to keep this from the public but had obviously decided to make the fact known. As Abdul was dead, he couldn't talk, and the colour of his skin was now in the public domain; the masses were jumping to the logical conclusion that it must be extremist terrorists. Things were still going to plan. He took another forkful of his kung po chicken. The trouble with Chinese is that, no matter how much he asked for extra chillies, it was just never hot enough for him. Still, it was pleasant, but he longed for a really good vindaloo. He had chosen the same meal as Annie had ordered to somehow balance things out from him ordering her drink. Somehow it made things even. Annie seldom talked much when they were eating. He guessed she wasn't used to company at mealtimes. All these restaurants were a far cry from dinner for one in front of the TV. She too liked to people watch. He noticed that she was watching the same people he was watching or had been watching. Her ears were probably more sensitive than his, she would be better at picking out their conversations than he was. He wondered if the years of listening to loud music had actually affected his ears. He was so blasé about things like that. In his game you seldom lived to be old enough to face the consequences. Was she copying his behaviour or was this what she liked to do? If she were copying him then why? To make herself out to be more like him? He still couldn't completely trust her. He'd never understand her, but then again, he had never fully understood any woman. Maybe he should still consider engineering a situation whereby she could be tested; a situation where Dom could know for sure what she was up to. There was still plenty time to dispose of her. During their walks on deck he had studied the ship's layout and the movement of passengers. Maybe the fishes wouldn't go hungry after all.

CHAPTER 56

Vincenzo had put the feelers out with his contacts in the UK to try and locate Montgomery to aid his location of Devizes. Whilst he didn't know where Devizes had gone after he left prison, the one thing he knew was the he would indeed have made plans to get the hell out of South Africa as soon as possible. And an English guy fits in best in his native England. He thought this should be a simple task. It shouldn't take long for his English contacts to track him down. But his contacts were telling him that they had nothing on him. For now, he focussed his attention on what he would do to him when he finally got his hands on him. There was information he needed before he could finish off his planned actions. He also needed to avenge himself for the scar Devizes had left him with. He vividly recalled stitching up his own wound in his cell and trying to act normally for the days after as the wound slowly healed. His men employed highly successful questioning techniques. They had only failed once to get the information they needed and in this case the subject had died of a heart attack when they were only just getting started. This type of accident couldn't be avoided. He had no way of knowing how people react to having their toes cut off. This guy had croaked at the sight of the bolt cutters and been disposed of fully intact. He knew Devizes wouldn't croak at the first hurdle. He would see many hurdles before he croaked.

It wasn't difficult in South Africa to get hold of false IDs with all the supporting documents. Officials could be bought off, as was the case in every country, but here more than most.

Devizes never got close to anyone inside, kept himself to himself. Never sharing anything that could be seen as a weakness and used against him. How the fuck he had gotten out of the country he didn't know or really care; he just knew deep down that Devizes had gotten out of the country and he hoped he had headed for London or was there already. He assumed that a lot of money had changed hands and he hadn't needed to dig a tunnel or climb the walls, both of which he knew were impossible. In the days immediately after he had realised that Devizes had switched identities and wasn't dead but had been released under another name, he'd focussed his attentions on the prison staff in the hope that one of them could be identified as having played some part in it all, but he'd drawn a blank. He'd been in there a couple of years so whatever he'd arranged he'd had plenty of time to plan it. It was now ancient history. Devizes was out and about, but not for long.

CHAPTER 57

Bill had been through all the available footage and noted all the vehicles where the registration plate was visible, and where it wasn't a match to the recorded make, model or colour, in an attempt to rule out some of the vehicles. He had three hundred vehicles in his spreadsheet all timestamped with known locations; but a lot didn't have legible registration plates. Some of the footage was so poor you couldn't make out clearly the colour of the vehicle or how many occupants there were. He was pissing into the wind. He knew it was a waste of his time and it wouldn't lead to anything, but he'd done it anyway. That's what policing is all about. Two long days of graft, his eyes hurt, and he needed a drink. Bob had gone home a couple of hours ago, he knew that he'd find him in the boozer. Sure enough, ten minutes later, as he entered the pub himself, he saw Bob sat at the bar, alone, with an empty beer glass in front of him in a world of his own. Even though Bob pissed him off so much of the time, deep down, he knew Bob was a good copper and always did the right thing. That's why he put up with all the shit that came his way. He respected Bob and he knew Bob respected him.

He walked to the bar and took a space beside Bob and ordered two pints. Bob didn't see him at first but when the pint appeared in front of him, he looked up and thanked him and, after a brief pause, asked Bill how he was getting on. Bill explained his findings but with a positive slant. "Well, that's as good as it gets, I think – well done. It's not easy keeping focussed on the slog, but it always pays dividends in the end.

One of those vehicles on your list might well be the kidnappers' and whilst we can't know which one or act on it now, when we get more information or possible leads, we can cross reference them to your list. Good work, you deserve a pint, the next couple are on me". Bill smiled and downed half his pint. Bob ordered him another one, he would need to drink a few more to catch up with Bob but he had nothing better to do. Their conversation inevitably turned from small talk to the recent explosions. "Shouldn't we be focussing our efforts on those groups most likely to perpetrate this kind of terrorist atrocity?" Bill said, looking at Bob to gauge his response. Bob's body language answered his question very clearly "We need to keep open minds on this and not be seen to take any action without a valid lead or cause….". Bill stopped listening and turned his attention to the girl collecting the glasses. She was heading their way from the other side of the pub. She looked about twenty, blonde, tight ripped jeans with exposed knees. She picked up six or eight glasses then took them behind the bar, returning for more. Bill knew that she could have done her job a lot more efficiently, but he liked to watch her move. She moved nicely, maybe she did this deliberately, they weren't the only two old men watching her with interest. As she got to their end of the bar, she looked at them both briefly but didn't smile or acknowledge either man. She clearly enjoyed her job. This type of kid always worried Bill, as they had their heads turned at the thought of a few quid for whatever. "Thanks." Bill said as she took away his first glass. She looked at him quickly and nodded. Then swept up a few more empties off the bar and took them away to be washed. Bob had finished offloading and he knew Bill wasn't really listening anymore. Bill felt a little bad, so he asked Bob if there was any more news on the body parts discovered under the Thelwall Viaduct. Bob told him that they wouldn't know until tomorrow at the earliest. After another pause, he asked Bill if he was hungry. Bill replied to say he was, so they decided to go for a curry. In for a penny in for a pound. Bill took one of his heartburn pills as they left the bar. He was used to the fragrant emissions from Bob's side of the desk. Tomorrow he could wage war.

CHAPTER 58

"You know that no one can know of our meeting like this – I mean no one. They'll kill my family first them come after me." Paolo was sitting and rubbing his hands together and moving around in his seat. He was visibly distressed. Everyone involved knew full well what he was risking and that this was Paolo's last resort to end the situation. "You know what I tell you is the truth – I've never lied to you. But I am telling you they smell a rat. And that rat is me. Any day now they'll turn to their own and it won't be long before they come to me and I won't be able to hide any longer. I need out – today – now. I need a safe place for the four of us, away from here and completely off the radar. No safe house is safe for me, you know that – he has contacts in his pocket everywhere you look. He's hit people in safe houses before even though it was never proven to be him. I need guarantees for my family's safety, and I need them right now.". Paolo was now facing the consequences of a lifetime of crime and greedy decisions and weakness. It was his weakness that would be the end of him.

After making a few phone calls to the various departments, some official, some unofficial, Detective Rethabile from the SAPS (South African Police Service) had made the necessary temporary arrangements to house the family. It was agreed that the four of them would be taken roughly a hundred miles away to stay with another police informant – he too had too much to lose. He wasn't in a safe house so there would be no records and he was still alive which meant the location was still secret. Only a very few people, all of whom Rethabile trusted implicitly, knew about this arrangement and he would make sure it stayed that way. Once they had the evidence needed to convict Vincenzo Dente, then they could put them somewhere more official. To be honest he didn't care much what happened to Paolo, but he did feel sorry for his family, even though they must have known that Paolo wasn't all he seemed to be. They were hoping to get most of his confidantes as well. Often when the big cheese goes down the lowlifes run or fall like dominoes – each trying to save his own skin at the expense of someone else's. The more the merrier. They'd been after Vincenzo for many years and each time they thought they had something on him either the witness changed their mind, wound up dead or evidence mysteriously disappeared. He didn't know who in the service was in his pocket, but he suspected there was more than one and at least one of these was a superior rank to himself. This was the joy of living in such a beautiful place. The constant paradigm.

Paolo was briefed on the arrangements and he seemed a little more comfortable. Conversation went on to Vincenzo's current activities, what he may be planning, where he may be going, much was informed conjecture. The police would need to plan their operation very carefully and ensure they picked him up in a place where things could go smoothly, damage limitation so to speak. In order to effectively plan ahead it was important that they had an idea of his possible movements. Paolo said he wasn't high ranked enough to be included in Vincenzo's inner circle, but he was a trusted member of his team. He knew that Vincenzo was after someone with whom he had shared a cell and that this person had gotten out of jail before Vincenzo, having left him with a nice leaving present. Rethabile thought it wouldn't be too difficult to track who he had shared a cell with and who had gotten out before him. If he could identify Vincenzo's target and they could get to him before Vincenzo did then it would offer an ideal opportunity to catch him. South Africa was indeed a large country, but he felt sure he could make progress on this front. Even better if they could catch Vincenzo or one of his cohorts trying to do away with said person. He had a plan formulating and percolating. He'd had many plans before and where Vincenzo was concerned none had come good. A couple had come good initially only to go away at the hands of his henchmen. This time they'd get him and bring him down.

Rethabile made some calls and within half an hour he had a list of the people who had been inside the same prison at the same time. There was no record of who had actually shared a cell with him. Of the four names, one was dead in a prison accident, two were still incarcerated there, which left only one. After investigating the remaining man, he had drawn a blank. He turned his attention to the other three. From his information he had mugshots of the four men. He noticed a passing resemblance between the man who was now out, whom he was sure wasn't involved, and the man who had died in prison in an attack a few days previous to the release. His name was Dominic Devizes. DoDe as the other inmates apparently referred to him as. He had been incarcerated for a five-year sentence but was killed after a couple of years sentence served and coincidentally only a few days before the fourth man was released, this being several months before Vincenzo himself was released. Devizes seemed to fit the bill – could he have swapped identities with the guy that was released allowing him to get out as the other when his sentence was served? It was worth looking into. The more he thought about this, the more he became convinced that Devizes was probably the target Paolo was referring to. He had no evidence to back this up and there would be none. Still he felt more and more convinced that his scenario fit the facts that Paolo had laid out. He made more calls to gather intel on this Devizes guy – who was he, what were his skills, what did his record look like and, most important of all, if he was indeed still alive and kicking, where would he likely be now?

The answer to that last question eluded him. No one had seen him or the guy he was pretending to be since his release from prison. He might even be dead after all. No flights had been taken using either name. No credit card usage. Absolutely nothing on either, which was to be expected. He'd seen this before and it usually meant one of two things. Most likely was that the guy had been taken out never to be seen again. The second was that he'd done a disappearing trick using an alternative identity. The latter made more sense for two reasons – firstly Vincenzo had been after him. Secondly Vincenzo was still after him – if Vincenzo had already found him, he'd be long dead and forgotten. He'd have to be damned clever and well off to elude Vincenzo. Like a mouse in a tiger's cage.

He knew full well that Vincenzo and his merry men had a lot of resources at their disposal. If they hadn't found him yet, then it wouldn't be easy for the authorities to find him either. He was a British national, he'd have to extend his search to Britain. He had all the flights to and from the UK checked again for anyone matching his description. Checking the sea routes would be more difficult as there were so many vessels, many off the official radar. He could have taken a boat to Madagascar and then hooked up with another larger vessel going to Australia, India or Singapore. That was a lot of places to check and a lot of flights! He could also have taken a boat to Brazil. Again, he didn't stand a cat in hell's chance of tracing him through Brazil if he'd chosen to go that way. This was gonna be a mammoth task, no surprise Vincenzo hadn't caught up with him yet. Maybe they'd need another way to get him – whatever happened they had to have him within two weeks at the outside, ideally much sooner. He couldn't guarantee Paolo's safety any longer than a few days. He wasn't even convinced anyone could guarantee it that long. He wasn't really bothered what happened to him so long as he got to testify. His family didn't deserve to die at Vincenzo's hands either. Detective

Rethabile wouldn't be getting much sleep tonight.

As a younger man, he would have sought solace in the local bar. However, when his drinking had gotten out of control and his wife had left, he managed to take hold of his life again and he hadn't had a drink in over ten years. His wife was long gone, married to another cop, apparently. Like so many cops he was married to his job. And his one-person marriage was no happier a marriage than most other marriages that involved two people. He set about checking all flights to London during the two-week period after Devizes left prison – this was the most likely time period in which he would have travelled. It would have taken him a week, maybe more, to organise a new identity, passport, get some cash together and set about his journey. He would have to focus his attentions to stand a chance of getting a hit. If the scope was too wide, he wouldn't be able to tread water. He hoped he wasn't putting all his efforts into searching for a dead man.

He circulated a description of Devizes, along with the most recent photograph they had of him, his mugshot taken when he started his sentence. A lot of criminals were of average appearance. A trait that served them well when witnesses later came to describe their assailants. Devizes was tall and English. This would make his job a little easier. You can disguise many aspects of your appearance but not your height, not if you are still walking. Devizes would have been careful but somewhere along the line he would have left traces of his movements – footprints in the ether. He needed to find them before Vincenzo did. He would have put a twenty-four-hour surveillance on Vincenzo but that had been tried before and failed. One cop had been killed whilst watching Vincenzo from the roof of an adjacent building. He had mysteriously fallen to his death. Detective Rethabile would surveil using technology not footfall. He had people watching the CCTV footage on the main roads around Vincenzo's home and office. Office – that's a laugh. A lock up where he and his cronies did their business. For now, he had done everything he could do. Now, like a spider, he had to wait until he got a lead on Devizes or they caught Vincenzo on the move. He wasn't a good waiter. He knew deep down that his best chance was to tag onto the shirttails of Vincenzo. He had more and better resources to track Devizes than were at his own disposal. But this was far from ideal and meant that if they were too late they may lose their quarry altogether. For now, they were one step ahead of him.

CHAPTER 59

Annie had wanted to go on to one of the liner's night clubs. Not exactly Dominic's scene but he went along quite willingly. They got a couple of drinks then Annie lead him onto the dance floor. The club was full of people – this must be where the majority of the younger end of the cruisers came in the evening. The rest sat on deck by the pool or in one of the bars they had been frequenting. The age group ranged from teens to forties. The teens looked like they'd escaped from their parents who were probably up on deck by the pool. The others looked like young, fairly well off, cruisers. Why a young couple in their twenties went on a cruise was beyond him. From earwigging a few conversations during the course of the evening he learned that many of them were actually staff. The club they had chosen was the favourite of the staff. Some were entertainment staff, some general waiters, waitresses, kitchen staff, porters, cleaners, engineers or contractors. They couldn't hear any conversation on the dance floor over the racket but by the bar the noise level was low enough to be able to hear those in the immediate vicinity. They had to shout into each other's ears to make themselves heard. Annie clung onto Dom's hand the whole time. Every so often she glanced down at her ring. Dom wondered if she actually believed that they were engaged to be married, or already married or just putting on a show for anyone watching them. He knew that he didn't want to have to do away with her. For one thing the sex was great. He didn't think he'd have a job finding partners on a boat like this but if Annie did find her way into the drink, he'd have to lay low, very low. He still had time to consider his situation but the more he thought about it, the riskier and more undesirable the thought of dumping a body overboard seemed to him. This wasn't a valid option, not really even another plan B.

Tomorrow they were to arrive at Casablanca. He'd never seen the film. By all accounts it was a classic. He asked Annie if she had seen it. "Yes." she replied. "It's about a World War II freedom fighter who comes across an old flame in a night club somewhere.". "Interesting." replied Dom. Her slant was different to what he thought the movie was about. But what did he know? He hadn't even seen it. He preferred titles like Alien, or The Blues Brothers. He didn't have the patience or attention span to watch long-winded films about politics or court rooms or small towns where every week several inhabitants get killed off by some random village local. He wondered how many villages in England had a zero population as they'd all been killed off, the police dying of boredom.

After a couple more dances and several more drinks Annie declared she was tired and they set off on their way back to their cabin. Dom suggested one more for the road, but Annie preferred to snuggle up and make love…. 'make love' eh. He'd thought of it as more of a good old shag. Still, he agreed and they did just that. Twice in fact. After they'd finished, and Annie had cuddled him for a few more minutes, she drifted off to sleep. Dom gently turned away and returned to his own side of the bed leaving her to sleep peacefully. She certainly didn't carry much in the way of a conscience. Every night since they'd killed her father, and countless other people, she'd slept soundly. He knew many criminals who, even though they were hardened, still didn't sleep that well at night. She seemed to be able to disassociate herself from her actions – compartmentalise. That was a very useful skill to have in his business. A conscience never bodes well if you tend to kill people in your line of work. Maybe they could make a good partnership in some sort of illegal venture. Something that would provide them a good income – her father's money wouldn't last long at this rate. Bonnie and Clyde. Annie and Dom. Bonnie and Clyde hadn't ended too well though. Or maybe she was just too young to understand what they had done.

CHAPTER 60

Chief Constable Owen Evans and his wife of fifteen years, Mavis, had worked hard all their lives. They hadn't taken a holiday in five years, in order to save up for the cruise of a lifetime. After a few unexpected situations it turned out that the money they had wouldn't stretch to the cruise of a lifetime they had in mind, so instead of waiting a few more years, they decided to take the best cruise they could afford now, whilst they still had their health. They were loving it so far. At each port of call they'd disembarked and taken in the sites and atmosphere of all the places. From Southampton, Lisbon, Cadiz, Gibraltar and Malaga. Mavis was particularly looking forward to Casablanca. Owen was enjoying being completely away from work. He had started on the beat and worked his way up to becoming a detective. He had worked homicide and was now on what the Americans would term homeland security. His area of expertise was travel – airports, shipping etc. and how the bad guys could secure their travel and how to track them. He'd tracked down many villains in his time. Kipper of the Yard. This was the first time they'd holidayed since the death of their son, James, Jimmy. He'd been a great kid. Worked hard in school, done well at university and got a job in the city. He had only been working there a couple of months when he was knocked down crossing Old Street on his way to a restaurant to meet his friends. He never got there. By the time the ambulance arrived through the busy teatime traffic it was too late to save him, and he had died on the way to the hospital. He was twenty-three years old. So much of life to live, so much that he never got to experience. Not an hour went by when they didn't think about him. At first, they suffered in silence – it nearly drove them apart. But over the past couple of years they'd overcome this, talked a lot and now openly talked about Jimmy. They still chose not to mention him in company, except to their old friends who had known Jimmy, or to Owen's colleagues. This type of devastating loss broke apart many couples, but not them.

Owen had had a great day doing absolutely nothing. Taking in the sun by the pool, drinking cold beers, and watching the women as he tried to read his book. As a cop he had a nasty habit of watching everyone, taking in the tiniest of details and suspecting evil deeds. He often saw the bad in people, picking out strangers and jumping to conclusions that they were drug dealers or prostitutes or worse. The trouble was, his intuition was very good. When he sniffed something bad about someone, he usually turned out to be right. His colleagues often asked him his thoughts regarding a suspect when they had absolutely nothing on him. If Owen had thought he was dodgy then they'd put more effort into researching him. He was like a sniffer dog, sniffing out the bad guys. One of the reasons he liked the cruise was that, compared to walking around the city, or spending time at a tourist beach resort, on the whole cruisers were straight, hardworking people. It felt strange to him, but it offered him a way to wind down and relax, recharge his batteries. He had just turned fifty. Mavis was forty-nine. So far, the only people who had attracted his attention were a waiter whom he had taken an instant dislike to – he'd seen his sort – finger in the till. But as Mavis reminded him, if that were the case, he wouldn't have taken a job on an all-inclusive cruise – he'd be bar hopping. But there were always tips. And even if he did find someone on the take, what was he to do about it? The ship had its own security services. Apparently, they vetted each and every one of the several hundred staff. He guessed the ratio was something like three or four staff to each passenger – that was a lot of staff, all living in confined spaces, working closely together on long shifts. Then they ended up spending their free time with them as well. He believed that the staff had some private places where they could relax, away from the passengers. He should put his suspicious mind to bed - it too was on its holidays. "Are we ready?" Mavis asked? "Yes dear." replied Owen, and with that they got up and ambled back to their cabin. Mavis was looking forward to seeing Casablanca and chatted about what to wear for the day. Owen just nodded.

CHAPTER 61

Annie was up early the following morning. They'd decided to have a walk around Casablanca and get some exercise and check the place out. They were due to arrive first thing that morning, so they'd get most of the day there. As Dom peered over the top of the quilt, he saw Annie was already dressed and putting on her earrings. "Hey, you." she said, looking at him in the mirror as she finished dressing. "Look at you, up so early." Dom replied. "You go shower, I'll grab a newspaper." she said, smiled and got up. She was wearing her blue shorts and white top. She looked lovely. The top showed off her figure very nicely. He wondered what she'd got on underneath as he'd missed that part this morning. He'd make up for it later. Away she went. Dom got out of bed, visited the toilet then got into the shower. The shower in the cruise liner was actually very good. It got warm quickly and the temperature stayed pretty constant. Once it had gone cold briefly, spluttered, then returned to normal but he guessed this was to be expected when God knows how many people are showering or flushing at the same time - all that water.

Dom was dried and dressed when Annie returned to the room with a paper. "You'll want to see this." she said. Dom looked at her with a shocked expression. Had the police somehow linked them to one of the attacks? Had they stepped up the kidnapping enquiry? He took the paper and looked at the front page. Light aircraft crashes into Old Trafford killing twelve people. Many more casualties. He looked at Annie. Everyone is talking about it – they all believe it is the next stage of the current spate of radicalist terrorist attacks. What's next? They were discussing at the shop. "What the fuck?" said Dom. He read the first two pages of the paper. A Cessna had flown over Old Trafford a couple of times, nothing new there, but then it had dived, crashing into the West Stand, which was pretty much full as United were playing City. Burning fuel had sprayed over the adjacent people and many had burns. Twelve were dead, eight critical and another twenty hospitalised. It went on to say that this was, by far, the worst of the atrocities committed in this recent spate of terrorism and no stones would be left unturned in finding the perpetrators. ISIS had claimed responsibility, apparently. This was good news if it was in fact true – the heat was off their doings and moving onto this attack. If they caught the associates of the dead pilot, then they would be blamed for the other bombings as well. This was a gift-wrapped solution for them. "We'll be in the clear." said Annie, in a very matter of fact but slightly naïve way. "Indeed, we may." replied Dom, keeping his cynicism to himself for now.

Today, they too could partake in the speculation as to why ISIS would do this, what should be done to them when they find them, and so on. It was as if a load had been lifted. But Dom knew that if they identified the pilot's co-conspirators the police may not be able to make the charges for his bombings stick. That said, everyone hated ISIS and any type of associated actions – the UK had to make a stand. He guessed that not many people would be bothered too much if those proven to be behind the plane attack were actually responsible for the bombings. As long as someone went down for these crimes then everyone would be happy. They weren't in the clear yet, but it was a good day for them. Maybe Casablanca was a good omen. They could eat, drink and be merry today. And they did just that.

They packed a small bag with everything they needed for a

day on dry land. Dom took plenty of cash and Annie packed a cardigan in case it got chilly. Dom didn't see the need. Shorts and tee shirt were good for him. They waited with the other passengers after the liner had docked and disembarked with the hordes of tourists. Everyone appeared to want to hit dry land today. Being younger and fitter than most, they soon passed most of the elderly coffin dodgers and managed to get a taxi from the port at Casa to take them to Quartier Habous. This was where there were several shops and places to eat and have a few drinks. It turned out that there wasn't an awful lot to see in Casablanca after all. The taxi driver, who spoke fluent English, told them that the finest tourist attraction was the Hassan II Mosque. Neither of them had any desire to go visit a mosque so they settled for the shops. The plan was to head straight to a bar, have a few drinks, chat, eat, then hit the shops in the afternoon for a couple of hours. No sooner had they gotten out of the cab than Annie spotted a sign for the Moroccan Artisan market. She was now on a mission, like a kid in a candy store, so off they went.

The shops, as you may expect, specialised in rugs, handmade metal items, handmade wooden items and, of course, jewellery. This is where Annie headed. It only took her five minutes to find a bracelet that she wanted. It wasn't expensive, so Dom bought it for her. She was like a child who had just got a new doll. She was more talkative, altogether more outgoing and open. She was now looking for earrings to match. After they'd tried half a dozen places, Dom saw a restaurant with tables outside offering a nice view. He said that he was parched, and as time was getting on they should get some food and drink. Annie agreed, and they headed for the bar. Bar Du Titan was the name. Who was Titan? Dom wondered. Their first bottle of Flag Pils went down almost in one. Their second took a little longer. The sun was hot, and the waiter had put up a large parasol to offer them shade. They ordered a selection of tapas. The waiter was very observant. When their beers were nearly empty, he brought two more. On a couple of occasions Dom drank both as Annie's legs weren't quite as hollow as his. The tapas were excellent. It took them an hour to work their way through the splendid dishes that were brought to their table. After one final beer they decided to have another hour or so at the shops and then grab a taxi back to Casa and their liner.

Annie found a bracelet for Dom in a similar style to hers – not matching but definitely with a his and hers feel. Dom wasn't really bothered about jewellery, but it made her happy and maintained the happy atmosphere. Annie found another cardigan that she liked and after they had haggled over the price and made the purchase, they made their way back to where the taxis were. There was plenty of time left before the boat sailed so most of the other tourists were either still eating or shopping. They had had a good head start on their more senior fellow travellers. As they waited, a slightly older couple, maybe aged around fifty, also arrived in the taxi queue. The lady smiled at Annie and then said "Hello, I believe you are on the same boat as us.". "Are we? How nice" Annie replied. Dom realised that they were angling to share a taxi. He knew there would be room enough for the four of them including their bags, so he said politely "Yes, would you like to share our taxi back to the port?". "That would be lovely, replied the woman. I'm Mavis and this is my husband Owen." It seemed a little out of the ordinary to Dom that the woman was carrying more bags than the guy who was a big, strong copper. He only carried bags in his left hand, his right arm just dangling by his side. Owen must have spotted Dom looking at his trailing arm and said "That's my bad arm, but it's getting better and I'm trying not to overuse it on this trip. These bags are quite heavy.". "Tell me about it!" Dom replied.

CHAPTER 62

It only took a couple of minutes before a taxi appeared. By then Mavis had told them it was their first cruise and probably their last, that she was active in their local community and that Owen was a detective. "That's nice." said Annie. "Have you caught any killers?". Owen looked slightly embarrassed. "It's not always about catching killers, there's a lot more mundane stuff to do, lots more. It takes a team of people doing mundane stuff so that one detective can catch a killer. It can take months.". "Annie smiled, then said "I'm glad I'm not a criminal." Dom remained silent, amazed at both the fact that Annie was being so cool and that Owen was lapping up the attention of a young, pretty woman. Mavis started talking about care in the community when they were spared further stories by the arrival of the taxi. It was the same taxi and driver as that had taken Annie and Dom earlier. The driver opened the doors to admit the four passengers then got in and headed back towards the port. He asked them if they had enjoyed the market, what they had bought, what they ate etc. as they drove. When they got out of the taxi Annie and Dom wished Mavis and Owen a good day and headed back to their room, ostensibly because they both badly needed a shower after all that walking in the shining sun. Soon they were back on board the ship. They went up top for a drink by the pool for a while dangling their feet in the pool as they recovered from all their walking. Annie was still in a very good mood from her shopping experience, "What if they see us here and not in our rooms." Annie said. "Fuck 'em." was Dom's reply. Dom was still in a good mood about the plane attack, and as soon as they got back to the cabin, they made love. It lasted a long time, not like casual lovers but much more than that. Dom had never been a victim of his own emotions. His EQ was low, his IQ well above average. Was this what love felt like? Was he falling for this girl? She was intelligent, very pretty, easy to get on with, not very demanding, she didn't look at other men and she seldom complained. Even when she had been locked in his cellar in Horwich she hadn't really complained. What a shit life she must have had before he whisked her off her feet. He felt good. Life was good at the moment. He had learned to enjoy the good times whilst they lasted. He had never put down roots, never held any type of normal friendship for more than a few months so he knew he had to make hay whilst the sun was shining down on him. And that it was.

He could feel a touch of sunburn on his head and neck. He had omitted to put suntan cream on that morning. He would need to apply lots of after-sun after he had showered later on. For now, they just lay in bed and cuddled for a while. Annie then asked Dom a question, one he hadn't been prepared to answer. "So how did you know my father?" Dom was taken aback. How did she know that he knew her father? Did she know? Was she guessing or testing him? From her expression it was plain that she was firmly of the opinion that Dom had indeed met him. He wondered what he had said or done to give her that impression. He had indeed met her father – he was the reason Dom was sent to prison in the first place. He was also the reason he managed to get out so soon. Should he come clean with her? What did he have to lose? After all, it seemed evident to Dom that she hated him even more than Dom did.

"I did some work for him in South Africa." Dom said. He was half hoping that that brief answer would satisfy her, and she'd move on to something more mundane like did he really like his new bracelet. "What did he do that pissed you off so much that you wanted to kill him?" was the next bolt from the blue. Again, he wasn't ready for this line of questioning either. Dom thought about his answer to this one. Annie looked into his eyes as if searching his soul to find out whether or not he would lie in his next answer. "Well, er, he was the reason I was in prison in the first place." Annie knew he'd been to prison, but she had never asked him why. She didn't say anything else, just continued to look into his eyes demanding more of an answer from him. "Look, diplomats are just legalised crooks doing the bidding for the real important ones who can't afford to get their hands dirty. One of his contacts knew something that he didn't want to get out. I was hired to lean on this guy, ensure he didn't say something he shouldn't." "Did you kill him? Annie said. He looked into her eyes. What was she hoping to achieve from this line of questioning? If he admitted that he had tried to do so would she somehow like him less? He didn't want to frighten her or drive her way. "I didn't kill him, no." Dom replied. "It was one big set up. I went where I was told to go with a weapon and the police were waiting. They arrested me and tried me for attempted murder. Once I was inside your father had the power to get me killed and out of his life for good. He chose to leave me there, but not to simply rot. There was a prisoner your father wanted dead and it was all set up to get me inside to do the job. Maybe if I'd served my sentence, he'd have had me killed the day I was due for release, who knows? All that matters is that your father set me up. He wasn't a nice person. He used people as pawns in his games. The people higher up used him in a similar way, except that they never got their hands dirty. Call it a prison? That place was hell. Once I was in, I had no choice but to cooperate. The guy they wanted me to kill was a real mean mother fucker. He bragged to his buddies in there how he had raped and murdered women. He was a nasty piece of work."

"So, did you kill this guy in prison? Is that how you got out? You did exactly what my father asked you to do in order to buy your own freedom?" She was still looking into his eyes.

Dom couldn't read her expression. He had already said more than he ought to have said. But he nevertheless felt compelled to continue.

Her stare was relentless. "God knows how many other people they have exploited. But no, I didn't kill no one. I got lucky – simple as that. Someone beat me to it, I just kept stum and your father assumed I'd done it. The same day I'd gotten into a fight with an Italian Mafia guy who thought he could take anything he wanted. I was sharing a cell with a young African lad who had apparently attacked a policeman. He told me that he had been set up as a punishment for his father because his father wasn't doing whatever the police wanted him to do; money, protection or something. I believed him. The Italian guy, Vince they called him, wanted this lad to run his errands – errands that would get him killed. So, I felt obliged to have a word with Vince.

I took a makeshift knife with me and ended up using it on him. He got the message. He didn't report the incident and never went to the sick bay for stitches. He laid low whilst he healed. I thought at that point that I was a dead man walking. As soon as Vince had recovered, he'd be back for me. Next thing I knew I was being released with instructions to walk to a place where I'd be picked up and flown back to England.

It was a Diplomatic car that picked me up. Took me to a private airfield where a plane was waiting to take me to Brazil. From there I was taken to a private jet that went to London with a stop to refuel – no idea where. No one asked for documents – hell, I didn't even have a passport. When I landed at London, I was told to wait for your father to meet me. As soon as they turned their backs I ran. Through the baggage handling bay where I managed to get out with some other workers finishing their shift. Your father must have been really mad but, so far as he was concerned, I'd done what he wanted and left no trace." Dom had now said way more than he intended to and most of it was true. He had always been a good liar. His story must have sounded convincing because Annie came and sat beside him and put her arm around him. "So, you know first-hand what a bastard he was. He used and controlled everyone around him, including me. I'm glad he's dead."

Dom thought she might start to cry at this point. She didn't; she just sat there staring at the wall. Dom had already let his guard down more than he had ever done in the past. He needed to put this chit chat behind him before he chit chatted something he'd later regret. "So that's why you took me – to get your own back on him. Did you just want the money, or did you intend to kill us both?" As she finished this sentence a smile came over her face, like a naughty schoolgirl. Dom thought about his reply for a few seconds then said, "I need a drink." Annie looked into his eyes and held his gaze for a few seconds and then said, "Me too." She stood up and took his hand. A couple of minutes later they left the cabin and headed for the bar.

CHAPTER 63

Owen and Mave were sat at the far side of the bar, beside the pool, enjoying their nightcap when they spotted a young couple as they walked into the other end of the bar holding hands. They weren't talking and looked a little sombre. The man was tall and rather dashing Mavis thought, unable to see his face clearly. The man was tall and hiding something Owen thought. The couple went to the bar and sat beside each other on bar stools. It was quite late and most of the tables were taken. Mavis knew that in thirty minutes or so the place would be much quieter. They recognised some of the people sat at the tables – they'd been walking around town all day and shopping, so they'd all be wanting their beds soon. Mavis and Owen had said that this would be their last drink before they retired for the night. Mavis's feet were killing her. "That's the couple we shared the taxi with." remarked Owen, "over there, just walked in." Mave looked a little more closely. "Is it darling? You're the observant one. I hadn't noticed."

"You've had it pretty tough." Annie said to Dom. "So have you." he replied. She kissed him on the lips. Dom felt a stirring in his underwear. Before he could say anything else, Annie said "Let's drink these and go and make love. It is our honeymoon after all." He'd heard this line before, but he liked it. She smiled at Dom who quickly downed his drink and off they went hand in hand. They took a bottle away with them to their room. Over the other side of the bar Mave and Owen watched them as they left. "They weren't here long." Owen said. "I'm not surprised given that they are just married."

Mavis replied with a knowing smile. "How do you know that, woman?" Owen asked. "I saw her lips say the word honeymoon dear." Mavis replied with a glint in her eyes. It had been a long time since they had made love. But Owen knew the meaning of this particular glint. Mave must indeed be pleased with the gifts she'd bought in town. They too drank their drinks and headed off to their cabin. By now the young couple were long gone. "I bet we don't see them again any time soon." Owen said with a smile. "She was very pretty Mavis. Just like you were dear." Mavis looked at him and replied "What do you mean were? And he was a real hunk too."

Annie pushed the door closed and locked it. She went into the bathroom and when she came out Dom was already in bed naked with two glasses of champagne and something for her to hold on to. "Happy honeymoon darling." he said. He knew this was just what Annie needed to hear. She slid her nightie off her shoulders and it fell to the floor. She got in bed and on top of Dom. They weren't as tired as they had first thought. Their drinks remained on the nightstand for some time.

CHAPTER 64

Annie was up first again the following morning. Once again, she kissed him. He opened his eyes and looked at her. She was already dressed and on her way out. "I'll go pick up some coffees and a paper." she said. He nodded and off she went. Dom had a quick shower, dried and dressed. Annie still wasn't back. After fifteen minutes he was getting a little nervous. What if she had been thinking about what Dom had told her the previous evening? What if she had decided to part company with him in fear of her life? She still had the "I'm an abductee" card that she could play, although it was a very risky one. She'd have to play it very well indeed to make it convincing after all this time and mayhem. And she'd have to explain her father's current situation. He doubted she could get away with all that. If she tried and the police saw through her then they may pick up on Dom's description. Despite the fact he had no criminal record in the UK, they would probably find out about his other exploits. Whatever the outcome it wouldn't be good. He decided to go look for her. He locked the door behind him and headed off to the shop where Annie picked up the paper. The shop was empty. He then went to the coffee shop next door where Annie was to pick up the coffees. There she was, sat at a table with an old couple, none other than Detective Owen and wife. They were chatting and exchanging pleasantries. What was she telling them? Should he go over to her? He waited and watched for a moment. He saw Annie push her chair back and stand up. It looked like she was taking her leave and everyone was smiling so he quickly headed back to their room, less concerned than a few minutes ago. He went into the bathroom and started to shave. He hadn't shaved for a couple of days. The cabin door opened and in came Annie. She bobbed her head into the bathroom and kissed Dom, getting foam on her lips. She laughed. He laughed too. "Me first." she said, and started to read the paper. "Anything about the Man U attack?" Dom asked. "I'll tell you in a minute" she replied. She was a quick reader. A minute or so later Dom came out of the bathroom smelling very nice. He sat on the bed beside her. "The pilot's dead, plus a couple more people have died in hospital. ISIS for sure they say. They had waited until the final attack before claiming responsibility. "Convenient" remarked Dom. She passed the paper to him. He looked over the pages and casually said to Annie "You were a long time getting the paper." "Sorry, I got talking to that same old couple in the coffee shop." she replied. "Apparently they were also in the bar last night and had seen us go in for our nightcaps. The lady, Mavis 'but call me Mave', asked if we were on honeymoon." "And?" Dom asked. "I said we were. She wore a hearing aid. I suspected she may have overheard us in the bar last night or read our lips. Remember – we are on honeymoon I said as we left." "Who's a clever girl?" Dom said and immediately regretted it. He half expected Annie to take the hump big style as he had referred to her as a girl, but instead she wore this really pleased smile and replied, "That's why you married me." She was such a good actress. Such potential with these old, rich couples. But he shouldn't forget they weren't that old, and he was still a serving detective. If she could pull the wool over their eyes, then the skies the limit. Still, better try to avoid them for the rest of the trip.

Owen and wife aside, the ship sure was full of lots of old, wealthy couples. Dom felt sure that they could carve a way for themselves moving across the world and feeding on couples like this. He would think about this at length and devise a potential storyline for how they could get money from the couples without them going to the authorities. Something whereby it didn't leave them penniless, more ashamed, and likely to keep it to themselves. Once he had his plan, he'd run it by Annie. Hell, she might even be able to suggest improvements. One long holiday if they played their cards right. He was always coming up with new options.

CHAPTER 65

Rethabile had got up early for the long drive. Upon his arrival he had parked a way down the street and walked up to the house and knocked on the door – three quick knocks followed by three slow ones then he rang the bell. He saw the flap move over the peephole indicating that the occupant was checking him out. Next came the sound of the bolts being removed and finally the door opened. He went in quickly and the door shut behind him and was swiftly locked inside. They went into the living room at the back. It was not overlooked, courtesy of the conifer trees that lined the perimeter of the garden. "You all OK?" he asked. Paolo nodded. "They'll be looking for me by now." he said. Rethabile also knew this to be the case. One of their informants on the street had heard that there would be something good waiting for the person that took Paolo back to them for his punishment. Vincenzo wouldn't stop until he knew Paolo was dead. They needed enough time to keep Vincenzo off their backs until they had built a case and arrested him and his entire gang. Rethabile knew that they couldn't hide Paolo for ever. Paolo knew what he had to do in return for his family's safe keeping. Now was the time for him to spill all the beans in great detail to Rethabile so he could start to build his case. It would be a long day. But the sooner they got this done the sooner they could pull the documents together, put them before the powers that be, and get the wheels in motion.

Paolo was keen to get things off his chest. His family were his number one priority. He knew this was the only way to guarantee their safety. They waited in a separate room whilst

Rethabile listened intently to everything Paolo had to tell him. He also set up a small video recorder to record the interviews. He frequently stopped and asked questions so he could add detail to the events discussed and ensure it was all clearly documented. By lunch time Rethabile knew that they could have a really good chance of charging Vincenzo and bringing him in whilst they gathered evidence. He hoped there would be a wealth of forensic evidence, and the key was knowing exactly where to look. Paolo had spoken of three killings and several attacks already, giving details that weren't made available to the public. He had also told him where Vincenzo stored his arms. Rethabile knew that these could link Vincenzo and his gang to some or many of his crimes.

CHAPTER 66

It was the first time Dom had thought about Vincenzo and their incarceration. He knew he had cut him bad. He reckoned that his makeshift knife, fashioned from a piece of slate he'd found in the yard, even though it wasn't particularly sharp, had gone quite deep leaving him needing fifteen or twenty stitches in a 6-inch jagged scar, maybe longer. It was difficult to tell with all the blood. A wound like that wouldn't heal on its own. Vincenzo must have sought medical assistance. But if so, how did he explain his injury? The authorities would have wanted to find the culprit and make an example of him. If Vincenzo didn't talk, they'd make an example out of him. He could so easily have blamed Dom, backed up by the testimony of any of his gang who would willingly lie for him, but he hadn't done so. Dom wondered why. He probably wanted to get his retribution himself as it was personal now. When Dom ventured out the morning after there was no indication of anything having happened. He wondered if Vincenzo was still in there. Maybe someone else had taken him out by now. Prison was full of murderers. He was surprised there were any prisoners left in there. Still, even if Vincenzo had survived and got out, he wouldn't be able to trace Dom's movements. Only the diplomatic services knew he'd been taken out. Montgomery wasn't going to tell anyone now. In his line of work, everyone had enemies. Funny how the difference between being a career criminal and a diplomat was so small. Different clothes and different perspectives on what constitutes a crime, and what is justifiable. In Dom's book, anyone who killed a killer was a good guy. He felt sure that his real name wouldn't have been used in any of the planning. And he knew he was lucky to have survived and even luckier to have landed where he was now. But a lucky streak, as any gambler will tell you, always comes to an end.

CHAPTER 67

Vincenzo had called his key people to see how they were getting on with tracing Devizes. So far no one had come up with anything. No trace of him from leaving prison. He was last seen walking into town, which was a fair walk, where a halfway house was expecting him. He never showed. Vincenzo knew that, in a place like South Africa, where walls had ears and eyes and noses, most of them connected to him somehow, that, were he still there and alive, then he would surely know about it by now. He was now convinced Devizes had got out of the country, and quickly. He had made this clear to his guys that were checking the ports and airports. He doubted Devizes had the funds or connections to organise a private plane or anything lavish. He felt sure he would have gone for a cheaper, slower, more freely available sea route initially. One his UK contacts was in the London Metropolitan Police – a detective. Vincenzo had gotten to him a few years ago and when he occasionally needed a favour, this particular detective was in no position to refuse. He had been tasked with looking into any reports relating to Devizes in the UK since his release. He'd been provided with photos and a full description etc. There was nothing on the UK criminal database about Devizes. But he could look into aliases. He knew this was a long shot, but he also knew that facial recognition technology could be extremely effective in picking out wanted people in any random CCTV footage that was scanned, regardless of the name. The police had been inundated recently with all the terrorist attacks. Maybe Devizes had arrived in the UK already and had somehow been picked up somewhere. If so, he needed to know. Devizes was his on his most wanted list.

So far in Vincenzo's career no one had ever lived longer than a few months after appearing on his list – let alone top of the list. This was business and it was personal to him. When Devizes was found he wanted to dispatch him personally, and slowly. He needed payback. He always got payback – it would just be a matter of time. He'd cut him good. But Vincenzo was wise, experienced in these matters and patient. He was a hunter. He had also put tabs on Devizes's known contacts including Montgomery. He knew Montgomery had played a part in Devizes's initial incarceration and he knew the practises of his country well. He wouldn't be the first person that was set up with a stretch and then encouraged to do something specific in return for release. If this were the case, then Devizes was connected to Montgomery and would be in some sort of contact with him.

It irritated Vincenzo that none of his contacts had come up with anything whatsoever in relation to either Devizes or Montgomery. Their work had been hindered due to the terrorist attacks in the UK. Bad timing for Vincenzo. It may slow him down in his quest but he would find one or both men soon and Devizes would be made to pay for what he had done to him. The wound still gave him pain. It hadn't affected his attraction to the opposite sex – the large, ragged scar was a well-chosen fashion accessory to a man of his reputation. He needed to see Devizes dead so that his enemies knew that they couldn't get away with crossing him. The longer it took, the more he appeared to be weak and a loser. But he was no loser. Devizes would be the loser. He had a good mind to cut off his head and place it somewhere public for all to see. Killing him was only the start. He needed a full PR exercise to recover his standing and send a statement out to his enemies and associates alike. No one fucks with Vincenzo Dente, the dentist. He'd remove his teeth before he killed him. That was a great message to send. He had boxes of teeth that he had acquired over his career.

PART 5

CHAPTER 68

Paolo's wife and two children had been picked up, along with suitcases, on the pretence of going away for a few days. They were indeed going away for a few days. Four hours later they were reunited with Paolo. His wife knew he was involved with bad people and she was relieved that he had had the guts to finally do something about it. Unfortunately, she had no idea just how bad these bad people were and the grave risk they were now facing. If she had known, she may well have cut him loose. Hindsight is a fantastic thing. From one blissful ignorance to another. From the lion to the snakes. It didn't come easy to trust the police in her birth country. But they had no other option. Paolo was in the other room with the lead policeman, who was asking him lots of questions. They were in the living room with two policemen and a policewoman who was to stay with the family at all times. The two men would be the security, remaining out of sight, offering twenty-four-hour protection. She could see that they were armed. Once the police had all they needed from Paolo they would also make video tapes of him – just in case he didn't live long enough to make the trial. Whilst he was reasonably safe at the moment with this level of police protection, once they had all they needed he would no longer enjoy the same level of protection. Whether this had been made clear to him or his family was questionable to say the least. In this world, everybody uses somebody else. Everyone is a user, and everyone is used. There would always be elements of the police who remained corrupt and in the pockets of the bad guys.

In the other room Paolo was being asked endless questions relating to various crimes and incidents the police had suspected Vincenzo, or his people, of being involved in. There were so many that this would take many hours to get down in detail. Paolo was cooperating fully. Where he had first-hand knowledge, he recounted who had done what, with particular emphasis on things Vincenzo had chosen to do himself. Unfortunately, when he did this, he usually worked alone which meant all he could recount was second or third hand knowledge. They needed something serious, like a murder, where Paolo could provide irrefutable eyewitness evidence that would secure Vincenzo's lifetime accommodation in one of the country's highest security establishments, where hopefully he would end his days, sooner rather than later. They also wanted proof of the involvement of other, minor players, ideally within the family. They would be the most likely to change sides once Paolo's position became public. They would have to choose which side they were on. One of them would be eying the vacancy. If they could get a couple more people to turn to the police for help, then their accounts would bear more weight under scrutiny. Vincenzo had some very powerful lawyer friends who were adept at playing the system, both legally and illegally, to get their clients to walk free. They were formidable foes.

CHAPTER 69

Bob was at his desk when Bill arrived. It was seven forty-five. They had both left the office at around eight pm the previous evening, stopping by the pub for a couple before getting some seriously needed sleep. The heat was off a little since the Manchester attack, as they now knew the group responsible was ISIS, and the media were in full swing once again. After making the coffees Bob called his contact in forensics to see if they had anything for him regarding the scene of Montgomery's demise. "Bob, I was just about to call you. We've taken DNA samples from the body parts recovered at the scene. We can now say categorically that Montgomery was a victim of the bombing. We have various chunks of him here but none large enough to tell us anything more than he was blown to bits." "We'd gathered that." replied Bob dryly. "We haven't found any traces of cash or of his daughter. As always, we'll keep working on it and if we find anything more, I'll call you straight away." Bob thanked him and put the phone down. Bill had been watching from his desk but couldn't hear the other end of the conversation. As Bob had only nodded and stared into space, he had no idea what had been said. "Montgomery was blown up. No sign of his daughter though." Bob said to Bill. "But what interests me the most is that no money was found either." Bill looked at Bob and then replied, "Maybe the kidnapper had already taken the cash and had gone away to fetch or release the girl." "Don't think so." said Bob. "Firstly, Montgomery wouldn't just give him the cash, even if he pointed a gun at him. He was too clever for that. Maybe he hadn't actually taken any cash, a double cross. Also, the kidnapper wouldn't be crazy enough to expect to get the cash then go away and return with the girl. It would have to be an exchange – bag of cash for girl. That's how these things usually played out."

Bill was nodding as Bob shared his thoughts. "So, you'd think that we would have found either the girl or the money along with Montgomery then." Bill said. Bob looked at him, thinking. "That's what I would have thought Bill." He replied. "There is something we're not seeing here. Something more to this thing than appears on the surface. It'll be difficult to get any more information on Montgomery with his diplomatic status but Bill, see what you can dig up on him anyway. Try the media archives too. Anything at all. See if you can pull any strings to access his financial details. If we could prove he had withdrawn a sum of cash that would be very helpful. He can't have had that much stuffed under his mattress. At the moment we have nothing to say he was actually pursuing the kidnapper and his daughter on his own. All we know is that he stopped speaking to us and ended up under the bridge. If he'd only stuck with us things could be so different." The thing that played on Bob's mind was that, so far, they had nothing to say his daughter was killed with him following an exchange. So, where the fuck was she? Did the abductor still have her? He had no reason to keep her alive. Either she was dead before this, or he would have killed her and dumped her body after the attack. But did the abductor know Montgomery was dead? If he was at the planned exchange point, then the abductor would know that the bridge had been a target. If he'd any prior knowledge of the bombings he would have stayed the fuck away. He'd know Montgomery could have been killed there waiting for him. If the kidnapper still had Annie alive then they needed him to know that Montgomery was dead, and no money was forthcoming, assuming he hadn't already gotten any in the hope he'd release her. This was the only scenario whereby the kidnapper might release Annie and drop his plan.

Maybe she had died at the scene but they hadn't yet retrieved anything to prove it. Same could go for the kidnapper. More body parts might still turn up, he thought. If Montgomery hadn't made the drop when he got blown up, then should they now release details of his death as part of the terrorist action in the media? That was the best way to ensure the kidnapper knew Montgomery was dead, assuming the kidnapper was still alive and well. He would have to think about this carefully before going to his superiors and offering this as his plan. It was risky. When the kidnapper knew his cash source had dried up, he may decide to cut his losses and kill the girl to avoid any comeback. It would tie up loose ends, assuming he had no conscience.

CHAPTER 70

Annie had her bathing costume on and was about to get into the pool on deck. Dom was reading the paper, once again studying anything relating to the ISIS attack at Old Trafford. He was still getting his head around the fortunate timing of this attack and how it would deflect any interest in the first attack's perpetrators. It was just too good to be true. ISIS – it must have been ISIS. ISIS I insist. What if it was nothing more than an accident and ISIS had claimed responsibility anyway? Still nothing about Annie's father. This both intrigued him and concerned him. With all the new DNA analysis they could identify a body from a small fragment so long as they had a sample to compare it with. He was under the impression that all senior public figures had samples for exactly this type of analysis – mainly for their protection. He felt sure that by now the police and authorities knew Montgomery was dead and where he had died. But did they know how he died? Surely, they think he was in the wrong place at the wrong time – blown up and buried. But they'd have found his car parked a way away and found this highly suspicious. That said, who cared what he was doing beneath that bridge? This one tiny piece in a massive jigsaw. One where there weren't enough policemen in the UK to put the pieces together properly. Humpty Dumpty Monty was no longer centre stage. They would have to focus on the bigger pieces. He felt pretty sure they were in the clear, thanks to ISIS.

"Are you coming in?" Annie asked as she tottered on the edge of the pool. Dom smiled and stood up. He then shouted "Coming!" and ran toward her as though to push her in. She screamed and jumped in before he got to her. He went in with a loud splash and came up next to her, where they kissed for what seemed a decade. That's what newlyweds do. Everyone loves a newly wedded couple starting out in the world. Especially older couples who have no children of their own, or who lost their children in tragic circumstances. Dom was still formulating his strategy for his and Annie's future career. They would have to move from town to town, city to city and not strike twice in the same place. At least not within a few years. If things got tricky it wasn't difficult to shut up an old person and make it look like a heart attack or accident. When old people were found dead it was only natural to assume the tragedy was age related. His strategy was taking shape. Annie had found an inflatable crocodile lilo and was trying to get onto it. Despite her being slim and fit she was struggling to get on and kept falling in, much to the amusement of the other people watching from the sun loungers. She was very attractive, and the bikini showed her off very nicely. No wonder people were watching. Dom gave her a hand getting on and she gave him a kiss. He pushed the crocodile towards the centre of the pool where she began to drift with the breeze. Dom swam a few lengths of the pool. It was more of an obstacle course, trying to avoid children and old people bobbing up and down. He preferred a pool to himself where he could focus on doing fast lengths in peace. He was a very strong swimmer and, as a child, could outswim all his friends. They would swim in the sea in the evening, daring each other to swim further out or dive deeper. He wondered what Annie's childhood had been like. He looked over towards her. She was lying on her back taking in the rays of the sun. Her skin glistened as the moisture evaporated slowly. He could see the outline of her nipples through the thin material of the bikini top. He felt a stirring in his swimming shorts. If he'd been wearing speedos he'd have had to stay in the water 'til he cooled off. Luckily, his swimming shorts afforded him some discretion. He decided to leave

Annie on the lilo for a while – she looked too relaxed. He would get out, dry off, and finish reading the paper. It was impressive how the cruise company could get papers that were typically only a day or two behind. Still, it didn't matter much as they still continued to view the British media via the internet and breaking news. Newspapers were becoming outdated anyway. But there would always be a place for them on holiday. But still nothing felt quite like sitting in the sun, on the deck of a beautiful boat, accompanied by a beautiful woman, with nothing more to do than read an English newspaper. The feel of the pages, the rustling sound they made as the gentle breeze rustled them.

Dom decided to get out of the pool. As he was drying himself, he spotted the elderly couple that Annie had been talking to in the coffee place earlier that morning, that copper and his wife. Dom draped the towel around his waist and got back onto his sun lounger donning his sunglasses hoping they may not recognise him. As they passed by, they both looked at him. He glanced up at them and said "Hello". He knew only too well that they had indeed recognised him and Annie in the pool. "Your wife looks lovely and relaxed over there in the pool", Mave said. Dom looked over at her and replied "Yes. We're newlyweds." "We know" replied Mave and her husband in unison, like it was some secret they were party to. They both wore wide smiles as they continued their walk. Coppers are dumb thought Dom.

He lay on the lounger exploring different ways of potentially getting a Mave and Husband to part with their hard-earned retirement money. They were obviously suckers for newlyweds. Suppose said newlyweds had an accident, or had their money and cards stolen. Maybe they'd lend them 500 dollars, or pounds, or Euros, to tide them over whilst they sorted their affairs and were able to repay the loan. Which of course they would never do. Was that sufficiently humiliating for them to part with the money and then, upon realising they had been stung, keep stum and not tell their family, friends or police? Possibly. They'd likely have more money than sense anyway. And they'd need to work hard at 500 dollars a time. Easy come, easy go. He suspected they needed something on these lines but potentially even more humiliating and lucrative. Maybe borrow the money, then engineer a situation where the old man is tricked into touching Annie in some way that he wouldn't want to be known by his wife. There's life in almost every old dog.

His thoughts were disturbed as his face was splashed with pool water. Annie was stood there giggling. She had gotten out quietly and sneaked up on him. In any other circumstances this would have annoyed Dom immensely. But today his sense of humour was in good form and he laughed with her as she giggled like a schoolgirl. He got up and started to wipe her down with her towel. His problem came back and so he poked her with it as he wiped her. She started to giggle again but this time the giggle was different. This particular type of giggle served to turn him on even more. "We'd better get back to that room pronto before your shorts split." Annie said with a wicked smile. They collected their stuff and headed back to their cabin.

As Dom finished his second shower of the day, he had worked up an appetite. Annie was drying herself as Dom left the shower. "I'm hungry." she said. "Meatloaf!" Dom replied. Annie looked at him with a puzzled expression. "You took the words right out of my mouth…" Annie replied but she had decided not to try and sing them. Annie smiled. "Clever." Dom said. Again, she smiled. "I fancy a full English!". With that they dressed and headed up back up through the decks in search of breakfast.

The restaurant they chose was more of a café, but it served an all-day breakfast. They took a table and sat down. After a couple of minutes, the waitress came over and took their orders. Two full English, two rounds of white buttered toast, two mugs of builder's tea and two beers. She didn't think anything strange about ordering two beers with breakfast. After all, they were British. They drank the beers first to cool down. Both red and brown sauce arrived with the breakfasts – and in bottles not sachets. Dom helped himself to a generous splodge of tomato sauce plus a splodge of brown sauce on the bacon. Annie looked at him – thought for a couple of seconds – then did the same. Dom watched her and then said, "Red is by far my favourite but bacon always needs a bit of brown." As Annie ate her breakfast, she had brown sauce on her lips. Dom couldn't help himself thinking of her giving him a rusty trombone. They hadn't tried that yet. He noticed that most of the customers in this café on the ship appeared to be British and elderly. The brits like their plain food and especially tea and all-day breakfasts. A happy hunting ground. Places like this were everywhere – on board cruise ships, on street corners and in almost every city in the world. Trouble is they didn't necessarily attract the affluent targets he needed. An upper-class restaurant attracted affluence. Cafés like this attracted almost everyone. You would have to know a bit about the punters beforehand – do your research. Every such scam relied on lots of research and preparation. He was always sure to do his. At some point he needed to have a serious chat with his wife about how she saw their futures panning out. Dom knew that he had fallen for her, so far as he was capable of, anyhow. He'd fallen hard. Harder than he'd ever fallen before. Life was so good. When life got this good it usually meant one thing – that a fall was on its way. The end of a lucky streak. He felt sure that this time it would be different.

CHAPTER 71

Bob had put a lot of thought into how he could recover from the situation. No kidnapper or kidnappers and no victim. Unless they moved quickly the daughter would die, as without the prospect of ransom money, she had little or no value. If she wasn't already dead, she soon would be. If she'd somehow escaped, then she'd have turned up by now.

"OK Bob. I think this plan of Bill's and yours might have legs." said the Chief Inspector. "But we can only put so much effort into this before it is deemed as gone cold. We'll give it a week and if nothing useful comes in by then we'll drop it.". "Yes, sir," said Bob, "thank you. I'm confident we'll get something useful back from this. By including the reference to his sister from Kensington, and the bogus online information we've posted, we're offering the kidnappers a new opportunity for obtaining the cash they need. We need to consider the option that she's already dead, even if they do get in touch. Detective Inspector Standing will have the phone with her at all times, so if they get in contact, she'll know exactly what to say and do. It's our only chance, sir." The Chief Inspector nodded knowingly. Nothing more needed to be said. They all understood this could be the last chance Annie would get, assuming she was indeed still alive. With that they left his office. A statement would be put together, short and sweet, and presented to the media later that day so as to make the evening news and papers. It would state that Montgomery was dead, where and how he died. His only sister was distraught, and his daughter was missing, with a reward for finding her. All they could do was to hope that whoever took his daughter saw it and tried to get in contact with the fictitious sister to collect the reward.

CHAPTER 72

Dom and Annie had spent the afternoon browsing the many shops on board and then sitting in one of the bars drinking cool beers watching the world go by. "What do you want?" Dom asked Annie. She looked at him with an expression of confusion. "Sorry, I mean, what do you want for yourself for the future – you know, after we get off this boat and, well, disappear." She looked like he'd brought her down to earth with a bang. After a pause she said "I'm just having such a nice time with you here I hadn't really thought about it. I don't want this to end." Dom smiled, and she knew from his smile that he had fallen for her. All was good. She took hold of his hand and squeezed it and then kissed him. "We should go somewhere away from Europe, that's for sure," Dom replied, "and definitely not Africa!". Annie smiled. She had no desire to go there either. "I've been thinking about how we can get by. We've still got a fair chunk of cash but that won't last forever. We need a way of, well, earning." Annie looked at him, not quite knowing where he was going with this. "I've never met anyone like you and I think we get on well together. I think we should stick together and disappear – together. Look at the way these oldies take to us – newlyweds. We could live on ships like this for a few months, befriend an elderly couple then on the last day we could, I don't know, get robbed, lose our cash and cards, and have to borrow some cash. Then disappear." Annie looked at him. "We'd need to borrow a lot of cash – to cover the cost of the cruise and make a profit." Dom smiled. "I wasn't really thinking of paying for the cruise. We could get new identities and cards for each trip. We'd be living all-inclusive for free and collecting cash at the end. Annie considered this and replied "But how long could we keep this up before they realised that someone was taking them for a ride? On a ship, even one this size, there is nowhere to hide. I want us to stay together but we need a better plan." Dom knew she was right. She didn't want to upset him, so she kissed him again and he smiled at her. "See what I mean, beauty and brains." She beamed at him the most beautiful smile he'd ever seen. "We've got a lot of tools in our locker, blackmail, con artistry, theft, with all these we should be able to come up with something that will keep us together and happy for a long time. Dom, for the first time, realised that he was no longer in full control of this situation. He had gone from captor with complete control to partner with what was now evenly shared control, if that. Only one thing for it. Dom waved to the waitress as she walked past indicating two more beers. She nodded. A couple of minutes later the beers arrived. Neither of them had spoken during this time. The waitress took away their empties and they both simultaneously took a long drag of the fresh beers. They looked at each other and smiled. Actions in unison – as one.

The next couple of minutes Dom spent people watching. He was particularly interested in a couple, probably in their late fifties, probably taken early retirement, not flamboyant but seemingly comfortable. They seemed to have plenty of money to spend, being on a cruise like this. One thing he had learned is that the flashier folk aren't necessarily the richest. What would be the most likely way to get them to part with a significant chunk of cash? Some sort of embarrassing scam? That had been his line of thinking so far. Steal their money in such a way that they were unlikely to go to the police or close family – or anyone else, come to think of it. He'd heard of old people, typically widows or widowers, where a friendly builder had knocked on the door doing them a favour by offering to fix a few broken roof tiles… only for the job to get big-

ger and bigger…. cash up front for materials for the new roof….
But Dom wasn't a builder. He needed something quicker than
that with less social interaction. A clever smash and grab
if you like. One featuring this beautiful and very vulnerable
young lady beside him. In all his plans she had been the bait. As
he continued to look around, his eyes were attracted to the TV
on the far wall. The sound was turned low, and it was the UK
news. The picture that came up on the screen grabbed his attention – it was Annie's father. What the fuck? He nudged her
and they both strained to listen to the dialogue over the other
customers' voices. After a few seconds the newscaster went on
to another story. Dom looked at Annie. "I didn't know your
father had a sister – you never mentioned her before." Annie
looked at him with a puzzled expression. "He doesn't. At least
not that I've ever met or heard of."

CHAPTER 73

It was gone seven and it had been another long day – the pub beckoned. Bill and Bob left the office for the real world – the outside world. Bob thought that he knew what it must feel like for a prisoner who has finished his sentence to get out of the institution and breath fresh air again. That's what it felt like after spending the day in the hot, busy office that was the nick. Beer awaited but they weren't heading for their usual haunt, as it didn't have a telly. They continued down the road for a few minutes until they found one that met their requirements – that being a telly that was showing the news. They went in, looked across the room to the large TV and saw that the news was already on. Bob went to the bar to get the beers in and Bill took a table close to the telly where they could see and hear it, despite the low volume setting. The TV was within reach, so Bill found the volume button on the side and eased the volume up a little. A few seconds later Bob returned with two pints. Both men downed a third of their pints straight away. The news had started and after yet more conjecture about the recent bombings and Manchester United crash, on came the piece they'd been waiting for. They watched the brief story about Montgomery – it only lasted around thirty seconds and the gist was that he had been killed by the bomb and his daughter was missing and everyone, including her aunty, wanted her back safe and sound. They showed a picture of the dead father, and another one of the daughter, who appeared to be young and very pretty with long blonde hair. Not one of those typical family photos where the person in question smiles up at the camera like they don't have a care in the

worked – in this one the daughter looked small, sad and lost...
unhappy even, but still pretty nevertheless. But it was the
best one they had found. Bill looked around as the article finished. No one else in the pub seemed remotely interested. The
guy or the daughter could be standing at the bar right here and
now, staring at their own images on the big screen and no one
would recognise them. The rest of the punters either chatted
or stared into their glasses. What a world we live in. All they
could do now was to wait – wait to see if the phone would ring.
If it did, they would be the first to know. The newspapers the
following day would leak news that the daughter had possibly
been kidnapped, hence the reward. It was a good plan – all
they could do under the circumstances really. Neither Bob nor
Bill now held much hope of finding the daughter alive and well
after all this time. The job made you cynical – that and age. She
was too pretty to come back in one piece. But they remained
hopeful to the end. The end being a body.
Bill got up and said, "Same again?" Bob nodded and Bill headed
towards the bar. Nothing to do but wait.

CHAPTER 74

Paolo lay in bed. Neither his wife, Maria, nor he, had gotten a wink of sleep and it was now 3am. The kids were fine, they had no idea of what was happening – it was all an adventure to them. Maria was only now beginning to understand what had happened and the seriousness of it all, and its life changing effects. She was on a downward roller coaster heading into a black tunnel with no idea what was inside, or whether she should duck her head or not. She was trapped. All her married life she had known Paolo was a player, but she enjoyed spending the rewards of his labours. She enjoyed the social circle and closeness of Vincenzo's extended family. They had eaten dinner in each other's houses, enjoyed weekends away, looked after each other's kids just like real friends. But it had all been something of a sham, a cover. Everything she thought she knew about these people was a lie. She was sure that their wives knew a lot more about the actions of their partners than she ever did. Was she naïve? The answer was a definite yes. But not any longer. Could she go back to her old life and cut Paolo loose? She knew the answer to this was no. So long as Paolo lived, they could be used as leverage against him, or simply killed as punishment. There was no way off this particular roller coaster – she had to sit tight and wait for it to come to a stop, then find a different ride.

Outside she could hear the sound of crickets, the odd bird and occasionally the cry of a larger animal. The two policemen, who had remained concealed, had made no noise. She didn't know where they were, aside from the fact that it was close by, with a good view of the house and exits, and close enough to act if needed. The policewoman was on the couch in the lounge. Their bedroom door was ajar. If the policewoman, Andrea, went to the toilet or the kitchen for a drink, Maria would hear it. The more she listened the louder the quiet noises became. The birds sounded closer. The footsteps – were they footsteps or was her automatic volume control playing tricks with her again? She thought she'd heard the sound of crunching beneath a shoe, like standing on a seed or a stone. It's probably one of the policemen looking around, she thought. But no more sounds were heard. If it were the policeman, he would have no reason to stand still or avoid being heard. He would naturally want to be quiet so as not to disturb them and not to be overheard, but if what she heard had been a footfall then the person with the foot was deadly silent now, not doing the rounds......

A minute, maybe two had passed and still no more untoward sounds. Maria was becoming confident that her imagination was playing tricks with her. Then it happened again. A muffled sound coming from the lounge – not a cry, not a thump but an ominous, quiet thud with what sounded like an exhale. Maria went rigid in bed. Her ears went up to max as she listened intently for further sounds. "Did you hear that?" whispered Paolo without moving. "Shhh" Maria said – she was beginning to sweat. Paolo was slowly sliding out of bed – he peeped though the open gap towards the lounge for a second then hid behind the bedroom door. Maria was desperate to ask him if he could see Andrea but she daren't. They both waited in silence. No more sounds, no movement. The door was ajar for security, but it didn't offer them any security now.

CHAPTER 75

Dom was confused. Firstly, why show Montgomery's picture on the news at all, given all the other things happening? Secondly why make up the fact that he had a distraught sister? Surely it couldn't be a mistake? Annie would surely have known about her, or met her at some point. He didn't believe she was lying to him. "He went to the police. He must've done. That's the only way they'd know about me being taken." Annie said. "They must know he's dead but they didn't find any money or me close by so they must think he was there under the bridge to make the drop. No bodies, no money – did he make the drop or not? They are trying to get the kidnappers, that's us… I mean you… to make contact with the so-called sister and try and get money from her because they think that you may not have got the ransom money because of the bomb or something. I reckon whoever calls the sister will be speaking to a policewoman. Clever." Dom doubted he would have come up with that scenario himself – not for a while at the very least! But it made sense. They knew Annie was missing and they still thought they had a chance of getting her back. This wasn't good news for Dom. It offered Annie a new way out if she chose to follow it. He'd have to be very vigilant from now on.

"Where would he have got the cash from Annie? Would it be traceable? Would the police know he had the cash with him?" Dom asked her. Annie thought about this for a moment. "If he went to the police and told them everything they wouldn't need to resort to this trickery. He must have gone to them at first, and then gone solo to the drop after your second call, where we met him, without the police knowing. If he'd got untraceable cash, they wouldn't know if he'd taken the cash or not, I guess. They don't know about the drop – they are just making guesses. No money was found, obviously, so that means he could have made the drop before that." After a few seconds pause Annie continued "They don't have a fucking clue what happened that day. The problem we face is that the police are still looking for me. But that said, it really shouldn't be long before they assume the worst." Dom thought for a moment then said "No one is going to contact the sister unless they are trying their hand, which will only confuse the police and slow them down, and that'll mean only one thing to them – that you are dead with or without the money. Fuck, we should have left a couple of grand at the scene to be recovered; they'd have assumed the rest went up in flames or was buried or washed away or something. We need to stay low for a bit longer than we thought, that's all." Dom had learned another valuable lesson from this, one that he would mentally store for the future.

They finished their drinks and went back to the cabin. Dom put the news on to see if there was anything else. He was beginning to feel that all the news was about him. It was feeding his ego. But it didn't make him feel special or powerful, something somewhere made him feel more vulnerable with each mention of any of his doings of the past few days. Annie seemed to be just fine with everything. She took everything in her stride – nothing fazed her. Whatever happened; kidnap, threat of death, bombs, killing, stealing, masquerading, she just got on with it and did it very well. She seemed to be born to this stuff. He wondered what would have become of her if he hadn't entered her life. Annie was lying on the bed on her back, arms crossed over her chest staring at the ceiling. Her hair flowed over the pillow, she looked lovely. He got on the bed beside her and lay on his side facing her and put his arm over her chest. She held his hand and a smile came over her face. They lay in silence for a couple of minutes then Annie said, "Any more ideas about what we'll do after all this has gone away?" Dom thought for a moment then answered honestly "No, not yet. Have you?" He almost expected her to have a plan ready to run by him. "Not really" she answered, "but I'm working on it."

CHAPTER 76

It happened so quickly that Maria, still lying on her back in bed, didn't have time to react. Paolo's scream lasted only a fraction of a second as it turned into a gurgle. She heard splashing sounds that confused her, then the door slammed shut and she heard footsteps going across the lounge. No other movements to be heard from Andrea. Then she heard the back door open and footsteps outside. She then heard gunfire – quiet gunfire – pops like maybe a silencer had been used. As she realised the attacker had left, she turned her attention to Paolo. He was slumped on the floor by the door. She turned on the bedside light and was greeted by a scene of red. Up the walls, on the ceiling, on the bedding and pools on the floor. Paolo was twitching slightly – on his back, hands clutching his throat where a wide gash extended from ear to ear with blood spurting upwards. She knew there was nothing to be done for him, as the blood left his body at such an alarming rate. His throat looked beyond repair. He was already unconscious, soon he would be dead. She got out of bed, her bare feet sliding in the blood, and falling hard on the floor, smearing blood all over her nightgown. She must have looked like something from a horror movie. She ran to the children's bedroom. Both her children were awake and unharmed. That couldn't be said of Andrea. She was unconscious in the lounge, but there was no blood. Maria cuddled her children, told them to stay in their room, despite their stares at her bloody attire, and went back to see if Andrea was alive. To her surprise it appeared that she had been somehow knocked out silently. There was a slight smell and she wondered if they'd used chloroform or something to knock her out quietly, rather than kill her noisily. She wasn't dead. After a few seconds she awoke with a start and threw up on the floor. She was confused at first, as though she didn't know where she was, plus it was dark. Her face was filled with horror when she saw Maria covered in blood. She looked into Maria's eyes for a second and then looked away, silently admitting that she'd let Maria and the family down. She said just one word "Paolo?" Maria looked at her and stood up. "He's gone but we need to get out of here. Where are those fucking guards?" Maria stood up and went outside.

A minute later she returned with only one of the guards. He was wounded. Maria had obviously briefed him. As he came inside, he was already on the phone saying to get backup, to search for the guy that had attacked them and downed an officer, and the urgent need for transport to move everyone right away. He ended the call and went over to Maria and said "I'm sorry, we let you down. Whoever did this was a professional. We saw and heard nothing until the person left the house. We chased him, but it was too late, and I was in no condition to give chase. But we know who was responsible, right? But rest assured, no one else was harmed, and it's unlikely they'll come after you or the children now. They wanted to silence Paolo and they've done that. They could probably have just killed all of us if they'd really wanted to." Maria started to cry. She broke down. Andrea offered to hold her, but she pushed her away and went to the children's room and closed the door. What would happen to them now? Would they still get new identities and a new home, or would they be left to rot? She was no use to anyone.

CHAPTER 77

Bill and Bob were briefing the chief. They'd had a few calls, but all were deemed to be from cranks. Three trying to arrange a handover for cash! But when pushed, none of the callers had any information that lead them to believe they were involved. Crackpots after a handout. "Should be locked up" Bob said. The chief said they'd give it a week then the case would be closed, and she'd be added to the long list of missing persons assumed dead. It wasn't as if any anxious relatives were on their backs, she could have just upped and left for all they knew. But of course, she hadn't. Of the three of them, Bob was the only one who thought there was a chance of Annie still being alive. And that was a slim one. That said, he knew in his heart of hearts that the next lead they would likely get, would be a body. The thing that still nagged at him was this whole handover scenario. How had her father come to be in such a remote location and on his own? It could only be for a pre-arranged exchange. There was absolutely no other reason to be down there. Unless he was meeting someone else for something completely different. But what? Montgomery had no record of drugs or anything illegal. He wasn't squeaky clean but there was nothing on record anywhere indicating anything untoward. Maybe he was unlucky – got there early, fell victim to the bomb and bridge collapse and the exchange never took place? That was the only possible scenario in Bob's head that made any sense. His phone records had been checked, both mobile and home, and no suspicious numbers had been found. There were a couple of untraceable, unregistered numbers on there, but it could have been PPI for all they knew. If this was a drop how had they organised it? Was there anything to trace? Did he have another phone? If he did then surely, if he was making the drop, he'd have had it with him. Nothing had been recovered, which was by no means a surprise, and given the circumstances probably nothing more would be recovered. The only course of action was to wait and see if the kidnapper had taken the bait. If he had arranged it and was late getting there then he'd know that Montgomery was under the bridge anyway, even before the news bulletin, assuming he'd seen it. Nothing made sense. And where was Annie, or her body?

CHAPTER 78

"Remember Pulp Fiction?" Annie asked Dom. "Never seen it, don't watch movies really." he replied. "At the start, this couple are in a diner and they suddenly stand up with guns and rob the place. Their logic was that nobody expects a diner to be robbed, the staff are only employees paid peanuts, so no one will be willing to risk their life to stop someone else's money being stolen. It's brilliant" "So you are suggesting we do a similar thing only in flash restaurants? Most people pay on credit card anyway." Dom replied. "No, silly. The restaurant doesn't matter, it's the fact that the money being stolen doesn't belong to the people you are stealing it from. Therefore, they won't put up as much of a struggle. They are only concerned for their own safety and getting out unhurt. They offer less resistance than someone who is having their own money or property stolen. It's like businessmen are quicker to spend company money on hotels and food than they would be if they were spending their own hard-earned cash." Dom thought about this. "Just like the old-time bank robbers in the Wild West... So, if we are to steal on a big scale, we target places where the staff are paid peanuts and there are reasonable volumes of cash on the premises." Dom said, thinking out loud. Annie smiled at him. "Well, it's a start." She said. "OK, so what types of business would work best then? Ones using low paid staff but taking reasonable amounts of cash. Not supermarkets – they have systems that take the cash and they are full of CCTV." Dom said, again still thinking out loud. He wasn't used to having a co-conspirator. He hadn't gotten used to this yet. "Also, we should look at places where the staff are mainly female – they are more likely to back off and not put up any kind or struggle." Annie said. Dom thought about this for a few moments, again there was logic in her words. Lots of cash, predominantly female staff, ideally no CCTV. After a few seconds Annie smiled widely at Dom and looked at him. Dom waited a few seconds, but her smile was infectious. At this point he would normally be getting angry at the possibility of being outsmarted by a girl. But instead he too smiled. "What have you got for me then? He said. Annie replied "Hairdressers, beauty salons. They charge a fortune, mainly staffed by women, girls, and take cash payments. The largest ones may accommodate six to ten clients at a time. By lunch time they'd have taken maybe a grand. More in upmarket areas. We'd need to do one a week to cover our costs. Dom thought about this and then replied, "That's a lot of jobs, the risk of getting identified or caught is quite high, even if we use different disguises." It's too small-time, nothing more than petty burglary. We're so much better than that. We could do with something where we make 10 grand or more. Annie looked at him intently for a few seconds and then said, "Leave it with me." After a minute or so she said, "What do you fancy for dinner tonight?" It was like she was two people – one minute the new bride, the next Annie Oakley.

While both Dom and Annie considered their plans on and off throughout the evening, neither spoke about it again. This was their penultimate night on board. They needed to make plans for where they went and what they did when they disembarked, as the clock was ticking. They'd had several conversations about this already. Dom's initial plan had been to leave the cruise and lay low for two weeks. His idea was to get the Red Funnel to The Isle of Wight and find a B&B or cheap hotel. By then no one would be looking for Annie anymore and the coast would be clear so to speak. They could then get an overnight ferry to France and start their new adventure. He hadn't shared this with Annie yet. Every day he had been with her she had shone more brightly. Not just in her beauty but her brains. She had both. He was keen to see what plan she would come up with. Whilst Dom had many years' experience of illegal activities Annie had none, bar this past week. They would see things from different perspectives. To plan a perfect crime, you needed to see things from the victim's perspective and to be able to predict their actions.

They'd decided to go for an Indian for their last dinner on board. The food was great, as was all the food they'd had. The Cobra lager, albeit bottled, came icy cold and complemented the meal nicely. Whilst Dom had drunk nearly two beers for Annie's one, they were both pleasantly inebriated by the time their desserts arrived. Gulab jamun. As they left the restaurant for the final time, they decided to have a nightcap up top in their favourite bar. Dom had a pint of lager, Annie had a vodka and coke. Annie was saying she daren't think about how much weight she'd put on during their honeymoon. So far that evening they hadn't engaged in conversation with anyone. Dom had been vigilantly checking so as to avoid Mave and Plod. The Indian restaurant seemed to attract more of the younger people than the older set. They hadn't wanted to be conspicuous or memorable. As they sipped their last drinks a younger couple went over to the bar. The bar was full now and there were no tables free. Dom and Annie had a table for four to themselves.

"I've decided what we'll do for the next couple of weeks." Dom said to Annie. She looked at him without saying anything. "We need to keep our heads down until this story of your father has gone away. By my reckoning that'll be a week, two tops. We'll lay low, call it the next part of our honeymoon. The Isle of Wight isn't far from where we dock tomorrow. We can get a ferry over there, book a place to stay for two weeks and make our plans from there." Neither of them had visited the Isle of Wight before. Dom didn't think this would be a problem. It wasn't a big place and they'd stay close by the town where they were staying. He'd been online and found a B&B in Cowes, within walking distance of the Red Funnel hydrofoil terminal, which was the means of getting from Southampton to Cowes, on and off the island. Annie seemed happy with this. Dom didn't dislike the idea of two more weeks close to Annie either. But they needed to make some firm plans in this period. No one joined them that evening at their table as they talked and they finally retired for the last time having avoided any further close contact with the other passengers.

Tomorrow would see the next stage of their journey.

CHAPTER 79

Bruce was now working on the fitting out of the upper floors. The basement, to all intents and purposes, was complete bar a few cosmetic things. Tim and Gavin had finished their work and the SSF had been sealed shut. All that was evident of that particular room was the door. It no longer looked like a cross between a large safe and a submarine watertight compartment door. In itself, it wasn't that outstanding. It was by no means apparent to the casual observer that a room of such a considerable size lay behind the door. This was exactly as it was meant to be. Bob was intrigued by the interior. He needed to get in there to examine it. His selected means of access was under the pretence of a safety examination for the building certificates. As the Project Manager he was required to undertake certain audits and document the findings. This was in his plan for later that week. If he was refused access it would cause problems. But his curiosity was getting the better of him.

All the contractors had exceeded their contractual duties, something that Bruce had never heard of or experienced before. Where he anticipated delays, things were completed quicker than planned. The building was shooting up nearly twice as fast as he realistically expected. How the owner had got every one of the suppliers to perform so well was a mystery to him. He must have been paying them very well indeed. They didn't appear to be cutting corners.

This project was unlike any other he'd been involved in. Normally his day was filled with interruptions from problems here and there, missing materials, accidents, errors of some sort. Here things went smoothly and efficiently, one big team. Outside, the weather had turned. He could hear the rain banging against the windows; people were rushing back inside soaking wet, but it only lasted a few minutes, then all was back to normal bar the wet floor.

CHAPTER 80

Vincenzo had heard the unfortunate news about Paolo. The primary objective was to kill Paolo, but they were also instructed to kill the wife, kids and cops and burn the house down. Sadly, they'd failed in this objective but no matter now. Paolo wasn't talking. His wife would disappear, and life would revert to normality, his team would be ever more vigilant having seen first-hand what happened to those who turned. He remained in control. Now he could focus all his attentions on his other mission. He could still take the family out if he so wished.

As he had gotten nowhere in tracking down Devizes, he was firmly of the opinion that he had indeed left South Africa and was already, or soon would be, back in the UK. He decided to widen his net. He put together a brief pack of information about Devizes, a couple of pictures of him, his height, weight, skill set etc. and circulated this to his circle of acquaintances, as he sometimes referred to them as. These included the people who occasionally did work for him in the UK, and the police officers that were also in his employ. Some of these did this to supplement their income. Some, mainly the higher-ranking members of his circle of acquaintances, had been coerced into assisting him by threats to their families, or through detailed knowledge of their nefarious affairs with both the opposite and, in some cases, the same sex. They were his. Loyal and obedient to the last. It would take some time. Each had a gmail or Hotmail account not in their own name that they were to check at least once per week. They were told not to do this even from their own computers or their work computers just in case anyone checked the access. Naturally, Vincenzo had a tech guru on his payroll. Full time in fact, such was the demand for his services. Every few months, when the techy had a gap in his workload, he'd get him to do some checking of where these web-based email accounts had been accessed from. Vincenzo had supplied the email addresses and passwords and his circle were told not to change the details or reset the passwords. The techy knew the IP address range of these people's employers who had fixed addresses and he could verify that the accounts hadn't been used at their places of work. It was more difficult to check home usage down to the dynamic IP addresses, but he had a script installed on each of their home computers, malware to anyone else, that sent their IP address daily, via a number of hops, to a place where the techy could pick them up, allowing him to check their home pc usage as well. Once, he had identified a policeman who had accessed the email from a computer in his local nick one evening. The said copper had been paid a visit a couple of days later to explain to him what he'd done wrong, along with a broken arm to act as a memory jogger for the future. He'd had two dozen Devizes packs zipped up and distributed to the relevant people. With this and his other enquiries he felt sure that he'd get a sniff of Devizes sooner rather than later.

CHAPTER 81

Disembarking had been a smooth process and both of them felt a tinge of sadness at leaving their temporary home. The Red Funnel was much larger than either of them expected. It also seemed to go much quicker than they expected. Whilst the ferry took cars, they didn't need a car just yet. They would get one soon enough. It took around an hour to get over to Cowes. The island looked beautiful as they approached. The sun was shining, and the sky was blue. There were lots of smaller sailing ships all around and they could see harbours with even more boats. If you liked boats and sailing this was definitely the place for you. All their newly acquired belongings had fitted into the case they had brought, and Dom was on deck wheeling it with one hand and holding Annie's hand with the other. They walked from the pier to the high street. Annie wanted to look in all the quaint shops, but Dom was keen to get rid of the case he was wheeling along as it also contained the money, so they tracked down their accommodation. It was too early to check in, but the lady let them leave their case. Dom had taken as much money as he could fit into the rucksack he had bought on the boat, so that in the unlikely event of the case getting stolen or simply going missing, they still had plenty of cash to see them through. He'd also given Annie a thick wad to keep in her handbag. Nevertheless, he didn't like the idea of leaving their case in some crummy B&B, with some old bat the only thing coming between his dosh and some scumbag thief. Still, they could check in in four hours' time. By the time they'd got their bearings, visited a couple of shops and grabbed a bite to eat and a couple of beers they'd be safely tucked up in bed with the money safely put away.

After leaving the bag and saying goodbye to Josie the receptionist, maybe even proprietor, they headed back towards the high street. Annie browsed in a couple of the shops but didn't buy anything. Dom bought a hipflask and a hunting knife. They found a nice boozer, suitably named The Anchor Inn. They had a good range of beer including Sharps, Fullers and Wadsworth. He hated London Pride. He really didn't see what people saw in that watery, warm, usually flat drink. He opted for a pint of 6X. Annie went for half a lager. The food menu was your typical pub grub but on a slightly higher level. They even did gluten-free meals. Dom went for the beer battered cod fillet. Annie went for the homemade Thai green curry. Dom was tempted but he always came away disappointed after having a curry in a pub. Nevertheless, he tried Annie's and it was pretty good fayre. There was plenty of time for him to partake in a Thai green curry over the coming days. He was sure there would be plenty of other nice boozers and restaurants in Cowes. It seemed like a nice place.

After slowly walking back to their B&B they collected their case, which was exactly where they had left it. Josie showed them to their room; it was on the first floor and at the end of the corridor. Wherever Dom stayed they always seemed to put him at the end of a corridor. Still, it meant neighbours only on one side. He was always conscious of places like this with rooms close together separated only by cardboard walls, with ears. But he had no reason to suspect anyone listening to them from the next room. Nevertheless, as the place was now full, according to Josie, he would try and ascertain who was occupying that room and give them the once over, just to be on the safe side. The room was pretty basic and not as nice or well-equipped as their previous residence but it had everything they needed for now. Annie unpacked their things, hanging their clothes up on hangers. "We'll have to find a cleaners at some point." she said. "No problem, they do a cleaning service here according to the sign at reception." Dom answered. "That's good then." Annie said. She made a pile of their dirty clothes and Dom took them down to reception to get them laundered. Josie said they'd be ready late tomorrow morning, all being well. Dom said that was fine and that there was no rush. He returned to the room and to Annie. They had plans to make.

CHAPTER 82

At the project meeting earlier that morning, Bruce had raised the issue of the safety certificate for the basement which included the SSF. He said he'd need admittance to check the facility in order to get the required certificate. He was told that this wouldn't be an issue. Fair enough, he thought to himself. It wouldn't be that day as he had too much on, but tomorrow morning was pencilled in for 8am – another early start. The rest of the day went by quickly, as the days did when you were busy. By the time he finished at shortly after 7pm most of the day shift had left and would be in the pub by now. Nevertheless, work continued where it could be done throughout the night. He went back to change his clothes then went down to the pub. Sure enough, there were three or four of the team in there laughing and joking about something. He noticed another couple having a game of pool. Bruce had been a keen pool player once. These days he never found the time. When he and his wife had been planning for the future, his dream home had featured a pool table. Thing was, it didn't feature in hers. As things ended up, Bruce didn't feature in it either.

He ordered a pint. The others must have just got a round in as their glasses were nearly full. That's lucky, he thought to himself. He listened to their talk about their day, what they'd like to do to the barmaid and how shit the other two were at pool. Before he knew it, it was ten pm. Given he had an early start, and a potentially interesting one tomorrow, he called it a night and left the others ordering another round. He walked back to his lodgings where he made a cup of tea and switched the telly on. Fifty-eight channels of shit as per usual. After flicking for a few minutes and watching more adverts than programs, he called it a night and retired with his book. He was reading a Simon Kernick novel featuring a DS Tina Boyd who he fancied, even though she wasn't real. This kind of summed up his love life. He should try and make an effort to pull, rather than drinking with his colleagues every night, he was missing his chances. Maybe he'd go into town on Saturday and buy a new shirt and a new pair of jeans too. And a new aftershave – in for a penny and all that. After reading for forty-five minutes he grew sleepy and put his book down and turned off the light.

CHAPTER 83

Dom and Annie awoke at 10am the following morning. This was the latest they'd slept in together up to now. They were quite relaxed. The sun was shining again through their closed curtains. The room was quite quiet given the proximity to the hustle and bustle of the high street. Whilst Dom was showering, Annie looked up the things to do in Cowes from the guest pack. There wasn't really much but she could find something for each of the next twelve days. Even if it was just mooching and going to the pub. And that's what they did, avoiding making any friends and not going into the same place too many times that they would be easily remembered.

They came to know the town quite well having visited nearly all the pubs and restaurants and shops. The time went by quickly and their plans developed with each day. By the time their last full day in Cowes arrived they had plans for the future. Dom had booked the Red Funnel for the following morning at 11. That would give them time to check out, grab breakfast and amble down there. From there they would get a taxi to Southampton Motor Auctions. There he would pick up a reliable, performant but non-descript car for them. He favoured a left-hand drive, given they would be heading across to France on the ferry initially, then on to Spain. Something with a bit of poke in case they needed it; that, and the fact that every man liked a fast car.

The sales took place at 7pm in the evening. Strange time, thought Dom. They got a late lunch in Southampton. Dom wasn't for traipsing around the shops with his large bag, so they sat outside a pub for a couple of hours. After exchanging some currency, they then got a light dinner and hailed a cab to the car auction. They arrived early. Annie let Dom do the car stuff. After all, she knew nothing about cars and couldn't drive. So, James Brook was the proud owner of a second-hand Audit TT with 24,000 miles on the clock. One lady owner, he was told. It went like stink and held the road like it was on rails. "So, you are no longer Annie but Charlie, you got that? I'll call you Charlie and you must call me James, not Jimmy, I hate Jimmy. We need to stick to this or we'll risk being caught out." Annie looked at him. "Oh James…. She said."

CHAPTER 84

The news of Montgomery's demise had reached Vincenzo a couple of weeks ago. He'd read the rumours of kidnapping and how he'd gotten blown to bits in one of the terrorist bombs. It just seemed too much to him that Montgomery would be under the bridge at the exact time the fucking bomb went off. Had he planted it and it had gone off? Unlikely, as other bombs went off afterwards. Maybe he was just another victim. That's what his inner circle thought. Just another victim. It was a shame as Montgomery was in a position of influence that Vincenzo may have one day needed to call upon. Not now. Apparently, his daughter was still missing, fuelling the kidnap rumours. He knew what Montgomery was like. He wouldn't be surprised if she had just fucked off to escape him, or simply topped herself. If she'd run away his team would find her, a naïve young girl on the run wouldn't elude him for long.

Over the past week or so, Vincenzo had heard back from over half of the people to whom he'd distributed the details of Devizes to. So far, no one had any sightings or information. As he was wondering what he could do next to speed things up, one of his people walked to him and said "Good news. I think we have a sighing of him." Vincenzo looked up at him. "Are you sure, are you absolutely sure?" The story was that one of the coppers that was onboard, a guy called Evans, had been holidaying on a cruise of all places and had reported seeing Devizes with a woman. They were purporting to be on honeymoon. They were very convincing, as he and his wife were taken in. "So how the fuck do we know it's him then? It could be some fucker who's just gotten hitched." "It's him alright, boss. I also got a description of the woman he was with. Now I may be wrong, but I think it's Montgomery's daughter." This took Vincenzo by surprise. "What the fuck?" he exclaimed. "Any pictures or proof?" "No boss just a description. The only thing was that her hair was brown not blonde. But her height and general description match. Vincenzo thought about this and he could only come up with two scenarios. Overactive imagination of an old man or.... "Fuck me." he thought, the sly devil. They've planned the whole thing together. Maybe it was a kidnap but an inside job. Devizes would be sure as hell that he had gotten away scot free. But how the fuck did this tie in with her father being blown up. All he had to do now was find the son of a bitch and he'd have his answers.

CHAPTER 85

It had been another long day in the nick. Ongoing investigations into the last attack at Manchester United had taken precedence, given there was more evidence to hand from the past few days and everyone knew it was part of the bigger sequence of events. There were much fewer loose ends now than prior to this last phase of the attacks. Despite the modus operandi being different, particularly in the fact that the last attack was a suicide attack, the big wigs and the media had convinced everyone that it was over. They knew the pilot's identity, and that of the bomber who had been spotted by the Clyde Tunnel. So far, they hadn't found any links, but it was just a matter of time. This still didn't satisfy Bob, but he'd had his fill of this episode in his work life. He'd had hardly any home life for weeks now. Long days in the office punctuated by evenings in the pub and the odd field trip. The thing that had intrigued him the most, and the thing that was playing on his mind now was the information he had gotten earlier that morning. And it wasn't to do with the attacks, but the kidnapping. After finally getting through all the diplomatic red tape the police forensic accountants had gotten into Montgomery's bank details and other financial details. Everyone had assumed that, due to his job, his lifestyle, and the apparent way he'd raised 250k or more in cash, that he was an affluent man. But from the records they had, this wasn't the case. His bank account had only a few hundred pounds in it. The modest place Annie had been living in had been paid for using his expenses as a London pad for himself whilst on business. This was his second home to all intents and purposes, but he didn't actually own it, it was rented. They were sure that a man of his means would have had cash stashed away in places they couldn't find, but they never put it all there. They had to keep a pretence of having enough money to justify their lifestyles and positions in society. Montgomery was something of a mystery. Did he ever have the ransom money in the first place? No money, no chance of finding his daughter alive.

The TV and media coverage of Montgomery's death beneath the bridge hadn't brought forward any information, just a few crank calls. No one had reported seeing him or anything suspicious like a getaway car or the like. He was an unknown in the UK. No cash had been found in the rubble. Even the most thorough looter, in the wake of the bomb, were they brave enough to go sifting through the rubble, couldn't have swept up every single note. He was convinced the cash had either been taken or was never there in the first place. It was entirely possible Montgomery had bluffed regarding the cash, maybe taken wads of paper with a note on top, something amateur like that, assuming the kidnapper wouldn't check thoroughly. Sadly, the media had been doing their own investigations into Montgomery. The rumours of a kidnapping and possible ransom drop had been. But this story had tickled the fancies of more than one Fleet Street editor. The police hadn't bargained for this. That morning one of the papers had a short follow-up article claiming that Montgomery had indeed been skint. Not only that, but they alluded that he had spent his fortune on nefarious exploits. Bob knew it was probably all bollocks. If they had any proof, like pictures, they'd have published without a thought for the potential damage it could cause to people – that said, which people? There was no one left who cared about Montgomery that they knew of. He remained deeply saddened that they hadn't found Annie. He knew now that she had probably died very soon after Montgomery had died. They'd done some initial, high level searches of the immediate area looking for possible sites for the quick disposal of a body. The canal seemed an obvious place, but it would have given up its secrets by now and they couldn't launch a search as they had no idea of a location. It was just too big and they had no resources as they were all tied up. Annie was down as missing assumed dead. He suspected someone in the nick, possibly his team, had been supplementing their salary by passing on titbits to the media. He hated loose ends. But on the upside, they had a lot of useful information from the brief interview with Paolo. It would help to build the case against Vincenzo if they ever got that far. He didn't know if they had enough to charge him with the confidence to put him away.

PART 6

CHAPTER 86

It was now ten pm and Annie was sat in the passenger seat, on the right-hand side, which felt strange to her, as Dom drove their latest acquisition down the M3 heading towards Dover – a 2014 black Audit TT. "It's a 2 litre, petrol, TFSI, S-line, quattro" he told her proudly. Dom had had a number of nice cars over the years, but he had never kept any of them for long. Many of them weren't purchased, but stolen. For now, he needed to be squeaky clean. He'd paid in cash using his new identity. He wanted to put it in Annie's name, but of course he couldn't as she had no license. It was quick and small and handled like a dream – this might come in handy at some point. It wouldn't be the first time he'd been in a car chase, but this one would certainly be more fun, and the handling would serve them well even if being chased by a faster car than theirs.

The ferry was booked at five past eleven and the crossing took around ninety minutes – it would be a long night. They only just made it in time – five more minutes and they'd have missed it. After parking the car, they went upstairs leaving their case locked safely in the boot. They found some seats and Dom sat down whilst Annie lay down with her head in his lap. He was going to get a couple of beers but within five minutes she'd nodded off. Dom didn't like to wake her, so he watched the people around him and soon he was asleep.

It was the hubbub of people getting up around them that woke them. The ferry had already docked and was in place. They were both a little groggy, but they made their way back down to the car and waited for their line to move. Dom was fiddling with the switches and flappy paddles. He'd found a button that raised the sat nav display revealing a DVD player and two SD memory card slots where they could load up their own music, if they had any. "Modern cars have Spotify." Annie said to him and raised an eyebrow. He smiled and said we'll make do with Radio three. They both laughed and the vehicles in front started moving. The next leg of their journey had begun. "Soon I'll teach you to drive." Dom said. Annie was glad he'd raised the subject. "But for now, let's find somewhere to sleep. I'll drive for a bit 'til we find somewhere, but I reckon it'll take us 24 hours driving to get to Nerja." Annie nodded.

The sat nav, loaded with European map, was taking them towards Arras. By now it was after one am but they spotted a small hotel on what appeared to be the main street that was still open. The name Arris made Dom chuckle; this was completely lost on Annie. There was a couple sat outside with a bottle of wine. Dom and Annie, or James and Charlie as they were now, both went in and rang the bell at reception. A French woman aged about fifty came through from what looked to be a small bar. "May I 'elp you?" she asked. The French had a nasty little talent of always being able to spot a Brit a mile off. Five minutes later they were in their room for the night. A small but well-appointed double bedroom with en-suite at the rear of the property. They were both tired, so they went straight to bed. "So far, so good.", thought Annie.

CHAPTER 87

That evening Vincenzo had been thinking about what he had learned recently – a possible sighting of Devizes on a cruise ship. This in itself was a little ridiculous, but being on honeymoon with a brunette who had a passing resemblance to Annie Montgomery was just too much to swallow, and worth following up. Plus, it was all he had. But by all accounts, Evans, the filth on the boat who was actually on holiday with his wife, had been certain that the man he had seen was in fact Devizes. He said that he had had his suspicions about the guy the minute he had first clapped eyes on him. Evans had been a good copper in his time – that was why Vincenzo had singled him out and ensured that he was now part of his team. He couldn't ignore this fact. He had set his techy guy to get the passenger manifest and check the names. He was hoping that he could get access to not only names, but ages or other personal information, allowing the list of names to be narrowed down to only those that fit Dom's height, age or the like. Even if they could do this, the chances were that there would be a quite a few men on board that would need to be checked out. His tech team would then spend many hours viewing passengers' social media in the hope of getting a shot of this couple. It would take time and resource. Was it worth the effort? But no expense would be spared in Vincenzo's mission for revenge.

Early the next morning, as Vincenzo was dressing, he got an email from his techy guy. He'd got the manifest and cross referenced with other information from the tour operator's database. Of the several hundred passengers on board he'd managed to reduce the list of contenders to just thirty-two, based on height and age. He'd ignored marital status as instructed. He was able to ascertain that of these thirty-two men, only two had paid in cash. After all, who pays for a cruise with cash? Normal, hardworking citizens paid upfront weeks beforehand. This was good, very good. He never replied, preferring to communicate only when absolutely necessary. He knew the techy guy would dig deeper into these two men and partners and by the end of that day he would know more. If he didn't, he would send someone out to find both the men. As it happened, he didn't get as far as organising any field trips. An hour later he received another email. One of the guys checked out. It was his wedding anniversary. The other guy, well he had drawn a blank. No history that he could find. This stunk of a false identity. He now had his assumed name, and this would make it far easier to trace Devizes. There was also the possibility that he had multiple identities, but now he had a lead, and a start to the trail, he wouldn't stop until he had his quarry in his hands, his bare hands. Today was a good day. And by four pm it had gotten even better.

CHAPTER 88

James and Charlie awoke early the following morning. They took a continental breakfast and hit the road by seven-thirty. Dom's first and foremost priority before breakfast was to exchange the number plates of the car. To do this he needed to steal some plates. He had left the hotel for a morning walk. It was still early and there were lots of cars around the sleepy backstreets. He spotted a Renault down a side street and off to the side where it was partially concealed. It looked like it hadn't been driven for some time. It had algae on the sides. No properties overlooked the spot and there were no cameras. He quickly removed both plates, put them into a carrier bag, and returned to the hotel. Once they had hit the road again, he found a quiet layby where he switched plates. He stowed the old plates where the spare wheel would normally be under the boot space, in case he may need them again. It only took him five minutes and they were on their way to sunny Spain. The thought of having no spare wheel concerned him slightly. Still, it had one of those temporary fixing pump things.

They drove solidly until noon. By then they had passed Paris, and the car needed fuel and they needed some food. Dom was careful not to drink any alcohol on this stage of his journey just in case they were stopped. Foreign speed limits could be confusing, and he didn't want any trouble. The plates on his car no longer matched the paperwork. Sadly, they wouldn't be able to keep this car for too long, but for now he was enjoying driving it. It made the journey less of a drag. After a light lunch at a roadside café they continued their journey heading towards Bordeaux. Dom knew they wouldn't get as far as Bordeaux that day. By six pm he was shattered, so they stopped at the next hotel they came across. Luckily it had a room. They checked in, ate dinner in their room and had an early night. Annie sorted out clean clothes for the following day.

CHAPTER 89

Vincenzo knew they'd likely lie low after the cruise to let the dust settle. He'd had his team checking airports and ferries and he now believed that Devizes, using the name James Brook, had booked a ferry from Dover to Calais with a car. Where had he been prior to this? And where had he got the car from? Had he stolen it? No matter. They had searched the records of all ferries leaving the UK daily on the hunch that Devizes would flee the country. He was so predictable. Although they had a day's head start on him and his team, he could smell blood. He dispatched one of his top guys, Dave 'Dirty' Dignam. Dignam had once held aspirations to join the police but they wouldn't take him due to his numerous offences during childhood and adolescence. Nevertheless, many of his acquaintances referred to him as 'The Filth' – an ironic nickname that had stuck. Dignam had flown from Stanstead to Paris using Ryanair. There he had hired a car, a BMW 435i, and was awaiting instructions.

They were now working on supposition. Vincenzo knew that, were he in Devizes shoes, he would get as far away from the UK as possible but definitely not Italy, for obvious reasons. He thought South of France or maybe Spain or Portugal. From the ferry booking they knew that Devizes was driving an Audi TT, which would be quite easy to spot, and they now knew the number plate from CCTV one of his cops in pocket had found. Still he knew the number plate wouldn't help them much as it would have been switched at the earliest opportunity. Still guesswork, but educated. He decided that the South of France should be their first place to focus attention on. They planned the route from Calais to the South of France – from looking at maps he knew they'd either use the A10 towards Bordeaux, continuing onto the A63 which lead all the way down to Central, and on to Western Spain, or the A75 towards Montpellier, which lead to the E-15 and Eastern Spain. By the time you got to Spain these routes were some two hundred miles apart. The Western route provided more options, so he told Dignam to drive South towards Bordeaux looking for Black Audi TTs. Meanwhile his techy guy would look for a trail to indicate where they had been on their journey. They may pick the tat up on CCTV somewhere, but it was a long shot. He was told to check the car parks of any hotels by the roadside as he headed South. He wasn't to stop, so he could catch them up. If he was on the right route, then they had sufficient time to catch them up. If they were lucky, Dignam would spot the car. He could only achieve this by driving through the night and continuing his quest. Some men needed eight hours sleep every evening. Dignam wasn't one of them. Vincenzo knew from experience that Dignam was up to the task. Dignam would have taken with him a supply of Red Bull to keep him going. Whilst they couldn't know how far behind Devizes they were, or even if they were on the right track, it was progress.

CHAPTER 90

It had been a funny morning for Bruce. Despite various stalling tactics he'd finally managed to get to inspect the SSF. The interior of the SSF was quite bare and plain. The only things of note were the overabundance of electrical sockets, plus other sockets that he assumed to be satellite TV – which is what the plans had stated, a large, walk-in freezer designed to store sufficient food for a pretty long time, but not necessarily a nuclear holocaust, and some sort of manhole cover in the floor. This really did interest Bruce as it hadn't been on the plans. A crude attempt at concealing it had been made by placing a rug and table and chairs over the top. This in itself had stood out to Bruce as strange and his curiosity had led him to look beneath the rug. He wouldn't make a big deal of this feature; indeed he wasn't going to mention it at all for now. He'd do some of his own research that evening and see what was on the site previously.

The following day was to be dominated by a visit from the owners – their first inspection of the new building. Mr. Vincenzo was impressed by what he'd seen. Bruce didn't get a chance to talk to him directly. By all accounts, they were very pleased with the speed at which it was coming along. The rest of the day passed quickly but Bruce's thoughts kept straying back to that manhole in the SSF. What was it for? Why was it hidden from him? Maybe he needed a second inspection. The door was kept locked at all times and he'd had to be let in by one of the guys who had commissioned the room – he couldn't remember which one. He didn't expect to see the inside of that room ever again. He'd sign the appropriate documents and continue with the rest of the project. After all they were paying him well.

CHAPTER 91

It was now eight am and James and Charlie were in traffic as they passed by Bordeaux. They were on the N230, part of the Bordeaux ring road, as it appeared on his sat nav screen if he zoomed out. They were approaching a river, the Garonne according to the signs. The bridge over the river comprised three lanes either side, just like a British motorway, especially in the fact that none of the three lanes were moving faster than ten miles an hour – stop-start. On the inside was a large wagon carrying large logs – tree trunks. The smell of diesel wasn't pleasant. Dom put on the air conditioning. Annie had been dozing in the passenger seat. There was something quite unnerving about being stuck on a bridge after they'd seen first-hand what it was like when a bomb went off below. For a few seconds Dom let himself wonder what it had been like for the innocent motorists going home only to find themselves dropping into an abyss. He switched the radio on. But it was all in French. He listened for a few seconds then Annie said, "It's the weather forecast, sunny all day but breezy." Dom looked over to her. "You never said that you spoke French?" She just smiled at him. "Don't suppose you can speak Spanish, too can you?" Dom asked. "No, yo no." she replied. Dom didn't know if she was taking the piss, she just continued to smile at him. The traffic started to move again. They were on the downward part of the bridge now, but he could see the traffic wasn't any quieter or quicker up ahead. Still, in the grand scheme of things, it didn't really matter.

In the car yesterday, they'd discussed other possible options for making money. They both liked the idea of cruising but had decided it was too risky. They needed something with no records of names or credit cards etc. to trace them. They both had experience of kidnapping. That could yield large sums, enough to last a few years. Fewer operations, less chances of being caught. But the heat would really be on. They'd gotten away with it once but there was no guarantee that they could continue to carry this off repeatedly. If things went wrong, they knew they'd have to kill the captive and even Dom didn't want to have to do this. He wondered how Annie would react if they were to get to this point. Could she step up into being a cold-blooded killer? He knew that your first kill changed you. He liked Annie as she was, he didn't want to see her make that change. Things would never be the same if she did. He also believed that she wasn't really capable of murder. To some extent she was putting on an act to please him. Little did he know.

They were still on the lookout for British newspapers. Once the peak time traffic had cleared and they had gotten moving again they drove until 1pm. They stopped at a small restaurant/diner place. They managed to buy a British Daily Express from the previous day. As they waited for their food Dom scanned through the pages. He seemed to stop at a small article on the third or fourth page. He read the article for some thirty seconds then looked at Annie. "It says here that they think your father was skint." Annie just looked at him. "It says he had bugger all in his bank account and he only rented your place and that was paid from his expenses." She continued to look at him. She didn't say a word. "Where the fuck did he get the cash from?" Again, Annie didn't say a word – she knew, of course, that he had money. What she didn't know was where it was, and if it was above board, and known to be his in the event of his demise. It seemed that his inheritance wasn't worth going back for after all. Dom could see that this had come as a bit of a blow to her. "I'm sorry." he said, not quite knowing why he had said it. After all, it didn't matter now, she was never going back, she would be assumed to be dead, and that life was long gone. Still, I suppose it would be a bit of a shock to find out your father was a fraud. Or worse. She was now just staring ahead. Dom took another forkful of his meal. Annie then did likewise and within fifteen minutes they'd paid the bill and were back on the road.

Dom stuck to the speed limit, despite the fact that most of the other cars went speeding past him. They were now approaching Bayonne which was quite close to the coast. Annie suggested they stop off somewhere for a few hours. She was getting sick of being stuck in the car. Whilst Dom's instincts told him to continue, he too was sick of being cooped up in this coupe. "There'll be a beach close by, let's go for a wander." she suggested, her brown eyes looking up into his. "OK he said, let's go to the beach. But we can't hang around, we need to get further South before we stop for the night. We can't stop here." She smiled at him saying nothing. Her mood lightened. She switched the radio on and found a music channel.

CHAPTER 92

That evening Bruce skipped the pub and went to his room. On his laptop he found the initial plans for the building and looked at the surveys of the land prior to the design and build. Now there was a thing. There was an old sink hole there, dating back years. Apparently, no one knew how deep it was. After studying the initial plans, it was to be have been sealed off. From scanning the sets of plans it became apparent that the hole was where the SSF was located now. Could it be that the sink hold hadn't been blocked off but had been used as a sort of disposal chute from the opening in the floor of the SSF? Bruce thought about this. For what purpose? He pondered this for several minutes. Then it hit him. Now he needed to do some research on Vincenzo. Who was he, what did he do, how did he really earn his money?

One of his old drinking buddies back home was a copper. It was a long shot but maybe Johnny had heard of him. Or maybe he could check up on him in the police computer database. It was only 9pm so he picked up his phone and called Johnny. "Brucey, how's it going mi old mucker?" said Johnny. "Good thanks. I'm working on the construction of a new office block and I was wondering if you'd heard of the owner?". "Who's that then? asked Johnny. "One Luigi Giancarlo Vincenzo" replied Bruce." The line went quiet for a moment. Then Johnny spoke "Do you mind if I ask why you are so interested in this guy?" It seemed a fairly normal question for a copper to ask. Bruce told him of his suspicions regarding the sink hole and its potential use and about the secrecy of the so called SSF in the basement, and about the two wacko's who were the only people ever allowed in there apart from his single visit. After another brief pause Johnny replied "Leave it with me, I'll do some digging tomorrow and if I find anything I'll be in touch. Seriously though, I wouldn't worry, it'll be nothing." Bruce thanked him and ended the call. Something wasn't right about this whole thing. He knew that he had felt this way since the first interview, the speed of his appointment and much more. Still if there was anything dodgy, Johnny would find out. "Fuck it, I'm tired." he thought to himself and retired for the evening, for once completely sober.

CHAPTER 93

The beach at Bayonne was larger than they had both imagined. Large hotel buildings lined the beach and the sea was blue albeit a little breezy. White topped waves rolled up onto the beach, but that didn't stop the avid paddlers and a few swimmers. Annie wanted them both to go for a swim, but Dom refused, saying it was too much hassle and they didn't have a room to get changed in. In the end she relented, and they walked hand in hand down the beach for half a mile or so then turned around. By now it was approaching four pm. Let's stay here tonight. It's too late to be getting going again. We've made pretty good progress so far and we aren't really in a rush, are we?" she said to Dom. His instinct was to keep moving, but nevertheless he relented. "Let's find a romantic hotel with a big bath." She said looking at him in that way which meant only one thing. They hadn't made love since leaving the Isle of Wight and Dom liked the idea of a big bath. "OK, you choose." he said. She clapped her hands and skipped a couple of times, then started to walk faster, leading him by the hand towards the steps that lead from the beach to the hotels. "Not one of these big things." Dom said. She led them away from the beach for some five minutes to a long road that comprised nice looking hotels and large summer houses for the affluent French. From the signage, they had realised that they were in Biarritz. This is where the beach was, a couple of kilometres outside of Bayonne, where the signs had led them. Funny how Dom hadn't spotted that on the drive in. Still, it didn't matter. Annie soon found a quaint hotel, off the beaten track, that looked quite nice. It had a nice restaurant with a few tables outside at the rear. They waited at the reception. "Bonjour, avez-vous une chamber double avec un bain desponsible?" Annie casually said to the receptionist.

Dom was taken aback. She could speak French. Mind you, that said, most decent schools taught French. It's not that unusual, he thought to himself. She looked at him and smiled. Her smile was different. Instead of a pleasant, loving sort of smile that she so often gave him, this was more of a 'I'm superior to you' smile. Her eyes seemed to have gone darker, but it must be the light here in reception. The receptionist spoke to Annie in French, none of which Dom could make head nor tail of, and she presented Annie with a key. "Pay on departure." Annie said. She headed towards the lift – their room was on the first floor of this two-story building. "She says the building dates back to the late 1800's." Annie said. "Nice." Dom replied.

They found their room and Annie opened the door with the large key they'd been given. "I need to go back to the car to get the bag. Maybe I should bring the car over. Did you see if they had a car park?" said Dom. "No car park, just street parking but the lady said it's better to leave the car where it is as it's nearly impossible to find a space here at this time." "OK" said Dom. "I'll go get the bag." Annie took his hand and lead him towards the bathroom. "Look at this big bath…." Dom knew the bag could wait a little longer. "You go in first and I'll follow you in a minute." she said, disappearing into the bedroom. Dom put the plug in and turned on the taps. The water came flowing out at a rate much quicker than his terraced house back in Horwich. The hotel had provided soap, shampoo and body wash. They could manage without their washbags for now. Once they'd made love in the bath, Dom could go fetch the case whilst Annie soaked and relaxed. Then they'd go for a walk and find a restaurant. He took off his clothes and got into the bath. It was already half full. He didn't overfill it knowing that when Annie got in, the level would rise. He couldn't speak

French, but he wasn't stupid. The head of the bath, where his head was, was looking towards the bedroom. The door was partly closed. He could see Annie by the window looking out. He hadn't realised how tired he had become. He closed his eyes for a moment. How his life has changed these past few weeks. And how he now had a promising future, featuring lots of fantastic sex, and plenty of money, and no one knowing who they were. They were making plans for the future. Working with Annie meant more opportunity for less risk. Life doesn't get any better than this, he thought to himself.

And then it happened. Suddenly he was sliding down the bath, his feet in the air. He could feel a tight grip around both his ankles. His face was under the water and he couldn't see his assailant. He immediately breathed in soapy water and started to panic. His mind flashed on Annie; had she been silently killed by the same person that was trying to kill him? His face was underwater and he hadn't had a chance to take a deep breath before being plunged underneath. He was now desperate for air. But however much he tried to raise his head out of the water, he couldn't. His head was at such an angle that water had run up his nostrils and into his throat. He couldn't resist the urge to cough and as he did so he exhaled, breathing in water. His lungs burned like they were on fire. Never had he realised how painful drowning was. As his already blurred vision faded to black, he wondered how they had found him, and who Vincenzo had used to kill them both. It was the last thing that went through his mind.

PART 7

CHAPTER 94

All enquiries into Montgomery and his daughter had, to all intents and purposes, ceased. The case was closed pending any new evidence. There were no angry relatives or friends demanding action and the media had forgotten them. There was still lots of work to be done on the terrorist attacks, but they had appeased the powers that be and the media. For Bob and Bill, it was back to gathering scraps of evidence for his previous case. The drudgery was welcome as it didn't require long days and sleepless nights. Nevertheless, he hoped a new case would come along soon.

CHAPTER 95

"Vincenzo, it's Johnny. You have a problem mi old mucker." The call was brief. Afterwards, Vincenzo called his on-site operatives and gave them instructions. This loose end would have to be dealt with first thing in the morning.

CHAPTER 96

It was approaching ten pm and Digby was now at Bayonne. This was the first place near to a beach and Vincenzo had suggested driving around Biarritz before continuing South. No sooner had he gotten onto the road by the beach than he spotted a black TT parked by the roadside in close proximity to the beach. The number plate was different, but they had expected that. TTs were far less common than your average car. He parked on lines a little further down the street and walked back to examine the car. Whilst he couldn't be sure it was the right car, the model was exactly right even down to the quattro four-wheel drive. He peered through the window to see if there was anything inside the car that could give him a clue, but it looked clean. He took out his newly acquired French disposable phone and called the number. Within a minute he was speaking to Vincenzo himself. "I think I've found the car, boss. Same make and model down to every detail. Nothing inside, no sign of Devizes. I can't be certain, what shall I do?" "Wait around and watch the car. If he comes back, follow him. If it isn't his car let me know immediately. It's late, he may have booked a room in one of the hotels. Let me get someone to check them all. Stay put and don't fall asleep." Digby needed sleep. But he walked up and down the street casually. When a car on the other side to the TT moved, he returned to his car and parked in the spot. It took him a few goes to get into the tight spot but it afforded him a good view of the car. His BMW had privacy glass so no fear of anyone spotting him. His only problem might be getting out in a hurry if Devizes showed and drove off. He'd cross that bridge when he came to it. He opened a Red Bull and switched on the radio and waited for news.

CHAPTER 97

Around an hour later Digby was woken up by the vibrating of his phone. He realised he'd nodded off, but the car was still there – phew. He answered the phone. "Write this down." Vincenzo said. Digby always kept a small notepad and pen in his pocket. "Go ahead." he replied, and wrote down the name of the hotel that Mr. James Brook had booked for the night. With a bit of luck, he'd be tucked up in his room, or in the hotel bar. They'd checked in earlier that evening for one night and it was a short walk from here, and that hotel had no parking. It seemed to fit and there was a strong chance it was Devizes.

He locked his car and, using google maps on his phone, walked to the hotel. It was a quaint, older hotel with just two stories with only street parking and no spaces that he could see. This must be why Devizes hadn't moved his car. He waited across the street watching the people inside. Even though Devizes wouldn't know or recognise him, Digby was, nevertheless, inherently very careful. He waited until there were fewer people in reception and walked into the hotel, past reception and headed towards Devizes room. The rooms, being old, were opened using a key, not the modern key card access of the newer hotels. He found the room number he had been given and stood outside the room, listening. He could hear nothing. He decided that Devizes was probably out in some bar somewhere, so he took the bold step of knocking on the door. His gun and silencer were in his hand beneath his coat. If Devizes answered, he would shoot him in the heart and push him back into the room, closing the door behind him and then depart quickly. Still no sound from the room. He put on his gloves and tried the door and, to his surprise, found it was unlocked. He opened it slowly, just in case it was a trap, and went inside. The bed hadn't been touched and there was no sign of luggage or anything personal to say the room was occupied. The bed was ruffled a bit, giving the appearance that someone had maybe sat on it. If the room had been turned around awaiting occupancy the bed would be immaculate, no creases. The room was an en-suite. There was a smell coming from the bathroom, like someone had bathed recently. The door was closed. Again, in an attempt to evade a possible surprise attack, he got his gun out and pushed the door open slowly to minimise noise, ready for a confrontation. His heart rate elevated.

There was Devizes, dead. He was in the bath, on his back, lips blue, eyes haemorrhaged just like he'd drowned. Drowned in the bath. Fuck, this was no accident, who had beaten him to his quarry? Who else was after him? What would he tell Vincenzo? He couldn't afford Vincenzo to know that someone had beaten him to it, he knew Vincenzo didn't accept failure. He didn't think he'd failed in his mission, but would his boss see it that way? He didn't have much time to think. He needed to call with an update and soon. He made his decision. He'd tell Vincenzo that he had killed Devizes. He'd take the credit. Not that he wanted the credit, he just didn't want the consequences of the alternative. Hopefully no one would ever be the wiser.

He knew he hadn't touched anything, or left any fingerprints. He checked that he hadn't left any footprints on the bathroom floor, but he noticed that it wasn't wet. There must have been a lot of splashing so whoever had killed him had used the towels to mop up the floor. He backed out of the room, gave the bedroom one more look to make sure he hadn't missed anything then exited the hotel. When he got to the road he started walking back to his car. His head was spinning. He took out his phone and called Vincenzo. "Yes?" he said. "It's done. He's dead." "And the girl?" he added. "No sign boss, nothing to say she was ever there at all. He was in the bath alone, he still is." After a brief pause, Vincenzo replied. "Good work. You've done well. Spend the night there on me, get yourself a nice girl and return tomorrow." "Thank you, boss." Digby replied. He thought he'd stay at a hotel by the beach where he could try and pick up a girl. If that failed, he'd procure one.

After a little walking to clear his head he found a suitable hotel and went in and booked a room. This place wasn't cheap, but it had parking. He walked back to his car, so he could move it to the hotel and get his bag before getting a well-earned drink. But as he approached his car something was wrong; something was very wrong. The TT was gone. What the fuck? Had it simply been stolen? He should have made a note of the new registration when he first found it, but in his excitement to report his progress to his boss he had forgotten to do so. Shit. Now he'd struggle to trace it. It could be anywhere. He knew the crime rate in these beach resorts was high, so he decided to assume it had indeed been stolen and hope no one asked about it. He hadn't been told to break into the car or move it or anything. He was OK. Just forget it, move his car and get that drink. But he couldn't get it out of his head. Maybe the girl had been with him and done a runner whilst he was in the bath and he'd just missed her? Could she have killed him? More likely she returned to the room, found him dead and she ran. Hopefully she'd disappear and there'd be no further questions regarding the car. Whilst it played on his mind it wouldn't spoil his evening.

CHAPTER 98

As soon as Bruce got to site the foreman said, "Someone's waiting for you, down in the basement by the SSF." Bruce acknowledged him and went down to the basement. Sure enough, the same two guys were there. "Bruce, it's about your survey, we have a couple of things to ask you." "Sure, ask away." Bruce said. He noticed the door to the SSF was open. "It'd be quicker to show you" said Gavin. Bruce immediately got a really bad feeling about this. "Can it wait guys, I'm late for a planning meeting with suppliers?" Bruce said hoping it may give him time to think or flee. If they were going to do away with him, they'd find him anyway he thought. "It'll only take a minute then you can go to your meeting." Came the reply. Tim pushed the door open and the three of them went inside. Tim then closed the door behind them. Bruce now had a sinking feeling in the pit of his stomach. With the door shut he was trapped. Before Bruce could say anything or ask any questions Gavin produced a gun with a silencer, quite an unnecessary precaution given where they were. "We hear that you've been nosy mate. Too nosy." With that he shot Bruce in the head and he fell to the floor. Tim moved the table and chairs, removed the rug and opened the door. Bruce would be the first deposit of many to disappear down this hole. No doubt there were several old skeletons already down there to keep him company. Two minutes later the door was sealed, the rug and table back in place and Tim and Gavin left the room. Bruce lay at the bottom of the hold, still warm, but very dead. His contract terminated.

CHAPTER 99

Vincenzo was quite ebullient that evening. He'd eliminated two loose ends that day, Devizes and Bourne. Both chapters were now closed. His new hidey-hole had been christened. In a few short months he could take up residence in his new penthouse apartment that would occupy the whole top floor of the building. From there he could expand his operations. He was already planning his next ventures on his way to the top.

CHAPTER 100

Rethabile now had more evidence and a lot more insight into Vincenzo and how he worked. He knew details of crimes that he had no proof of. He also now knew about his links to Rimmer and his attention turned towards an office block that Rimmer was building. He was in it for the long haul, but he knew he was on the way to catching a very large fish.

The only thing that played on his mind was that Digby had made no mention of the girl. If she'd been there, he would have killed her too and reported back. She mustn't have been with him. Strange. Maybe Devizes had already killed her somewhere along the line having served her purpose – this looked the most likely scenario. Still, he'd find out more tomorrow. In the grand scheme of things, she really didn't matter to him and was of no value.

The End

Acknowledgements

I'll be very brief. Thank you to my wife, Diana, for supporting me now as always. Thank you to David Brankley for proof-reading the manuscript for this edition. And finally thank you to you for purchasing and reading my story. I hope you enjoyed it.

To follow my progress and to find out about my further books please visit my web site www.roberthpage.co.uk or my Facebook page - simply search for 'Robert H Page Author' from Facebook.

Printed in Great Britain
by Amazon